HONEY CHASER

Published by Almondhue Press
ISBN: 978-0-9839243-0-2
Library of Congress Control Number: 2011919228

Simone, Zori.
Honey chaser, the trustafarian / by Zori Simone. -- Carlsbad, CA :
Almondhue Press, c2011.

p. ; cm.
ISBN: 978-0-9839243-0-2
Summary: When Sheila, a haunted beauty, meets Darren on a
cross-country trip, they begin a passionate affair. His demands for
a commitment challenge her to choose love over fear.

1. Man-woman relationships--Fiction. 2. Commitment
(Psychology)--Fiction. 3. San Diego (Calif.)--Fiction.
4. Albuquerque (N.M.)--Fiction. 5. Love stories. I. Title.
PS3619.I56282 H66 2011
813.6--dc22 1111

Printed in the United States of America.
Edited by Jessica Walker
Book design by Brion Sausser

HONEY CHASER

The Trustafarian

ZORI SIMONE

ALMONDIIUE PRESS

CARLSBAD, CALIFORNIA

Dedicated to Jason, my hero.

PROLOGUE

"Run Liz!"

The sound of boots pounding the cement in pursuit made her obey the command. "I'm going to get you, you little—" an explosion drowned out her attacker's voice and she ran several feet before taking a chance and looking back.

The hefty man had fallen and he'd taken down someone with him. "Grandpa!" Fear rooted her feet to the ground and she whipped her head around. *Where was Rick?*

"Get out of here—" Grandpa said. The attacker threw an elbow into her grandfather's face and the old man lost his grip on the gun. She screamed again when the second shot rang out.

"Miss Washington!" someone called. The voice penetrated her dream and Sheila awoke with a gasp. Someone was banging on the bedroom door, and she blinked several times before remembering where she was. "Miss Washington, are you OK?"

"Yes," she said. Reaching for the lamp on the night stand, she flinched when her hand brushed against a tissue protruding from its box. "Yes," she said again. "I'm here." Her voice was more convincing now that the light was on and she could see her surroundings. Columns of dusty pink roses came into focus on the wall opposite the bed. Their cheerful faces mocked her.

"Miss Washington?"

Pulling her attention from the wallpaper, Sheila grabbed a quilt from the velvet chaise and wrapped it around herself before unlocking the door. Mr. and Mrs. Crandall, the owners of the B&B, stood in the hall in their robes.

"We heard you screaming from the third floor," Mrs. Crandall said.

"Bad dream," Sheila said. "Sorry to wake you."

"Are you all right, dear?" the old woman asked.

"Yes," Sheila lied. She made a show of covering a yawn and apologized again. When the couple left, the young woman peered at the tangled sheets and blankets. She couldn't go back to sleep—nor did she want to—but the room was chilly. She kept the quilt around her shoulders and slid between the sheets before lifting her phone from the nightstand.

It was 1 AM on the West Coast. Dr. Baldwin's answering service would put her through to the psychiatrist. However, that privilege came with a condition and she hesitated over the number. Instead of dialing, she opened the mp3 file he'd recorded and found herself relaxing at his reassuring words.

"I am safe," she repeated. "I am safe in this moment. I get to choose environments where I feel safe and in control..."

She'd stayed in Maine for a month; two weeks too long. The nightmares only flared up if she stayed in one place too long. Tomorrow she would get back on the road and leave Liz's nightmares behind.

CHAPTER 1

SHEILA HAD NOT PLANNED TO STOP IN ALBUQUERQUE. BUT WHEN SHE saw a sign for the Rio Grande, she acted on an impulse and exited the freeway. The car stirred clouds when she steered it over the unpaved parking lot of the vista point. She left her purse on the floor of the passenger side and grabbed a granola bar from the snack bag.

Squinting at the shallow river bed, she thought the Rio Grande should be renamed. Last May she passed up an opportunity to view the famed river when driving through Colorado. Now Sheila decided she wasn't missing much.

The embankment was dry and cracked where the sun had licked the moisture from the dirt. Fluffs of seed lingered in the air and she sneezed. Shaking the granola crumbs from the folds of her dress, she shoved off the picnic bench.

Albuquerque was too hot and too dry. After two scorching days in Texas, she intended to traverse New Mexico and find a hotel in Phoenix. Tomorrow afternoon she'd arrive in San Diego.

San Diego was a place of healing for her, the Pacific Ocean in particular. She loved to listen to the constancy of waves against the shoreline and bury her feet in the cold, wet sand. For hours, the sand pipers would amuse her, their spindly legs working constantly to keep them just out of reach of the approaching waves.

Driving had become her avocation, and she relished the freedom of getting behind the wheel and going, anywhere. In the past two years, Sheila had visited all forty-eight contiguous states.

She heard a scurrying noise and glanced over her shoulder in time to see a road runner dart from the chaparral to seize a lizard. It amused her to think of the cartoon rendition of the road runner she'd grown up with, and how different it was from the real thing. She had the same reaction to pelicans when she saw them on her first trip to San Diego.

San Diego, she thought, and her mouth watered in anticipation of dining at her favorite taco shop.

When she turned the key in the ignition, the engine rumbled and coughed. "Don't do this now," she pleaded. "We're almost there!" For ten minutes she poked under the hood, and coaxed the car to start.

During the endless nights she spent in hotels, Sheila read. Alternating between fiction and non-fiction, she read the manual for the old Mazda twice. Sweaty and frustrated—a bad starter wasn't something she could fix—she slammed the hood closed and called for a tow truck. She missed her Mercedes SLK but the faded green RX-8 better fit her cover story of being a vagabond.

Fanning herself with the tow paperwork, she thought the nearest shade must be in Colorado. The truck driver spent more time glancing at her than working the levers to lower the flat bed. Sheila ignored him and glared at the river.

"All set," he finally said, opening the passenger door of the cab. She wrinkled her nose at the smell of fried food. With a sigh, she climbed onto the greasy cushion and pulled out her phone.

"Excuse me while I call my boyfriend," she said. Sheila didn't have a boyfriend but she wanted the leering driver to think she did. She called her own number, staging a request for the pretend boyfriend to pick her up.

"You want me to give you a ride honey? I'll do it for free," the driver said. He winked and she rolled her eyes. Her bangs flapped in the wind from the open window and she kept it down, even after the driver cranked the AC to maximum.

The waiting room at the repair shop was greasy and crowded. Sheila left her keys and phone number and meandered over the gritty sidewalks. When she came upon a park with a grassy lawn so green it looked artificial, she nearly skipped across the street to sink her toes into the shaded, spongy grass.

Families clustered around a small stage. They arranged blankets and chairs; the band members set up instruments. Sheila watched a pair of squealing toddlers chase after bubbles.

"Hi," someone called.

She started at the greeting, and turned to find a man grinning at her. The late afternoon sun hovered around his shoulders and she tented her eyes. He moved to the right, blocking out most of the light. When she could make out his face, her lips parted but made no sound.

"You forgot it's BYOB?" he said.

"Excuse me?"

"Bring Your Own Blanket, for the concert. I have a big one if you'd like to join us," he said.

Sheila blinked at the sun-kissed man and he grinned again. She wondered if he could hear her heart racing as she drank in his six-foot frame. He wore a hunter green polo shirt, the collar upturned. It clung to his broad shoulders and her eyes swept over lean arms, to his dark jeans, and long legs before returning to his face. The skin around his eyes crinkled when he smiled and she guessed that he had more years on her than height.

"Darren Abruzzo," he said, flipping the Z's as if there were a T in them.

"Sheila," she said, and cleared her throat. "Sheila Washington." She took his hand automatically and when he squeezed, shock waves traveled up her arm from their contact.

"Do I detect an East Coast accent?" Darren asked. She nodded and retracted her hand. It was tingling. "What brings you to Albuquerque?"

"Starter replacement." Sheila slipped her feet back into her sandals. She adjusted the purse strap on her shoulder and looked away. She came up with numerous fabricated replies to give the people she encountered on her cross country trips. This man caught her off guard with his casual manner and his dazzling smile. She didn't like that she'd answered honestly.

"Enjoy the concert," she said and turned to leave.

"If you're getting it fixed at old Sam's you won't be leaving till morning," Darren said. "You're lucky he was even open this Sunday. And it would be a shame to miss the Sandia Mountains at sunset."

Her neck prickled when she looked back at him. "How did you know I came from Sam's?"

"Sam's Auto is walking distance from here. You're welcome to join our picnic when you change your mind." He pointed to a partially shaded area where a bearded man and blonde woman were spreading a quilt.

Sheila resisted a smile. She didn't answer his invitation; instead she gave Darren a little wave and crossed the street. Although she had walked for only an hour, the shop was clear of customers and all employees but one.

"We tried to call you, Miss," said the repairman. "We should be able to get your part tomorrow, first thing. The car'll be ready by 10 o'clock, twelve at the latest."

Sheila grabbed a backpack from the trunk, stuffing her toiletries and little purse into it. Then she sat on the bench outside, rubbing her thumb over the corner of her cell phone. The map app showed a La Quinta Inn within walking distance but after ten minutes of staring at the route, she couldn't get her feet going in that direction.

"You need a ride?" the repairman asked. He hung out the window of a pockmarked Ford Pinto.

"No thanks, I'll walk," she said. He nodded and took off. The car rumbled onto Central Avenue.

Sheila worried her bottom lip between her teeth while the two halves of her brain duked it out. Picnicking with Darren Abruzzo would probably be more interesting than reading the McMurtry novel buried at the bottom of her bag, in yet another anonymous hotel room. *Ya think?*

Her eyes drifted closed. She recalled his full lips curled in a self-assured smile, his artfully tousled black hair, the shadow accenting his square jaw. But she shouldn't get involved.

Opening her eyes, she shook Darren's face from her mind. She'd met lots of guys with fantastic smiles and she hadn't broken her rule for them. *But sharing a blanket and conversation at a very public concert were not "getting involved."*

She stood. If she was stuck in this dusty city for the night, she would make the best of it. After all, she loved live music. When the concert was over, she'd call a cab to take her to a hotel.

Walking back toward the park, she heard music before the bandstand came into view. Her heart rate sped up again and she had to work at keeping her feet at a slow, casual pace. The band played Santana's *Oye Como Va* and Sheila returned to her original spot under the jacaranda tree.

She forced herself not to search the now crowded park for Darren. An elderly couple danced with panache over the cemented area serving as a dance floor and she focused on them.

"*Ciao, bella.* You've returned in time for sunset," Darren said. He'd come up behind her again and Sheila turned slowly toward him. "The Sandias and I have been waiting for you."

Despite the 90° temperatures, a shiver skittered over her when she met his smiling eyes. She found her voice and hoped it sounded cool. "The Sandias are oblivious to what I do. How do you know I'm not meeting someone else?"

"Nonsense. Dance with me." Darren held out his hand and Sheila looked at his long, expectant fingers. She dropped the bag off her shoulder and he took it, placing it against the tree. When his hand closed around hers, she got another jolt of excitement.

The Santana song ended before they reached the dance floor. She froze when the next song started. "I don't swing dance."

"Don't worry, it's all in the leading," he said.

Sheila shook her head and withdrew her hand. "Maybe the next one."

Darren studied her for a moment, then strode to the tree and picked up her bag. Returning to her side, he said, "I have a delicious Bourgogne you must try. Or if you prefer white, I have a pinot grigio. Come, I'll introduce you to my friends."

She gazed up at him and forgave his cockiness when he smiled. His smile made her feel like she was the only woman in the crowded park. "I prefer red."

"Great." Darren led her over to his friends with his hand at the small of her back.

The group, assembled on blankets and chairs, was only a couple hundred yards away. In reality, it took less than a minute to reach them but Sheila felt like she was moving in slow motion. The pressure of the man's hand on her back was doing *something* to her besides guiding her up the slight hill. Searing her, exciting her, startling her.

Before she could step from under his palm, Darren raised it in the air. "The lovely Sheila has returned!"

One of the women spoke. "I love that shade of green."

"Thanks, Alex," Darren said.

Alex's black hair was loosely restrained in a pony tail. She dressed in cut-off shorts and a worn t-shirt. When she pushed her sunglasses onto her head, Sheila was surprised by the intense blue eyes. "I was complimenting the 'lovely Sheila,'" Alex said, earning a chuckle from Sheila. Both she and Darren wore green. She chuckled again when she saw how close in shade her dress was to his shirt.

"Of course you were," Darren said. He slung an arm over Sheila's shoulders, turning her away from Alex. "This is my main man, Stan," he said gesturing to a bearded man. "We go way back to undergrad at UNM. And this is Liz," he said and the blonde smiled. "She's new to the neighborhood." Sheila's stomach seized at the name but she made herself nod hello.

Darren released her and lifted a wine bottle from the array of food and drinks to find it empty. He uncorked another one, poured a hearty serving of red into a glass, and presented it to Sheila. "Welcome to Albuquerque," he said.

"Are you sure she's old enough to drink?" Stan said.

"Stan, Stan, always the comedian," Darren said and held up his glass. "Salud."

The wineglasses clinked together and Sheila forced herself not to squirm. Under Stan's searching eyes, she wished she weren't wearing something from her wardrobe of loose-fitting, thrift store finds. Her hair was tight against her head in a French braid and she wore no makeup. On driving days, like today, she usually felt invisible.

At Chase Manor—she no longer thought of the family estate as home—Mother insisted that Sheila wear her thick, auburn hair curled around her shoulders and dress in the silk suits which made her feel like a walking trust fund advertisement.

She could feel Stan's eyes focus on the hem of her dress where the stitching had come undone and she was annoyed at his scrutiny. Then she was annoyed with herself. So what if some guy wearing Teva sandals, with socks, was assessing her. She was purposefully dressed so no one *would* recognize her.

Turning away from Stan, Sheila spotted a brawny man approaching. "Would you care to dance?" he asked.

Darren, who had been arranging hors d'oeurves on a plate, scowled. Sheila was about to decline, but when Darren stood up and moved toward her with a fixed smile, she accepted. "To whom do I owe the honor?" Sheila asked.

"Kevin Montgomery," he said, extending his hand. Sheila reached out and instead of shaking it, Kevin kissed the top.

"Montgomery, you old dog," Darren said.

Kevin kept a hold on her hand, leading her to the dance floor. "I saw you standing under that jacaranda tree a bit ago and I thought, Helen of Troy has reincarnated and come to Albuquerque."

Sheila laughed and he spun her out quickly then pulled her back into his right side, surprising her with how gracefully he moved.

"I don't stand much of a chance with the ladies once Abruzzo works his Italian mojo so I have to goad him when I can."

"I don't know *Abruzzo* any better than I know you but seems he's about due some humble pie," Sheila said. Kevin laughed and drew her closer.

When she'd risen with the sun in Texas, she'd planned to make it to Arizona. She couldn't believe not only had she broken her rule of avoiding men, she'd caught the attention of a pair who seemed to be old rivals.

Kevin kissed the back of her hand when the salsa song ended, then pressed his business card into it. Walking back to Darren's group, she folded it in half and withdrew a bottle of water from her bag. When she didn't immediately spot Darren, she dropped the sweaty card and reached for her phone.

"What's he up to now?" one of the women said. Sheila followed the woman's gaze to the band where Darren was sauntering up to the lead singer. After a brief silence, the band began again with Darren at the mike. At the familiar drum line of an 80's song, Sheila groaned. Not *that* song.

"Oh, baby let me love you right..." he sang.

"That man must be drunk," Sheila said. Her face grew warm under the stares she felt from his friends.

"Oh Sheila, oh oh Sheila let me love you 'til the morning comes..." Darren sang.

"No, that's Darren, always the center of attention," someone said. Sheila looked around to see it was Alex who had spoken.

"Don't listen to Alex, she's just jealous," said a brunette.

Alex stood up. "I'm not jealous. Sheila can have the louse." She turned to a man Sheila hadn't met. "Take me home Nick."

Sheila watched Nick and Alex depart. "One of Darren's exes?" she asked the brunette.

The woman smiled behind her beer. "Back in our UNM days. I'm Jen and you're quick." Jen patted the empty seat next to her. "Where did you meet Darren?"

"About an hour ago, right over there," she said, pointing. Jen raised her eyebrows but said no more.

Darren had a good voice and Sheila wondered if he'd pulled this stunt for other girls, namely Alex. Was this part of the Italian mojo Kevin mentioned? The song ended and Darren jogged over and pulled Sheila to her feet. "Ladies and Gentlemen, Sheila," he shouted. The concert crowd applauded and whistled when Darren swung her into a dip and kissed her. Sheila was so shocked she nearly fell when he released her. Everyone cheered wildly and she tried to shake the nasty, familiar feeling of being used.

CHAPTER 2

Darren bent to pick up their wine glasses but stopped when he heard Sheila's voice.

"Is there a bathroom around here?" she asked. He looked up to see she was addressing Jen.

"You can use the one at my house," Darren interjected. He smiled in anticipation of getting her alone and kissing her properly.

"Thanks but my Momma told me not to go to strange men's houses," she said.

He hid his chagrin and joined in the laughter. Jen offered her house and Sheila accepted, without another glance at Darren.

"Nice singing, Casanova," Stan said, clapping him on the back. "Does this mean we're getting the band back together?"

Darren gave him a half smile without taking his eyes away from Sheila and Jen. They slowly crossed the lawn. "*Look back*," he said silently, hopefully.

"You sang in a band?" Liz asked. Darren let out a soft curse when the two women disappeared around the corner.

"I'm sorry, what?" Darren said.

"Liz was asking about *Los Globos*," Stan said.

She wrinkled her penciled eyebrows. "You named your band after balloons?"

"Pretty corny but it worked," Darren said. "We couldn't name our-selves after the U's mascot, *los lobos*, so we used a word that rhymed."

Liz stood up and brushed off her shorts. "What did you play, Stan-ley? No wait, let me guess, the drums?" Stan grinned and shook his head.

Darren withdrew his cell phone from his pocket and fired off a text message to Jen. Liz guessed again and she giggled when Stan said he'd been the bass player. Earlier, when Stan stopped by his house suggesting they invite Liz to the concert, Darren had been unenthusiastic. Watching his old friend banter with the blonde, he wondered.

Last year, Stan moved back to Albuquerque to take a job at the firm where Darren worked. He'd overheard the secretaries gossiping about Stan being in the closet. The gossip aroused an old suspicion. Stan was a workaholic and used the long work hours as an excuse for why he rarely dated. When Darren tried to broach the subject a few weeks ago, his friend had sputtered as if choked. Then he knocked a beer over into his lap, leaving Darren's question unanswered.

"Stan, you should show her the videos," he said and turned to Liz. "He had the coolest hair in the band, better than Bon Jovi's."

"I would like to see that," Liz said. "I used to be crazy about Bon Jovi."

"Oh man, those old VHS tapes are so bad," Stan said.

Darren hit the back light button on his phone and frowned. No reply from Jen. Were they talking about him? Would Sheila come back to the park? He looked in the direction of Jen's house.

"Thanks for inviting me," Liz said. She extended her hand and Darren shook it.

"Thanks for coming. It was Stan's idea, though. Are you gonna go check out the videos at Stan's place?"

Liz flushed. "I uh, don't know..."

"She's not really interested," Stan mouthed. He was standing behind Liz and Darren made his eyes go big at the guy.

Liz patted her pockets. "Now where is my house key?" She knelt and patted the quilt.

"She's totally into you," he whispered into Stan's ear.

"I think I saw a key in the basket," Stan said, seeming to gather confidence. He reached for it at the same time Liz did. Darren covered his face when their heads collided.

What was he doing here, anyway? He should have left these two and gone after Sheila, but he hadn't wanted to look desperate.

He was being a simpleton, worrying about Sheila when she rejected him. But he couldn't shake the girl from his thoughts. It didn't matter that she was probably ten years his junior and didn't live in Albuquerque.

None of the women he knew would look half as sexy as Sheila did in her threadbare sundress. She intrigued him with her natural beauty and her coy manner. His lips twitched into a half smile. He wanted her even more *because* she had walked away from him.

"Earth to Darren," Stan said.

"What?"

"I said, 'Do you want me to drop you off at home?'"

"He's going to wait for her," Liz said.

Darren couldn't stop the smile from spreading across his face. "You think she'll come back?"

Liz smiled too. "If she doesn't, you know where her car's getting fixed."

"Wouldn't she think I was stalking her, if I showed up at Sam's tomorrow?"

"Not if you took some flowers and told her you hadn't meant to embarrass her." She shrugged a shoulder. "I thought the singing was kind of sweet but apparently she didn't."

"Thanks," Darren said.

"See you tomorrow," Stan said. Darren held back a laugh at the lump growing on Stan's head where he'd smacked into Liz. At least she had bangs to cover up her bump.

Darren took the corners of the quilt and lifted it from the ground, snapping it into the air. Something fluttered onto the grass and he shook the blanket again then folded it before stooping to pick up the paper.

"Damn him," he said. The business card read:

KEVIN MONTGOMERY

CIVIL ENGINEER FOR THE CITY OF ALBUQUERQUE

Darren examined the embossed black lettering, the official seal of the city, the hand written phone number, and the underlined words, "my personal cell." It was creased in the middle and Darren tore it there first, then matched the halves and tore it again and again. He stalked over to the overflowing wastebasket and dropped the confetti inside an empty chip bag. Darren's phone chimed and he let out a relieved sigh.

SHEILA CAUGHT A GLIMPSE OF THE MOUNTAINS, BETWEEN THE ROWS OF houses, glowing a deep red in the last light of the sun. The color made her pause.

"Beautiful, isn't it?" Jen said. "Sandia means watermelon in Spanish." Sheila nodded.

In less than a minute, the slim disc of the sun disappeared. They watched the mountains fade to pale pink, and started walking again. Sheila hugged her arms around her waist, trying to still the butterflies that started when she heard her name sung from the bandstand. She hoped her face wasn't still the color of those mountains.

She couldn't believe Darren had sung to her, much less kissed her. She'd noticed Kevin shaking his head, as if impressed but angry, when Darren released her from the dip. Kevin's expression confirmed her suspicions about he and Darren being rivals and Sheila decided she was glad she'd be leaving tomorrow.

Jen chattered about the adobe houses they passed in the four blocks it took to get to hers, stopping often to point out her favorite design elements.

"Sorry for monopolizing the conversation," Jen said. "I'm an architect and I get a little carried away when I have a new audience." Sheila waved her off. She'd been happy to keep the conversation off of herself.

"I'm much obliged," she said when she emerged from the bathroom.

"You don't sound like you're from the East Coast," Jen said.

"Who said I was from the East Coast?"

Jen regarded her with a puzzled expression and Sheila recalled Darren's guess at her accent. She felt angry with herself for slipping up. Momma always said, "Better to slip with your feet than your tongue."

"My mother is Southern," she said, calling on one of her fabricated answers. She declined Jen's offer to take her back to the park. It was full dark now and she walked forward like she knew the way to Menaul Boulevard. The repairman said the hotels were there. Jen's street was poorly lit and Sheila dropped the bag off her shoulder when she felt she was being followed.

"If I sang to you, would you give me a kiss, Sheila?" a voice called from behind. She didn't look back at the snickering.

"I'm fresh out of kisses," she said, glancing over her shoulder. "How about a kick in the teeth?" She counted three figures and quickened her pace.

"Ohhh," one of the boys said.

"How you gonna treat me like that?" the first boy called out. She heard more chortling and she began to swing her bag.

An approaching car turned the corner, illuminating not only the boys behind her but also the park to the east. Sheila corrected her route. Damn near three thousand miles I've traveled, she thought, to find trouble in Albuquerque. *Stupid Rio Grande.*

She crossed the lawn to the bandstand, pretending to watch the sound man disassemble the equipment and the boys fell away. The band members were gone, and in the nearly vacant park, she was sorry she hadn't waited thirty more minutes for the toilet. Darren had surprised her with the kiss and as usual, her instinct had been to bolt.

"You didn't finish your wine," Darren said.

Sheila stiffened at the sound of his voice and he wondered if he'd blown it with her. Liz must have been right; Sheila had been embarrassed by his serenade. However, she'd come back, so he thought he could salvage the evening with her. He rose from the cushion of the folded quilt and carried the two wine glasses over to where she stood. He was relieved when she accepted the glass.

"I guess I got a little carried away with the singing. I'm sorry if I embarrassed you," he said. Sheila arched a brow but said nothing. "I'm glad you came back. Again."

She stared at him for a long moment before looking away. Her lips twitched and he decided that she was fighting a smile.

"To Sam's Auto, for bringing us together," he said. Sheila didn't raise her glass and Darren flashed another grin. "It's bad luck if you don't drink."

"It's even worse luck if you slip me a mickey," she said.

Darren threw his head back and laughed. Sheila raised her glass but instead of drinking she poured the wine into the grass. "That's a vintage Bourgogne," he said.

"Then you should share it with someone who'll appreciate it," she said. Sheila set the glass on the stage and slung her back pack onto her shoulder.

Darren hesitated a beat before snatching up the empty glass and the quilt. "How considerate of you to choose the path to my house. Would you mind carrying the basket?" The corners of her mouth pulled up. "This quilt is cumbersome," he said.

"Your grandmother would have a fit if she saw that quilt on the grass," she said and took the basket.

"My grandmother didn't make it, I did," he said and Sheila scoffed. "I'm serious. When I was in grad school I couldn't afford a diamond, so I made this 'wedding ring' quilt to present when I proposed."

"The lady declined on account of it being too heavy to wear on her finger?"

Darren stopped walking. "No one has ever made a joke about that."

"You expect me to believe that line?"

"It's not a line," was all he said when he caught up to her. If Sheila heard him, she made no move to acknowledge his defense.

They arrived at an intersection and she set the basket down after crossing the street. "I guess I've carried this empty basket far enough. Good night, Darren Abruzzo."

"Would you join me for a night cap?"

"Thank you, no."

Darren jogged in front of her and turned around. The quilt bounced on his knees as he walked backwards. "My house is the tan bungalow right there." He pointed to a house with a black car in the driveway.

"A bungalow, how charming."

"It *is* rather charming. I think you'll like it. And I tell you what, you can have the keys to my Challenger and leave any time you want." Darren rested the quilt atop his mailbox. "One drink, no mickeys," he said. "Please?"

over her hair again. "You look Italian. Are you?"

Sheila ignored the question and turned to the last photo. "And this one?"

"This is from my most recent vacation," he said. "I went to Havana last year. I wanted to see Cuba before it gets ruined with imported American culture."

She peered at the image of an elderly man smoking a cigar. Something in his face reminded Sheila of her deceased grandfather and she turned away, draining the water bottle. "Thanks for the drink," she said. "I'd better get to my hotel."

"What? Water isn't a 'drink.' Come here." Darren took her hand and led her to the wine racks in the dining room, describing each section. He laced his fingers through hers, his thumb rubbing jerky circles over hers. She liked the nervous gesture and she was glad the bravado Darren showed in front of his friends softened without their audience.

Sheila chose a Malbec and sipped slowly while Darren finished the tour. The house was larger than it looked from the outside, with three bedrooms and a spacious backyard. She was about to protest when Darren refreshed her glass, but then he asked where she was headed after the starter was replaced in her car.

She took a gulp, then put her wine glass on one of the tall speakers. "I love this song," she said and turned up the stereo. "Her voice is so sensual."

Darren looped an arm around her waist and pulled her close. Sheila let a sigh escape and rested her head on his shoulder, drawing in his scent. It was musky, sweat mingled with some kind of soap. Something familiar she couldn't name. They danced in slow circles around the living room for the rest of the song.

"Why don't you set those keys down?" He didn't wait for her response before plucking the keys from her grasp and sweeping her into a dip.

"Wait a minute. You promised I could hold onto your keys and drive off in your car any time I felt like it. Are you a liar as well as a thief?" she asked, looking up at him.

"Thief?"

Sheila pushed on his hand and he pulled her out of the dip but did not release her.

"You stole a kiss."

"What?"

"At the park," Sheila said. "I guess you're so used to taking what you want it never occurred to you to ask?"

Darren laughed and his breath tickled her eyelashes. "That was only a little peck."

Sheila broke the embrace and retreated into the bathroom. Inside, she rested on the closed door and groaned. *Why hadn't she let him kiss her?* The cold water she splashed on her face was useless.

She told herself she would stop torturing them both and leave right after she peed. But then the song changed in the stereo. Billie Holiday, her favorite vocalist, crooned a melancholy tune and Sheila swayed to the music.

She stretched her arms and rolled her neck. The French braid had to go. It was long past when she usually freed her hair. She loosened it, rubbing her fingers over her scalp. That felt so good she unbuttoned the top of her dress to slip off her bra.

Pausing with her hand on the hook, she wondered if Darren would notice. The dress was two sizes too big, so probably not. Sheila unfastened the bra and sighed. She'd slip it into her pocket before leaving the bathroom.

"Wash your hands and call a cab," she mumbled. They'd met a few hours ago. She had no business imagining whether or not Darren would notice her lack of underwear.

Underwear.

The flush in her cheeks had little to do with the two glasses of Malbec.

Several months ago, when she'd driven through the Carolinas, Sheila ran out of clean panties. She discovered then she liked going commando. It had felt illicit at first, and she often wondered what it would be like for a man to discover her secret. Now she smiled, imagining Darren's reaction if he reached his hand under her dress and—

DARREN WALKED DOWN THE HALL TO LISTEN AT THE BATHROOM DOOR. Was she talking to herself? "Sheila? Are you okay in there?" He tipped the glass to his mouth and finished the wine.

"Do you have anything for mosquito bites?" Sheila called. He turned the knob, pushing the door open. It was immediately shoved back at him. "Hello? Ever hear of knocking?" Sheila said.

"What?"

"Miss Manners 101: a closed door indicates a desire for privacy."

Darren shook his head. "I don't believe I've ever been given an etiquette lesson on how to behave in my own house."

"No wonder you're so bored with the local girls, they let you get away with too much." Her voice, muffled through the door, sounded annoyed but then he heard her giggle.

"Do you want the chigger cream or not?"

"Never mind, I've found it."

Darren heard the door on the medicine cabinet click back into place and he turned the door knob again, opening slowly. When she didn't immediately shove the door back at him, Darren eased his body into the bathroom.

Welts had risen on her neck and shoulders, scattered like pink polka dots on her fair skin. "Don't put that stuff on your neck, you'll taste like medicine when I kiss you."

"You've just failed Miss Manners, TNME," she said in a haughty voice.

"TNME?"

"The New Millennium Edition: At no point is a woman supposed to stop caring for herself, in the event that it may bring a man discomfort."

The bantering was driving Darren crazy. She was right about the local girls whom he known since coming to Albuquerque for undergrad. Sheila was stunning and enigmatic. The sight of her on the edge of his bath tub quickened his blood. Her hair, wavy from the braid, was longer than he'd guessed and swept over a bared shoulder. But it was the sight of her black bra discarded on the white tile floor that had him teetering at the edge of control.

"*Dio aiutami!*"

"I'm sorry, what—" Sheila looked up at him and Darren forced himself to stay in the doorway.

"I said, *God help me.*" He shook his head. "I'm usually quick to learn from my mistakes but I'm having a hard time not pulling you into my arms and kissing you." He watched her eyes go wide.

"It was wrong of me to steal a peck at the park." He held out a hand and waited until she took it and rose to her feet before he continued. "I've been thinking about kissing you from the moment I saw you but now I know I can't be satisfied with a kiss."

Sheila's smile faded. "Why?"

Darren still managed to keep his body in the doorway.

"*Perché?* Why? Because *bellissima*," he leaned in and lowered his voice. "If I kiss you now I'm not going to stop until I have your legs wrapped around my hips and your moans of pleasure in my ears."

SHEILA LICKED HER LIPS. "I HAVE TO GO." DARREN DIDN'T MOVE AND she realized her lusty voice didn't sound very convincing.

"I'll call you a cab," he said.

"Say it in Italian," she whispered.

"*Io te voglio.*"

Sheila closed her eyes. "Yeah, I have to... call a go, I mean go a taxi. Why didn't you tell me you spoke Italian?"

Darren chuckled and his hand slackened on hers. Sheila forced her eyes open and she knew it was ridiculous to feel disappointed when he stepped back to let her pass. "You forgot something," he said.

She whirled around and gasped when she saw him holding her bra. "I forgot about that." Sheila reached for it and knew she must be turning the color of the Sandias when he brought it to his cheek.

"I guess I won't get to see the matching panties, so I'll have to use my imagination. Are they silk?"

"I'm not wearing any panties," Sheila blurted. She hadn't made it out of the bathroom and she gasped when Darren seized her shoulders and backed her against the door.

"Is that true?" Darren growled.

Sheila swallowed at the primal look in his eyes. Darren was definitely *not* calling her a taxi. She hoped he didn't see the trembling in her hands when she brought them up to his shoulders.

"Don't you want to find out for yourself?" she said.

CHAPTER 4

DARREN DEVOURED SHEILA'S MOUTH. HE MEANT TO BE GENTLE BUT the taunt that she was bare under the thin dress made the kiss urgent. When she opened for him and he got his first, sweet taste of her, he couldn't restrain himself. He delved in, groaning when her tongue met his hungry thrusts.

I'm not wearing any panties.

He pulled back. "Is that true?" Darren didn't wait for her answer. He nipped her plump bottom lip then sucked it into his mouth. Sheila's voice echoed in his head again and he scooped her into his arms. He had to get her to the bed before he found out for himself.

She linked her arms around his neck and he smiled. Never had he felt more relieved to have a woman call his bluff. Offering to get her a taxi had been risky and Darren had summoned his best courtroom finesse to pull it off. "God Sheila, you're the most beautiful—"

She pulled his mouth back to hers, and he groaned in approval, angling her down onto the bed. Darren cupped her breasts through the dress and she arched into his touch. He brushed a thumb over one of her nipples and stopped abruptly.

SHEILA HELD HER BREATH. DARREN TUGGED ONE OF THE DRESS STRAPS over her arm to bare her breasts. "Nipple rings?"

She flushed and brought her hands up to cover herself. Darren was the first man to see her jewelry and his bewildered reaction was not what she'd anticipated. He captured her wrists and said something in Italian, brushing his lips over one taut peak and then the other. He could have been saying, *I'm sorry* or *they're hideous* but she lost interest in the translation when his tongue flicked one ring, then moved to the other. Six months after getting pierced, she was still tender. It was worse during her periods but she loved them. They made her feel sexy. Darren tickled them with the tip of his tongue and she arched again. He released her and Sheila ran her nails over his shoulders.

She moaned when he sucked a metal ring into his mouth. In the shower, she'd discovered the pressure of the massage setting could make her climax. That was nothing compared to Darren's hot tongue. It was so incredibly intense, she felt like a dam had broken between her legs. As if he sensed the wetness pooling there, Darren's hand moved under her dress.

"*È vero!*"

"What?"

"It's true," Darren said. His fingers brushed over her sex. "Ahh! You're so wet for me."

She meant to pull his hand from between her legs. She should stop, she thought, but then he began rubbing her swollen cleft. She bit her bottom lip, and pressed her hips against him.

"Oh, Sheila."

She gasped when his hand left her. "Don't stop." Darren chuckled and the sound of his belt buckle hitting the floor brought her eyes open. He pulled the polo shirt over his head and dropped it on top of his jeans. His chest was carpeted in black hair that tapered to a line over his navel and fanned out again over his stiff sex.

"You go commando too?" she said. Sheila tried to keep her eyes off his cock and failed. "I don't think that will fit."

He bent to run his fingers over the swell of her breast before slipping a hand behind her back. He lifted her torso off the bed to remove her dress. "It will fit," he said.

Sheila knew she should protest but then he took one of her nipples into his mouth again and pressed her back onto the bed. Instead of protesting, she was wishing he would put his hand back to releasing the orgasm that was painfully close.

Darren skimmed his palm over her stomach and she wiggled her hips. She was relieved when he took the hint, pressing his fingers onto the spot where the pressure was the greatest.

"Yes," she breathed and clutched his shoulders. His mouth made a tiny popping sound when he released her nipple. His tongue was so hot that without it, the air felt cold on her moist nipple. Sheila kept shifting, turning, urging more and more of her body into his knowing hands.

"I want to taste you, here," Darren said. He slowed the rhythm of his fingers stroking her clit and she met his smoldering eyes. The idea of his hot tongue on her most sensitive flesh sent her over the edge. She squeezed her thighs together, crying out. The pressure melted into waves of pleasure.

"You're *so* beautiful," he whispered. Darren brushed his lips over hers and parted her legs; they felt heavy and useless. "I have to be inside you, Sheila."

Something tickled the back of her mind but it was so foggy, still reveling in the orgasm, that she couldn't process the thought. *The shower head didn't deliver anything like that.* What was it she needed to say? She wasn't easy? They should stop—

"Look at me, Sheila."

She forced her eyes to focus on Darren's face and saw the primal look in his eyes. It made her swallow a breath.

"It's been a while..." she croaked. Her cheeks grew warm and she started to turn her face but his palm cupped her cheek.

"WE'LL TAKE IT SLOW." HE BENT TO KISS HER WITHOUT MOVING FROM between her legs. The tip of his cock pressed against her damp heat and a shiver passed between them. "You surprised me with these but I like them," he said. He took one of the nipple rings between his thumb and index finger and twisted it. Sheila pressed her head back into the pillow and moaned.

The sound was like a purr in her throat and it deepened when he latched onto the other nipple with his mouth, caressing the peak with his tongue. "That's right," he murmured when she sighed. "Relax, honey." He throbbed at her opening but he forced himself to wait, even as she grew slicker against him again.

"More."

"More? More of this?" he asked, raking his teeth over her nipple.

Sheila mewed and rolled her hips. "That," she said. It was Darren's turn to growl when she took the tip of him into her body.

"*Dio aiutami.*"

"Oh God, yes! More Italian."

Sweat bloomed on his forehead and he gripped her hips. "You're so tight," he said. He switched back to Italian, telling Sheila he wanted to make love to her gently and slowly but—

She tried to wiggle her hips free of his grip. "Now Darren, give it to me now."

He ground his teeth. Her demand made him want to abandon restraint but he didn't want to hurt her. He slid his hands to her thighs and spread them wider. When he withdrew, he wanted to smile at Sheila's frown. He felt triumphant when he reentered her slick heat with the tip of his cock, and her sheath clamped around him. "Oh Sheila." He tightened his grip on her.

"Oh Darren," she giggled.

She flexed around him, teasing. With another groan, Darren relented and surged forward, seating himself into her completely. Sheila screamed and he forced his body to go still. "Are you okay? Did I hurt you?"

"Yes, I mean no. Don't stop." She dug her nails into his ass and Darren obeyed. He began to surge and retract, then surge again. His head fell onto her shoulder and he tried to maintain a slow rhythm until Sheila started to contract around him again. He panted against her cheek, trying to hold back through her orgasm but as she peaked, Darren gave into the pleasure. His body made slapping sounds against hers until they both cried out.

HERRERA CRUSHED THE EMPTY CAN IN HIS LEFT HAND THEN CHUCKED it onto the floor of the passenger's seat with the other empties. He hadn't been following the subject closely because of the hidden tracking device in her vehicle. Every half hour he checked her status on his laptop. At 3 P.M., he was surprised when her transmitter was signaling east of him, in Albuquerque.

Backtracking nearly sixty miles, he'd found the vehicle but not SW. For sixty sweaty minutes, Herrera paced in the shade across from the repair shop. His boss would be furious if his daily report said he didn't know where she was. He was relieved when SW had returned, but now Herrera was camped outside a residence instead of enjoying a hot meal and a hot shower.

Who the hell was the man? And why after all this time had she decided to go home with some hooked nose fool who thought he could sing? Herrera didn't care but the boss would want to know.

He downloaded the pictures he took of them talking in the park and walking to the man's house. Not very good images, but at least they were something. Herrera gritted his teeth. He wasn't a goddamned PI. The only reason he took this assignment was to get his ass back in San Diego.

Herrera watched a shadow pass in front of the window, and the lights were extinguished. The Subject hadn't strayed from the expected route for eight days. Now that they were a day's drive from his hometown, he was stuck in New Mexico. He cursed and punched the dashboard.

CHAPTER 5

DARREN IGNORED THE NOISE COMING FROM HIS BLACKBERRY. HE breathed in the faint, floral scent of Sheila's hair. It felt silky, trapped between his head and the pillowcase. His cell phone pinged again, alerting him to another email and Sheila twitched. He should retrieve it from the pocket of his jeans and at least check in with his secretary, but he couldn't pry himself from Sheila.

He loved the feel of her delicious body. One of her legs was tangled between his, and she faced away from him with her head nestled in the crook of his right elbow. Darren lifted his free hand to stroke her hair. She sighed and his erection stirred against her back. He slid his hand over her shoulder and down to her hip. Should he call in sick? Spend the day making love to her? He mentally ran through his calendar and decided he could probably take the day off.

His hand halted its exploration. Sheila hadn't revealed her travel plans. He didn't know when her car would be fixed or if she would be in a hurry to get back on the road. He didn't know where she was headed either, and the unknowns had Darren tightening his arms around her.

"Mmm," Sheila said. She stretched her legs and Darren kissed the side of her neck. "What time is it?"

"*Buongiorno, bellissima.* It's almost 9."

"Really?" Sheila sat up.

"Where are you going?"

"The bathroom."

"I meant after you pick up your car. Are you headed back East?"

"Oh... no. West. I'll be right back." Darren dropped his arms. Sheila stood up and yelped.

Darren jumped off the bed. "What's the matter?"

"There's something alive over there."

He laughed when she pointed to a black mass on top of her dress. "I wouldn't have pegged you for a Star Wars fan." Then he cleared his throat at her murderous look. Apparently she wasn't quoting Luke Skywalker. "That's my cat, Charlie."

"Don't let him lick my dress!" she said. Charlie hissed and she screamed again.

"It's okay, Sheila." Darren picked up the animal and she darted past them into the bathroom. He shook his head and pulled on a pair of Jockeys before opening a can of food for the cat.

"Do you prefer tea or coffee?" he called down the hall.

"Coffee."

He dropped a pod into the Keurig and pressed the start button on the coffee maker. Standing before the French doors, Darren didn't see the patio furniture or the hot tub in his backyard. He was lost in thought, hoping he could persuade Sheila to stay.

Where was she headed? It dawned on him that he knew almost nothing about her. He was sure he'd never met a woman who talked so little about herself. Sheila had a quiet, unassuming manner but she wasn't timid, he decided. Whenever she spoke, her words were direct and often sharp.

Darren turned to check on her and was surprised to find the beauty standing before the coffee machine. Sheila wore his wrinkled polo shirt, and her eyes were closed. She leaned over the coffee pot, sniffing.

"You have to be the best-looking woman I've ever seen," he said.

"I get that a lot."

He laughed and pulled her into his arms. Her beauty was more than the fresh bloom of youth, he thought as she smiled up at him. The more he looked at her, the more beautiful she seemed. Her cheekbone, jawline, lip line, the dark ring around her pale green irises—everything—was flawless. "I enjoyed being with you last night. Will you play hooky with me today?"

He brushed his lips against hers. Then he touched them to the mole below the corner of her left eye, her right cheek, her nose, and finally her lips. Darren pulled her closer and set to exploring her mouth as if he had all day to do it.

She made the little mewing sound that drove him crazy last night, until the beep on the coffee maker had them both jumping. Sheila stepped back. "Why did your engagement end?"

He tried to hide his surprise. "Do you take cream?" he asked, turning to fill the creamer dish. He put it in the microwave and set the timer.

"Well?"

"Don't you want to hear my cocktail party answers first? What I do, where I'm from, my favorite type of music? I want to hear yours. We did this kind of backwards, you know."

"You already told me you went to law school; you're some kind of attorney. Immigration, judging by the books on your desk. You also told me that because of your dad's job, you moved around a lot growing up. And your CD rack is filled with mostly jazz."

Darren's amusement turned to annoyance when his home phone rang.

Sheila opened one of the French doors and flinched from the

warm air rushing in. It carried the spicy scents of creosote and sage. An air conditioning unit kicked on, humming, and a dog barked. She shut the door and turned back to the counter, filling a mug with equal parts coffee and cream.

Darren returned to the kitchen. "I don't want to leave," he said. "But there's a 'fire'—" he made air quotes with his fingers—"at the office. I'll try to get back home as soon as I can. Will you stay?"

"You didn't answer my question."

He took a sip of her coffee. "Wow. You like a little coffee with your cream, huh?" She gave him an expectant look and he relented. "Wendy blamed our breakup on my temper but she had an abusive childhood. She carried around a lot of pain and anger..."

"And you broke it off," she said.

"I wanted her to go to therapy. I offered to go with her but she wouldn't face it." Sheila nodded. He looked out the window while his jaw clenched. "Will you stay?" he asked.

"I haven't decided."

Darren looked like he wanted to say more but nodded instead. He took her hand and she followed him to the bedroom.

"Do people often comment on the intensity of your eyes?" He brushed a lock of hair out of her face.

"Do my eyes bother you?"

"No, they're my favorite color. I guess what's unnerving is... how you seem to see everything."

"Oh, I miss a lot," she said. *Like how we didn't use a condom last night.* She scooted back on the bed, balancing her coffee cup, and winced at the soreness between her legs.

In spite of herself, Sheila thought about saying more, explaining, but Darren turned to the closet and the words got stuck in her throat. She wanted to tell him she didn't have sex with random men; she never, ever had sex without a condom. And yet she had. Her stomach flipped and

Sheila shut down her imagination when it started with all the what-ifs. Darren went to the bathroom to shave and she sipped from the mug.

When she looked up again, he was dressed in a navy pin stripe suit with a pale blue shirt. The color made his olive skin glow. She felt his eyes on her and she looked away, into the open closet. It was neatly organized, like the rest of the house, but a tube of blue balls on the floor seemed out of place amongst his shoes. If she had yielded to her father's plans, she would have been married to a racket ball-playing attorney back East.

"What are you thinking?" Darren asked.

She met his gaze. "You clean up well."

"The suit makes the man, or the man makes the suit?" he asked.

She walked on her knees over to him. She folded the silk tie into a perfect knot then smoothed the collar over his neck. "The man definitely makes the suit."

Darren captured her face between his palms. Her body responded to the kiss instantly. When her hands went to his waist, he pulled back. She flushed when she realized she'd been going for his fly.

"I don't want this to be a one nighter," he said, his voice rough. "Stay, Sheila. Help yourself to whatever's in the fridge. Take a bath if you want. I'll try to get back by lunch time."

"The office will be ashes if you don't get to that fire," she said. Darren winced and she felt a stab of guilt for not saying yes.

She wanted to stay but she didn't trust the feelings he stirred in her. Yesterday, she'd told herself that going to the concert was not "getting involved." Then she'd agreed to one drink, which had turned into two... which had led to breaking her rule.

No, she hadn't broken her rule, a rule she'd enacted to keep herself safe. She'd annihilated it. *Unprotected sex.*

If she spent any more time with this man, with his delicious lips, his expert hands, and his irresistible body, Sheila worried she wouldn't be able to go back to her life on the road. She would want more of Darren and more of the cataclysmic orgasms he'd coaxed out of her.

A shiver ran through her at the memory and his face darkened. He stepped back. "Wait." Before he could turn away, she grabbed his tie and kissed him goodbye.

CHAPTER 6

DRIVING TO WORK, DARREN'S HAND KEPT GOING TO HIS TIE. IT WAS crinkled in the middle where Sheila had used it to pull his mouth back to hers. The kiss had left them both panting and it made him hopeful she would be there when he got home, but he wasn't sure.

He was accustomed to directing the pace with women. Not knowing what she would do irked him. Last night he'd been caught up in the chase but in the Monday morning sun, the attorney reminded himself he was too old to play games.

"She's too young for me," he said aloud. The traffic light seemed to stay red forever. "And I don't do long distance relationships."

He ran his fingers over the tie again, fighting the notion that Sheila was toying with him. Yes, she was young but he didn't sense any pretense about her. He considered her shrewd attention to detail and felt certain there was more to the girl than her knee-buckling good looks. He hoped he'd get a chance to find out.

Darren sighed and glanced out the window. The driver in the car to his left wore a bemused expression. He realized his window was down and she'd overheard him. Ignoring her tittering, he removed the lid from his travel coffee mug. The steam fogged the lenses on his sunglasses when he blew into the mug.

He whipped off the Oakleys, only to wince at the sun glinting off a couple balloons tied to one of the storefronts. The signal turned green and Darren accelerated slowly, smiling at the silver mylar balloons, and the idea they inspired.

SHEILA TURNED ON THE SHOWER, THEN SHUT IT OFF AND PLUGGED THE bath tub. It took nearly a minute for the water to turn hot and when it did she'd changed her mind again. She left the bathroom and knelt on the living room floor, opening her Coach purse.

The tumbled leather handbag was one of her few indulgences from her old lifestyle. She wondered, if Stan had seen it, would he think the thousand dollar accessory was a knockoff? Smiling wryly, she withdrew her phone, and fingered the business card Darren gave her before he'd left.

The first of three voicemail messages featured a female voice. "Sheila, I wish you would call me. I didn't know your father was going to pull that stunt with Neil Fitzgerald. I promise—"

Sheila deleted the message without listening to the rest. She already decided Mirabelle Chase wasn't a part of the scheme. Mother probably didn't know Father had lured Sheila back to Chase Manor last April, to try to coerce her into marriage. As if she would marry a man named *Cornelius.*

The next message was from Sam's Auto. *Should she be relieved or annoyed that the repair was delayed until 2 p.m.?* She had four hours to kill. Would Darren return before then? She recalled his aggressive, masterful touch. Her nipples begin to tingle. "I shouldn't stay," she said aloud.

The final message was a made-up song. The words *call me* were repeated a dozen times by a soulful voice. It made her ache for her oldest friend, Andrea Washington. Sheila hit the call back button and left a long voice mail. She had an agreement with Andrea, to check in every couple days, to keep her from worrying. It had been three days since their last chat. Sheila grinned, imagining Andrea's face when she heard the update.

Opportunities to shock Andrea were scarce because of the stark rules Sheila had made for her new life. Avoid attachments and stay on the move to keep the fear and the nightmares at bay. Her last surprising bit of news had been a teary recounting of the fiasco at Chase Manor.

Neil had reacted poorly when Sheila rejected his proposal. He'd snatched her arm, twisting it painfully, and threatened her to reconsider declining a Fitzgerald. The anger in his beady eyes had shocked her.

Later, Sheila learned Neil had crashed in the stock market. She was sure Michael W. Chase promised him a hefty pay off if he married her. The scheme had renewed Sheila's belief that she couldn't trust her father and she vowed she'd never see him again.

Three years ago, she'd adopted Sheila as her first name. On the rare occasions when she saw them, her brothers and mother addressed her as Sheila, but her father refused to honor her request. She hoped legalizing the change and dropping her last name would punctuate the point that she wanted nothing more to do with Michael W. Chase; Sheila disowned *him*.

It took her about two minutes to decide on adopting Andrea's last name. In their hearts, they *were* sisters. In a few months the paperwork would be completed and she would officially shed the identity of Elizabeth Chase. If only she could rid herself of Liz Chase's memories, she thought with a shudder.

What would it be like to have a normal life? To have a permanent address again? To live without the fear of one day, being murdered by the man who had killed her grandfather and her boyfriend?

Before her world had been shattered, Sheila had dreams of becoming a surgeon. She'd planned to travel throughout developing countries and repair damaged clefs on children. Now she suffered horrible dreams if she stayed in one place too long. She broke into a sweat at the sight of blood and she could barely contend with her irregular periods. There had been so much blood on her grandfather, so much blood—

"I am safe," she said loudly. She closed her eyes, repeated the three words, and focused on keeping her breathing slow and even. Her psychiatrist would be proud of her, she thought. But then she *had* been working on this for three years. Sheila wondered if Dr. Baldwin would show his surprise when she saw him for her check-up in two days and told him about Darren.

Dropping her phone back into her purse with a sigh, she returned to the bathroom and unplugged the tub. A misshapen bar of soap lay in the holder. It made a slurpy sound when she pried it up with her fingers.

Sheila inhaled deeply. It was Darren's scent. Her lids fluttered as she imagined him naked, in the shower. She tossed the slimy soap back in place. "He's a complication you don't need, Sheila." With her clean hand, she turned the spigot on again and opened the valve for the shower head.

The doorbell rang, and she shut off the water. It rang again, followed by a heavy handed knock. Sheila crept around the corner toward the front door. She didn't know if she should answer it and after a third ring, retreating footsteps could be heard. Peeking through a slit in the curtains, she saw a messenger ride off on a bicycle. She was tempted to call the number on the card Darren left but the street was empty of vehicles except a white van parked a few doors down.

Sheila dropped the curtain and opened a closet door to look for a towel only it wasn't the closet. On last night's tour, Darren had skipped the garage. When Sheila flipped on the light switch, she made up her mind to stay another day.

IT WAS 3 O'CLOCK BY THE TIME DARREN LEFT THE OFFICE. THE MESSENGER had returned the envelope containing the spa pass he'd sent Sheila as an enticement to stay. He was still hopeful when, arriving home, he tried the front door and found it was locked. But the house was empty.

The attorney went through each room, hoping for a note. Her bag was gone, and he realized with a start, he didn't even know her phone number. He cursed himself for not getting it from her before he left.

The only evidence of Sheila's visit was the rumpled bed sheets and her half empty coffee cup. "Dammit," he shouted.

The refrigerator didn't have much to offer but he stood staring into it. All day his mind kept coming back to Sheila. Each time the phone rang, he answered with the hope her coy voice would be on the other end.

Charlie meowed at the back door. "She didn't even leave a note," he said. Staring into the yard, Darren wondered how she left the house if the front door was locked. Still hopeful, he checked the hammock on the side of the house and tried to remember if the French doors had been locked when he let Charlie into the house. He fed the animal and carried last night's wine bottle and the cat food can to the recycle bins. He turned on the garage light and stopped short.

"What the hell?" He stood staring at Sheila's bag. It sat on the ground next to the spot usually occupied by his motorcycle.

The Norton Commando first belonged to his father, who bought it new in 1969. Darren had inherited it after his dad died. It was expensive to bring back from New York but Darren liked the idea of restoring it. So far that's all it was, an idea. The thought of Sheila riding it made him smile, then grimace. It was hardly in running condition.

As if to contradict that thought, he heard the motorcycle rolling up the street, purring like a well-fed kitten. Darren opened the garage door and watched Sheila ease out of his helmet, still straddling the Norton.

"What's with the applause?" she asked.

"You're amazing. How did you get the thing running?"

"Oh, she's okay. She just needs a little lovin'." Sheila dismounted and ran her gloved hand over the cracked leather seat.

Darren grinned and bit back the quip that leapt to mind. "Did you put a new battery in it?"

She shook her head. "Spark plug and air in the tires."

"I'm glad you stayed." He went to hug her and realized he still held the recycling. When he emptied his hands, Sheila had picked up her bag.

"I need to pick up my car," she said.

"Oh." He wiped his hands on a towel. "I can drive you over to Sam's. Or we could walk."

Darren held his breath while Sheila deliberated. "We can walk," she said finally. "Is the building still standing?"

"What? Oh, the fire. Yeah. It probably could have been handled by someone else, half of the staff is working on this one case. I left my files with Stan and moved a few things on the calendar so I could take tomorrow off." Darren reached over and took her hand. "How are you?"

"Fine. You work with Stan?"

"Yep. Where did you ride?"

"When I bought the spark plugs, a guy at the auto parts store told me about route 536."

Darren stopped walking. "Route 536? You didn't go out to the Sandia Crest, did you?"

"No, the guy said the twisties were sweet out there but I stuck around town. The clutch cable probably needs to be replaced."

"Oh." Darren began moving again and his thumb rubbed her knuckles. "There's great hiking out there. Do you like hiking?"

"Sometimes." To herself she was thinking, *hiking in this heat?*

"One of my favorite spots isn't far from town. It has a natural hot springs tucked in a beautiful vista point. I'd like to take you there tomorrow."

Sheila didn't answer and he didn't press her because they arrived at Sam's. The owner was standing in front of the shop, smoking a cigarette. Sam greeted Darren in Spanish, and shook Sheila's hand. He showed her the old starter and ran down a list of suggestions for future work.

"If you're driving to San Diego, you'll need new tires."

Darren bent to examine the tires and nodded in agreement.

"These will make it," she said and followed Sam back inside. Darren waited by the door while she paid and held it open when she exited.

"What's in San Diego?" he asked.

"The Pacific."

Darren ran his hand over the curve of the car's headlight. "A Mazda RX-8. I had one of its predecessors in college. Manual?"

"Of course," she said.

"Sounds like it needs a lot more work. You sure you can make it to San Diego?"

"Yes, Dexter will make it. And I can do some of the repairs myself."

"Dexter? You're supposed to give a car a girl's name," he said.

"Well, since I'm the owner, I get to pick the name and this here is Dexter."

Darren leaned against the driver door and took Sheila's hand again.

"I thought about you all day, Sheila, and I kept hoping to hear from you. When I came home and you weren't there, I felt like a kid who'd missed Christmas. And then you roll up on my dad's old Norton. What other talents do you have?"

"None. Unless you count being a professional vagabond as a talent."

Darren tugged her closer. "If all that's in San Diego is the Pacific, stay with me for a couple of days. Tonight I'll make dinner for you, and to-morrow we'll go hiking."

SHEILA FOUGHT A SMILE AND FORCED HER GAZE TO A HUMMINGBIRD flitting around a cactus flower. "I guess the Pacific will keep," she said finally. Darren's arms came around her shoulders. When he squeezed, and Sheila breathed in his earthy scent, she battled the urge to beam with delight.

"Mind if we go by the store to pick up dinner ingredients?" he asked.

"I'm feeling kinda grungy after messing with the bike and riding all day."

"Well," he said, smiling. "Although I'd hate to miss the opportunity to shower with you, what if I drop you off at my place and you clean up while I shop?"

Sheila handed him the keys. Darren asked about her food preferences and teased her when she declared herself a pescatarian.

"Is that the new PC term for fish eater?"

"I don't know about PC," she said archly.

"If you like sushi, there's a great place in Santa Fe."

Sheila wrinkled her nose. "Sushi, in New Mexico?" The traffic light turned red and Darren leaned over the center console to capture her mouth. He nipped her bottom lip before shifting into first gear.

"Hey now, don't knock New Mexico. It may not have the Pacific Ocean but it *is* the 'Land of Enchantment.' We've got rich history, cultural diversity, *and* good sushi."

When they arrived at his house, Darren kissed her so long and so deeply Sheila thought he would forgo the grocery store. She felt giddy as she undressed for the shower. She threw the sweaty jeans and t-shirt into the washer, along with a load of her other road clothes. The water pressure was poor, so she ran back to the garage naked and turned off the washer. Once the temperature and pressure felt right, she stepped into the shower and set to shampooing her hair.

The motorcycle ride was fun but she was sore from the Norton's poor suspension; it was bad enough to rattle a filling loose. Sheila rinsed her hair and set the shower head to the massage setting. It felt good on her arms and legs. She was combing conditioner through her hair when she heard, "Hi honey, I'm home."

"That was quick," she said and worked the conditioner to the ends of her hair. When the door opened, she was ready to chide Darren and remind him of the rules for a closed door.

"Want me to wash your back?"

The shower curtain pulled back to reveal Stan, a look of shock spreading over his face. Sheila clutched her breasts and Stan jerked the curtain back into place.

"Sheila—sorry," he sputtered. "I thought you were Darren. Sorry."

Still covering her chest, she peeked out the curtain but Stan had gone. Why is he here? she wondered. When she emerged from the bathroom in Darren's robe, she found Stan awkward and Sandia-red on the sofa.

"Sorry. I thought I was pulling a gag on Darren. He left the office in a hurry and now I know why."

"He went to the store," she said flatly.

"Oh. Well. I stopped by to see if he wanted to play racquet ball but I guess he'll be busy." Stan walked to the door, trying to look normal. "I'm uh, sorry about the shower."

Sheila watched him walk off and locked the front door.

CHAPTER 7

SHEILA WATCHED DARREN FIDDLING WITH THE PASTA ATTACHMENT for the Kitchen Aid. "You're making the linguini from scratch?" she said.

"Italian, remember? I grew up in my grandmother's kitchen. She wouldn't approve of the machine, but I like my modern appliances. Do you like to cook?"

"No, but I like to eat."

"Oh good," he laughed. "You're going to eat well tonight. Why don't you choose a bottle of wine while I get started on the dough."

Sheila's phone chimed. She could feel Darren's eyes on her and she suddenly had the compulsion to tell him it was Kevin Montgomery sending her a message.

"My best friend, Andrea, is surprised I haven't arrived in San Diego yet," she said.

"Does Andrea live there?"

"No, she lives in Nassau," she said.

"Nassau? Wow. Do you see her often?"

"No."

"What's she like, Andrea?"

"Beautiful. Bossy. Brilliant." Andrea was the single person from her past with whom she still had a relationship. Andrea and her mother, Momma.

"How did you become friends with Andrea?" Darren asked.

"I've known Andrea my whole life. Her mother was my nanny and—" Sheila stopped suddenly. "Let me get that bottle of wine," she said.

"You had a nanny?"

"Lots of people have nannies," she said from the hall. She wanted to kick herself for letting that slip. Darren would be asking about her family next.

She hated referring to Momma as the hired help when the ebony-skinned woman had been more of a mother to her than Mirabelle Chase had. All four Chases were cared for by Charlotte Washington but Sheila was the only one who revered Momma.

Maybe the difference had been that the first three Chases were boys or maybe it had been Andrea. Growing up, the two girls were inseparable. They were only a year apart and their sisterly connection often got Sheila into trouble. She sighed at the memories of being scolded for shirking her parents' high society rules.

She often felt it was because of the time she spent with Momma and Andrea—*normal people*—she was able to "disguise" herself. It would be more difficult for her brothers to forsake the full complement of cooks, maids, and chauffeurs.

"Yeah, you're right. My grandmother was sort of our nanny," Darren said. "So where exactly did you grow up back East?"

"Maybe we should start with a white wine," Sheila said.

"There's some cold in the garage fridge."

"Okay. I'll be right back." In the garage, she paced around the Norton. Staying longer was a bad idea. Darren would be asking lots of questions she wasn't prepared to answer. This is exactly why she made the rule to not get involved.

"Did you find something you like?" Darren's head poked through the door, and Sheila faked a smile.

"I got distracted by the bike. It wouldn't take much work to get it back into shape, you know."

"I definitely want to restore it, but I haven't made the time." He came through the door and Sheila forgot her angst when he reached for her. "I still can't believe you got it running. It was incredibly sexy when you took the helmet off and shook out your hair." His mouth came down on hers and they were both breathing heavily when he pulled back.

"Mmm," he said. "I love that sound you make."

"What sound?" she breathed.

Darren chuckled. "I'll tell you later. Let's get back to the kitchen. I told myself I'd behave tonight. Come." Sheila allowed him to lead her back into the kitchen. "You were going to tell me where you grew up," he said.

"The DC area."

"I love Washington," he said. "Where's home now? San Diego?"

"You know what? We forgot the wine." She pulled her hand free from his and returned to the garage, grabbing the first wine bottle she saw in the fridge.

"Nice choice."

"How can I help? Would you like me to cut these vegetables?" She looked down at an assortment of mushrooms, onions, and garlic on the counter.

"Nope." He wiped his hands on a towel and opened the wine. "I want you to relax. And I want to hear about you. Do you have siblings?"

"Three brothers but we're not close. I'm estranged from my family so I'd rather not talk about them. How about you? Do you see your mother and sister often?"

"I'm sorry to hear that." He turned from the mixer and she squirmed under the sincere look on his face. "My sis is busy preparing for a gallery opening but we still talk about once a week. She's great. Beautiful. Bossy. Brilliant." He winked and turned back to the dough. "She's a lot like Ma, only taller."

Darren turned on the mixer and Sheila let out a breath. She was surprised when Darren looked up. "I'm sorry if I made you uncomfortable. I didn't mean to pry."

"I'm not used to talking about myself," she said. "Andrea gives me grief for spending so much of my time alone. Which gives me an idea. Say *formaggio*."

"You speak *italiano*?"

"No, I just know how to say *cheese* in 15 languages. It's my favorite food."

"Mine too," Darren said. "So how do you say it in Czech?"

Sheila swatted his arm. "I've never been there. Hang on while I send this to Andrea."

For the hundredth time, Darren resisted pulling Sheila off the stool and into the bedroom. Her damp hair hung on her bare shoulders, and he wondered how she could make a simple tank top look so damned good. *Behave yourself.* He turned off the mixer, shaking his head at how he felt like a randy kid. He sprinkled flour on the counter, then rubbed some between his hands before transferring the dough.

"What did she say?" Darren asked when Sheila giggled behind him.

"She says you're cute for a white guy and you get extra points for knowing how to cook."

"'Cute for a white guy?' Did you tell her I'm Italian and Filipino? What's Andrea's ethnicity?"

"Don't be offended, she was being playful. Andrea's Bahamian. Here's her picture."

Darren wasn't offended. He knew he looked more Caucasian than Asian but still he teased Sheila. "Bahamian? Looks like she's got a little cream in her coffee too." He gave her a quick kiss before he returned to the dough. "Tell me what you love about Andrea."

"She's funny and smart, strong and beautiful, loyal and funny."

"You already said funny."

"Andrea is *really* funny. One time we got caught sneaking back into the house after a party, and I thought we were dead. Her mother, well *Momma*, has the temper of a Chihuahua, but somehow Andrea talked us out of it. She started to tell Momma how lame the party was, how the host hadn't even had the sense to invite the neighbors so they wouldn't rat us out, and all of a sudden Momma was laughing. Stuff like that happens all the time with Andrea. There will be a situation that looks impossible, and then Andrea starts talking and somehow it works out."

Darren regarded her with a tilt of his head.

"Okay, so the story wasn't funny in the retelling..." She brought the wine glass to her lips.

"Sounds like she'd make a great attorney."

"I never thought of it like that but maybe. She just started her own clothing line."

"She's a fashion designer?" he said.

"Yeah. Her clothing is fun and sassy."

"What about you, Sheila?"

"What about me?" she said.

Darren turned around at the sharpness of her tone. "What's your passion? What do you do?"

"I uh, I'm in between ventures right now. Taking some time off, traveling the country, that kind of thing." She slid off the stool. "How about some music?" She didn't wait for him to answer and Darren frowned after her.

He put the rolling pin down. Why was she so defensive? He dusted off his hands and found her bent in front of the stereo.

"Sheila?" he said, and her head snapped up. "What's up? I keep getting the feeling you don't like me asking you questions."

"You're right, I don't." She crossed her arms over her chest. "I'm not good at this," she said. "I should go..." she looked toward the front door.

"Don't." He stepped forward. "I don't have an agenda, Sheila. Really." He brushed a hand over her cheek. "This is going to sound corny as hell but I don't usually go to bed with women I don't know. So I'd like to get to know you. And I want you to know me better, too. Last night was amazing but I haven't been that impetuous in a long time.

"When you agreed to stay, I vowed to behave tonight, see if we had something in common besides an attraction that could burn down the house." Darren felt relieved when she met his eyes.

"Since we're making corny confessions, I might as well tell you I've never, uh gone to bed with a man I didn't know. And I'm pretty rusty at the whole get-to-know-you-dating thing. I spend a lot of time alone and... there's a lot I don't want to talk about."

She shuddered and Darren pulled her closer. "OK, I don't want to make you uncomfortable, Sheila. I need to know one more thing before we go any further," he said. "Do you *like* garlic or do you *love* garlic?"

CHAPTER 8

A HORRIBLE SOUND INTERRUPTED SHEILA'S DREAM. SHE FOUGHT against the noise—good dreams were so rare—but the noise grew more insistent, pulling her into consciousness. She opened her eyes and scooted close to Darren, the subject of her dream.

"I think someone is trying to kill your cat," she said. When he didn't respond, she rolled over and gave him a nudge. His eyes were bewildered for a moment and she repeated herself.

He blinked several times. "What?"

"The cat is *dying*."

Darren lifted his head from the pillow and laughed at the yowling. "He's not dying, he's hungry." He got up to let the cat inside and Sheila's eyes bulged at the erection straining his briefs. She heard him sprinkling dry kibble into a bowl which elicited more yowls.

"That's it," he said to the cat. "You're out of wet food." He shushed the animal again and returned to bed. She was very aware of his length pressing against her backside when he spooned her. "It's too early," he mumbled, nuzzling her neck. "Mmm, you smell good." Darren's hand brushed over her hip and the length of her thigh, stopping to circle the bend of her knee.

"That tickles." She turned to her back to hide the sensitive skin.

After they'd gotten past the awkward conversation, the rest of the evening had gone wonderfully. They'd stayed up till midnight eating and talking about places they'd traveled.

Sheila was disappointed when he hadn't done anything more than kiss her goodnight once they'd gotten into bed. She wondered if Darren's reference to *behaving himself* meant he was going to let her make the next move. She wondered if she had the nerve.

"Good morning, gorgeous." He leaned over her mouth and she flinched when he prodded her hip.

"You're up early."

Through his laughter, Darren asked, "Do you want a shower before we go hiking?"

"I don't have any hiking boots."

"That's OK, you can wear sneakers." He sat up and pulled back the sheet, examining her feet. "What size do you wear?"

"Nine, why?"

Darren took one of her feet between his warm hands. "I have an extra pair that might fit you." He began kneading the arch of her foot. She tried not to look at the bulge in his Jockeys and failed.

"You like?" he asked.

Sheila's eyes flickered up at him and they were nervous at being caught staring. "It's kind of obnoxious," she said.

"I meant the foot massage." Darren pulled on her toes, each of them popping except the smallest one. "But you think my manhood is obnoxious? It's not every day I wake up with a stunning woman in my bed."

"Hah."

"It's true. You can ask Charlie."

She tensed at the mention of the cat. The animal took the sound of his name as an invitation, lithely jumping onto the corner of the bed. Sheila screamed and scooted to the opposite end. Charlie hissed and leapt back off the bed. He raced out of the room, his claws loud on the hardwood floor.

"Hey," he said. "Charlie only wanted to say hello."

Sheila narrowed her eyes at Darren, who looked like he was trying not to laugh. "I don't like cats."

"I noticed. Are you okay?" She nodded and he continued, "Shower time?"

"No thanks," she said quickly. "I'll wait."

Darren hesitated. She knew she looked ridiculous, perched on the balls of her feet at the extreme corner of the mattress.

"Would you mind making the coffee?" he asked. When she nodded yes, he left her on the bed and strode into the bathroom.

The pipes groaned when he turned on the faucet. Sheila listened to the first of the water sputtering its way through the shower head and she stretched her legs. She was still a little sore but soreness wasn't what kept her from making the first move.

Her inexperience made her feel awkward. Without the help of a couple glasses of wine, she worried Darren would scoff at her attempts at being sexy. He began singing, "Oh Sheila," in the shower and she sagged on the bed.

"I should get in the shower with him," she muttered.

A phone rang in the office, and she moved toward the noise. When a recording of Darren's voice rang out, she stopped in the doorway.

"What?" Darren called over the sound of the shower, and Sheila missed the name of the female caller. The woman spoke in French.

He poked his wet head from the shower. "Did you call me?"

"No, someone else did."

"What?"

"Telephone," she said sharply.

"Oh, the machine will get it. I'll be out in a minute."

Sheila listened to the last of the message. The woman was saying how excited she was for Darren to visit her in New York. Well, what do you expect? Sheila asked herself. Darren was a sexy, single, attorney. Of course women would be calling.

"Hi," he said.

Sheila started at the proximity of his voice. Darren was grinning at her from the open bathroom, and rubbing a towel across his chest. She hadn't heard the shower turn off. She'd been wondering about the French woman. *She* probably wouldn't have declined joining Darren in a shower.

"The message was in French," she said and realized she'd given her eavesdropping away. "Why do you still have an answering machine? I thought you liked your modern appliances."

Darren quirked a brow at her. "I do," he said. "Most people call my cell but I have an analog back-up line. Ma is the only one who calls me on my home phone."

Sheila tried to quell the annoyance she felt with herself. "You have plans to go to New York?"

He nodded and she didn't miss that he was fighting a smile again. "To visit my mother and sister. Ma's taking French classes. She likes to show off what she's learned with me." Darren wrapped the towel around his waist. "So you speak French too?"

"A little," she said.

He brushed his thumb over her mole. His skin was damp and the smell of the sandalwood soap was strong.

"Ma would get a kick out of you thinking she was my girlfriend. I don't have a French-speaking girlfriend calling," he said. "Yet."

SHEILA SMILED SHEEPISHLY AND DARREN FELT MESMERIZED AGAIN. "I love that mole," he blurted. When he'd seen it from afar, he had wondered if it was real. Up close, it was obviously not a tattoo; the skin was slightly raised and tinged the same reddish brown color of her hair. It sat an inch below the corner of her left eye and raised up on her cheek when she smiled. Staring down at her, he felt an odd satisfaction at Sheila's little display of jealousy.

"Kiss me," she said. Her voice was soft and when he leaned down, Darren made the kiss soft too. Sheila sighed and closed the distance between them, pressing her breasts into his bare chest. He could feel her piercings through the thin t-shirt she'd worn to bed and he sighed too. He bent his knees, then ducked his head to capture her ear lobe between his teeth. Sheila jerked to the side and squeezed his shoulders.

"You don't like that?" he asked.

"Yes." She angled her head. "Do it again."

She melted against him when the tip of his tongue traced her ear. Darren wasn't prepared for her weight and he staggered back, to keep them both upright. The opposite door jamb caught him but he lost the towel.

"Uh oh, there's that obnoxious thing again," he teased.

"Oh my gawd, I think it's bigger."

"Oh Sheila. You say the nicest things."

Sheila stared down at him with an unfathomable expression. He was ready to reach for the towel when she grabbed his penis. "Ahhh..."

"Sorry." She withdrew her hand and stepped back.

Darren was surprised to find her blushing. "Don't be sorry. You surprised me." He bent to reclaim her mouth but stopped at the thought tickling his brain. "Sheila you weren't a..."

Her blush deepened. "No." She tried to hide her face against his chest but he stopped her.

"What is it?"

"Ugh. I can't believe I'm going to say this... but you can obviously see how inept I am..."

"Inept?"

She groaned and he wondered if her face could get any more red. "I told you I haven't been with a man in a while and you're not my first but..."

Darren smiled encouragingly.

"You're my second, OK? My first was my high school sweetheart and he was a virgin too. We didn't do a lot of experimenting before he—" Sheila buried her face in her hands.

"It's OK, Sheila. I get it."

"No, you don't get it." She tightened her arms around her middle. "You've obviously been with more than two women. I haven't been with a man since Rick was killed—Oh, shit. I said that out loud, didn't I?" Sheila turned for the bedroom and Darren followed her. "Yeah, that was definitely TMI. See, *this* is why I don't get involved. I'll, I'll go."

CHAPTER 9

"Wait, Sheila." Darren stepped in front of her, blocking her from reaching her open bag. "I'm sorry about your boyfriend. I can't imagine losing your first love tragically." He took her hand and twined their fingers. "I'm glad you told me. And I'm honored you chose to be with me." Sheila stared down, blinking rapidly. "Do you want to talk about it?" he asked.

She shook her head. "I didn't mean to blurt that out. What a buzz kill, huh?"

"Don't worry about that," he said, lifting her chin.

She brushed at the dampness around her eyes. "You have furry feet," she said.

"What?"

"Hairy toes."

"I'm part Hobbit, on my mother's side. Do my 'furry feet' offend you?"

"No. Does my ineptitude offend you?"

"I don't think you're inept, Sheila." He tucked a lock of hair behind her ear. "I was hoping it was nervousness or inexperience and not that you thought me *obnoxious.*"

She reddened again. "Sorry, I—" Thunder struck outside the bedroom window and Sheila screamed.

"Wow," Darren said. "You should have been born a couple decades earlier. You could have given the woman in Michael Jackson's *Thriller* video some serious competition."

Sheila laughed uneasily and moved to the window. "I guess hiking is out for today. Look at the rain!" She heard a drawer opening but kept her eyes on the backyard. Rain droplets ricocheted off the cement patio and she wondered how long the steam rising off the slab would last.

"I overheard some people talking about a place in town that makes killer cinnamon buns. I think I'll stop there on my way out," she said. Her breath fogged up the window and she swiped the mist with her finger. It reminded her of the sketchy defroster on Dexter.

"The Frontier—wait, on your way out? You're ditching me because it's raining?" He came up behind her and nuzzled her neck.

"You're prickly." She giggled and shrugged her shoulders.

"I can shave."

"No, I'll go. I'm really hungry and I get kinda woozy if I wait too long to eat."

"The Frontier is less than a ten minute drive from here and the service is quick. They have the best fresh squeezed OJ too. Or I can fix something for you. Do you eat eggs?"

"You don't have to do that."

"Do what?"

"Pretend you want me to stay."

"Sheila." His hands came down on her shoulders and he used his hold to turn her around. "There's a lot of jokes about lawyers being liars but I'm not one of them. Honesty is crucial for me. I rate it right up there with sex. I told you last night, I want to get to know you. And I want you to be honest with me."

He rubbed his hands over her shoulders in gentle circles. Sheila swallowed, hoping it didn't look like she was swallowing a frog.

"I'm not worried about your inexperience. All you have to do is smile at me and I'm ready to strip you." The corners of her mouth turned up and he continued. "And there was nothing inept about the way you made love to me on Sunday."

"I had a couple glasses of Malbec. And you... you did all the work."

"Not true. You weren't passive at all. When I touched you, your breasts, you let me know how much you liked it. That's such a turn on for a guy." Sheila shivered at the memory of his mouth, hot and skillful. "You were over thinking it this morning, worrying too much. All you have to do is relax and do what feels right."

Do what feels right. Darren's hands on her body felt right, it was *her* hands on *his* body that worried Sheila.

A soft smile played on his delicious lips and sincerity burned in his brown eyes. He continued to rub his hands over her shoulders in a soothing caress.

She expected rejection and his kindness surprised her. Whenever Sheila tried to imagine having any kind of relationship with a man, she feared they'd bolt if she opened up the Samsonite she was toting. And any of the men who knew about the past, like the poser Fitzgerald, also knew about her family's fortune.

"Darren, I..."

"It's OK, Sheila." Darren drew her against his body, enveloping her in a warm embrace. His compassion made her want to tell him everything. Last night when they discussed traveling, they shared memories of fun places or interesting people they encountered. She had been careful to skirt the why of her travels.

Most people felt safe, rooted in familiarity. For Sheila, familiarity beckoned the menacing voice of a murderer in her dreams. And fear. The fear that one day the Butcher would find her and kill her too. Another thunderclap struck the backyard. She nearly knocked Darren to the floor, scrambling to get away from the noise.

"I thought lightning wasn't supposed to strike the same place twice," she said. To herself she chanted, *I am safe. It's just thunder. It's not the sound of a gunshot. I am safe.*

"Are you OK?" Darren asked.

"Yeah. I expect thunderstorms on the East Coast but not in the Southwest," she said. "Let's go eat."

DARREN DIDN'T WANT TO LET GO OF SHEILA BUT HE FORCED HIS ARMS to drop from her sides. For a moment, she was relaxed. Kneeling in front of her suitcase, she was guarded again. The terror on her face at the thunder ate at him and Darren cursed the storm.

What had happened to her? Did she think he would be put off by her inexperience? He'd been drawn to Sheila because of her beauty. After last night, he was captivated by the stories of her extensive travels, her sense of humor, her sharp eye for details. She was an irresistible puzzle. "You have to go to San Diego tomorrow?"

"Yes."

"There's a lot of noise about global warming but I don't think the Pacific Ocean is going anywhere. At least not this week," he said.

Sheila pushed her hair from her face. Darren was glad he'd donned underwear while she was at the window so she wouldn't see how easily she excited him. "My date isn't exclusively with the Pacific," she said.

He tilted his head. "Your date?"

"Appointment. Oh shoot. I forgot the load of laundry I started while you were at the store yesterday."

He brightened at the thought that they might not be going out. She turned on the spigot in the bathroom and he yelled down the hall. "I've got plenty of stuff for breakfast."

"Don't go to the trouble. I'll throw this on and we can go," she said.

Darren turned from the closet where he'd pulled a pair of chinos from a hanger. "Let me iron that for you," he said. The dress she held was similar to the one she'd worn on Sunday, only the tiny floral print on this one was difficult to see for all the wrinkles.

"That'll take too long," Sheila said. She gave it a shake, then stopped when she saw him slipping a leg into creased chinos. "Oh well, I've got one of Andrea's new creations I haven't worn yet and it doesn't need ironing." She pulled a bra and something green from her bag and retreated to the bathroom.

When she returned, she was brushing her hair and Darren wished he'd kept his mouth shut about the wrinkled dress. "Are you sure this isn't a bikini cover up?" he asked.

The brush paused mid-stroke and Sheila narrowed her eyes. "You don't have to go anywhere with me if you don't like the way I dress." She threw the brush at her suitcase.

Darren reached for her. "I don't want to have to hospitalize any men for drooling on you." He pulled her close and skimmed his hands over the tiny dress. It hugged her everywhere except her shoulders, where the extra fabric drooped off. Below the curve of her sweet behind was a flounce for a skirt. He imagined it could be something one of the Williams sisters would wear at a tennis match.

"I'm sorry," he said, trying to kiss her. Sheila turned her face and Darren got her cheek. He offered the apology in Italian. "*Sono spiacente, bellissima.*" He pressed his lips into the curve below her jaw. "You look good enough to eat, Sheila. Tell me you're not bare under here." He sneaked a hand under the flounce.

She backed away. "Food."

"*Dio aiutami,*" Darren muttered and grabbed his keys.

CHAPTER 10

SHEILA RAN FROM THE HOUSE AND PLOPPED INTO THE PASSENGER SEAT of Darren's car. She landed on a stack of papers and raised up to gather them while he slid into the driver's seat. She was prepared to give him the silent treatment but her name was written on the top envelope. "What's this?"

"Open it," he said.

She set the other papers on the floor between her feet. The manila envelope tore across the middle, spilling two more envelopes into her lap.

The first one was simple and bore the return address of the law firm where Darren worked. The second was pink and embossed in the left corner with a fancy B. Sheila gave him a curious glance. Inside, the handwritten note read:

Dearest Sheila,
Bella's gives the best massages and my secretary raves about the Sea Mud Body Masque. I've called ahead and asked the owner, Térese, to take good care of you. I hope to see your beautiful, smiling face again. I hope to hold you in my arms, and bury my face in your silky hair. I hope...
Baci,
Darren

The second envelope held a gift card for unlimited services at *Bella Day Spa.*

"I tried to have it delivered to you by way of messenger," he said, rubbing his hand over her thigh. "There's the spa."

Sheila looked up in time to glimpse the fancy lettering of the sign. Emotion swelled in her chest and tightened her throat. She closed her hand over Darren's. When she felt sure of her voice she said, "Thank you."

He squeezed her hand, then backed into a parking spot. The rain slowed to a drizzle by the time they arrived at The Frontier. He still insisted on using an umbrella.

"Isn't that Stan?" Sheila asked when they got in line to order.

A short man beside Stan called out. "Yo, Abruzzo, what're you up to?" Darren's arm tightened around her waist. He set the umbrella against the window and Sheila wished she had on the wrinkled dress. Andrea's creations were skimpy and she usually staged a photo for her best friend, rarely wearing them in public. She'd received this dress via general mail delivery in Austin.

The man who'd called out to Darren didn't attempt to disguise his appreciative stare and she felt other men staring, too. Most of the customers looked like students of the college across the street. Some were business types like Stan and the gaping man with him. One of the bus boys swabbed a tabletop with a dingy towel, his hand cupped at the edge to collect the crumbs but his eyes were on Sheila and the crumbs fell to the floor.

Stan was the only one watching Darren. He gave them a little wave and Sheila waved back. Then it was their turn to order and she half expected Darren to request the food to go but he didn't.

"Let me get this," she said.

"Don't be silly," Darren said. He released her waist to retrieve his wallet and she didn't miss the glare he gave to the male cashier. "Good morning," he said to Stan.

"I guess it *is* a good morning," the gaper said.

Darren groaned and she fought the feeling she'd done something wrong. "Sheila, you remember Stan. And this is Philip Morris," he said with a nod. "One of my coworkers."

"No relation to the tobacco company," Philip said with a grin. "Sheila, I *love* that name. You're not Australian, are you?"

"What a shame," Sheila said. "You seem like you'd do well in the tobacco industry."

STAN TRIED TO HOLD BACK A LAUGH BUT IT FOLLOWED DARREN'S SNORT and then they were both chuckling. Philip cocked his head and laughed belatedly. He was impressed; Sheila didn't crack a smile.

"Hey Phil, would you mind taking these back?" Stan asked. He collected a box of cinnamon rolls from the counter and pressed them at Phil. "I promised them to Doris and the ladies but I need to talk to Darren a minute."

Philip gave Sheila a long look before turning for the door. Stan thought the girl would probably have bruises on her hip from the way Darren clenched her to his side. He wanted to offer her his suit jacket, and he stopped himself from asking D how he'd let the girl out the door dressed so scantily.

"Thanks," Darren said. "That guy is such a jerk."

"I guess I should hang out here a minute, give him time to spread the word on your hot date." Stan glanced sideways at Sheila. "What're you guys up to today?"

"We *were* going to go hiking," Darren said. He guided them to a table by the window, pausing to listen to the number called over the speaker.

"I can get it," Sheila said.

Darren shook his head. "Have a seat." He pulled out a chair for her and waited until she was seated before he strode over to the counter to retrieve their food.

"How long will you be in town?" Stan asked.

Sheila turned her gaze from the window. The girl looked different, he thought, and guessed the difference was more than her skimpy attire. She was beautiful of course, Darren's women always were.

When he'd first seen her, Stan teased that the girl was too young to drink. At the park she seemed skittish. Now, she didn't seem entirely relaxed in the skimpy dress, but she didn't look as young either.

"I leave tomorrow," Sheila said.

"Not if I have my way," Darren said. "I intend to tie her to my bed." He slid the tray of food onto the table and Stan watched a blush spread over Sheila's face.

Stan tried not to imagine the scene his friend had suggested. He felt his own face growing warm when Darren sat beside Sheila and angled his mouth over hers.

Well, hello to two surprises for the morning, Stan thought. Since Darren had begun serving on the city council, he was practically a teetotaler and he became a lot more conservative with his women.

Stan didn't know which was more surprising, that Darren would be seen in public with Sheila in a clubbing outfit or that D was now kissing the girl breathless. His discomfort grew when his friend snaked his hand under Sheila's hair and gripped the back of her neck. She made a little whimper and he pulled her to the edge of the chair.

"Rent a room," Stan muttered. "You're going to get a citation for lewd conduct, Senator Abruzzo."

Sheila broke the kiss and Darren threw a creamer at him. "Senator Abruzzo?" Sheila asked.

"Future Senator Abruzzo. We're thinking 2014—"

Sheila's eyes widened and Darren interrupted. "Take a bite of this," he said.

Stan watched Darren lift a forkful of the gooey cinnamon roll to

Sheila's mouth. "Hasn't he told you? Darren made a name for himself with the Gonzales case and—"

"Stan," Darren said. "It's poor manners to discuss politics at breakfast. Isn't that right, *bellissima*? Isn't that in your Miss Manners, TNME book?"

The girl covered her mouth and giggled around the cinnamon roll. The rapt expression on Darren's face had Stan wishing he hadn't dragged Darren to the concert on Sunday night.

HERRERA LOOSENED HIS BELT, SURPRISED THE HUEVOS RANCHEROS were so good. He was so hungry he ordered enough for three people. After he polished off the cinnamon bun, he phoned in a report.

"Vasquez here."

Why does this idiot think I need to be told who I'm calling? Herrera thought but he didn't say it. "Yeah, so I'm outside this restaurant and I know you said she don't know the guy but she's definitely fuc—"

"Keep it tight, Herrera. These calls are being recorded."

Herrera slurped on his OJ, drawing on the dregs at the bottom.

"I observed the subject in a restaurant," he said in a starchy tone. "She, the subject, spent the night with the man again and they appear extremely familiar. Is that better?" Vasquez was a pain in the ass for following protocol. He wanted Herrera to refer to Sheila Washington as "the subject" not her, or she, or the girl, and especially not by her name. In his mind, however, Herrera called her SW.

Vasquez exhaled. "I've looked through the files and I don't see how the subject can know the man whose name appears on the title for the address you provided. The subject has never been to Albuquerque."

Herrera had been surprised when SW went home with the man from the park. In the weeks he'd been trailing her, SW had turned down better looking men. He shrugged, women never did what he expected.

"Well, I bet you the subject *knows* him now. Look, I ain't had a shower and my back is killing me from sleeping in this van. I overheard the subject saying she ain't leaving till tomorrow. Can't I get a break?" According to protocol, Herrera wasn't supposed to follow the subject into buildings but he'd been starving and he was glad to pick up a part of her conversation.

"Is the tracking device still in place on the subject's vehicle?"

"Yeah. Her vehicle is parked in front of the man's house. They drove his car and man it's a sweet—"

"All right. You're authorized to take a two hour break after which you'll phone in another update."

"Two hours?"

"Starting now."

Herrera stared at the phone in disbelief. Mr. Protocol had hung up on him. Snatching up the spring-loaded hand grips, he decided he needed a workout. With a few strokes of the GPS, he soon found a boxing gym and was pounding his frustrations out on a 100 lb. bag.

The old man at the desk who had checked in Herrera was watching him intently. When the sweat was steadily dripping off of the tip of his nose, the old man called over his shoulder, "Hey Pea, you wanna work out?"

Herrera looked over to see the door behind the counter open. A young Asian woman appeared.

"Just had a workout," she answered, looking between Herrera and the old man. "Thought you didn't want me to beat up the customers anymore."

"This one looks like he needs a whipping."

Herrera knew he was the only customer in the gym. Still he said, "If you're talking about me, I don't fight little girls."

The old man and the woman laughed; not little chuckles but deep belly laughs.

"Well mister, in case you hadn't noticed, I'm not a little *girl*."

Herrera removed a glove, swabbing a towel over his face, and took the invitation to assess her. She was short but she was solid muscle. She folded her arms over her chest, and he noted that her biceps were bigger than her breasts. A white ribbed undershirt covered her sports bra and checkered nylon shorts rode high on her muscled thighs. He couldn't see how far the black braid stretched down her back. Pulling deeply on a bottle of water, Herrera shrugged.

The woman chose some gloves from behind the counter and sauntered over to the competition ring. Herrera flipped the towel around his neck and followed. She looked barely five feet tall and her lithe movements resembled a cat ready to pounce on its prey.

He was about to tell her to forget it, deciding he was right and she was too little, when the woman leapt onto the corner of the ring. Her feet bounced off the mat as her body arched backward over the ropes. *Well damn, was she a gymnast, too?*

"You want some head gear?" she asked. Herrera ducked between the ropes and let out a snort. "All right. We don't want your wife calling up complaining about your pretty face when you get home."

Impatient, he tapped his gloves together and she nearly put him on his ass with a right upper cut.

"Don't knock him out with the first punch Pea," the old man cackled.

Herrera righted himself and threw one back but she anticipated and danced out of reach. She hit him again, a quick jab to the ribs and hopped back. Herrera pivoted to the left and connected with his right. The woman took the blow but before he could grin at it, she hammered him with a one-two.

Wincing at the power behind her hits, Herrera spotted a sizable scar on her neck and she hammered him again. *Dammit, she was nailing his ass 'cause he was too busy scrutinizing her appearance.*

"Ohh, not the candy cane," the old man said, describing the Sugar Ray Robinson move.

The mat rose up to meet him and Herrera blinked at the florescent lights, his ears ringing. No not his ears, he thought after a second, a telephone.

"Peach hold up a minute," the old man yelled. "The kid's had another attack."

She jumped from the ring. "Joelle?"

Herrera sat up. "Peach? Your name's Peach? You gotta be kiddin' me." At first glance, he'd dismissed the woman as a dyke, but her face, flooded with motherly concern, lost its hardness when she yanked the phone from the old man.

"How bad is it?" she demanded into the phone.

Herrera ducked under the ropes and dropped to the floor. His ribs ached as did his arms but it was a good ache, he decided. Peach surprised him and he felt a stirring in his shorts when he looked at her ass leaning over the counter.

She slammed the phone down and yanked off her gloves. "Tom—"

"Go. Call me when you get to the hospital," he said, handing her an old leather purse.

"You're the best, Tom," Peach said. She sprinted out the door.

CHAPTER 11

Darren pushed open the Museum doors and guided Sheila to the Sculpture Garden.

"Listen," Sheila said. She tugged on his arm, pulling him toward the rumbling noise. "I bet it's an old z28." She craned her neck around the sculpture and let out a whistle. "I knew it. Looks like a '74."

"74 was a good year," he said but shook his head.

"What?"

"You're full of surprises," he said. "How do you know so much about cars? Is your father a car enthusiast?"

Sheila snorted. "Not my father, my grandfather. Were you born in '74?"

Darren nodded and blinked at the sudden reappearance of the sun.

"A rainbow," she said.

He shaded his eyes and instead of following her outstretched arm to the break in the smoky clouds, he studied her face bright with excitement.

"Stay another day." He didn't give her a chance to answer. His mouth covered hers and he felt her laughter against his chest.

"I can't," she said.

"Why not? I thought you said you were a vagabond." His lips found hers again, and he squeezed her against him even tighter.

"Mmm."

"Is that a yes?" he asked against her mouth.

"Mommy, look! A rainbow."

Sheila tried to pull back at the sound of the child's voice. "Darren," she said. Her own voice was low and breathy. She put a hand on his shoulder and pushed. "Darren, we're not alone. We should go."

He moved his lips over her jaw and said into her ear, "Where do you want to go next?" He tickled her earlobe with the tip of his tongue.

"Your place."

"Do I get to take this off of you?" He skimmed a hand down her back.

"Yes," she breathed.

He laced their fingers and his feet didn't touch the sidewalk as they made their way back to his car. "Want to drive?" He offered her the keys.

"I'm going to show you how this car is supposed to be driven, Mr. Abruzzo."

He chuckled. "Is that right?"

"Did I tell you I helped my grandfather rebuild a '71 Challenger?"

"No, you didn't."

"He loved muscle cars. And I learned how to drive with that car; cherry red, 340 V-8 engine..."

Darren already suspected Sheila was more versed in car mechanics than the average woman. He couldn't help grinning stupidly as she unfastened her sandals and snapped the seat belt into place. After adjusting the mirrors, seat, and steering wheel, she looked at him expectantly.

"How do you say, 'hold on' in Italian?"

"*Tenga su.*"

Sheila shifted the Challenger into reverse, angled the nose of the car, and pulled out of the parking spot, executing a sharp U-turn in the process.

Darren rubbed his hand over her bare leg. "Do you drive Dexter like this?" They approached a traffic light that turned from yellow to red and although the car was roaring at 50 mph, she applied the brakes smoothly.

"Dexter is sportier than—What's your car's name?"

"I haven't gotten around to naming it yet."

She took her foot off the gas pedal. "How long have you had this car?"

Darren shrugged. "A couple of months."

"A couple of months. Oh no."

"What's the matter?"

"That's bad luck. She's gotta have a name."

He cocked his head. "What do you suggest?" They stopped at another red light and Sheila ran her hand over the dashboard, the steering wheel, the leather upholstery. "General Lee?" he said.

"It's not orange," she said.

"How about Leigh?" he said and spelled out the name. Sheila shook her head. "Christine?" he said.

"Now you're teasing me," she said.

"What was your first car's name?"

Sheila smiled wryly. "Silky." She didn't tell him her first car was a Mercedes SLK.

"Silky?" he repeated and ran his hand over her leg.

"I didn't name it, Andrea did."

"I can think of something that's *silky*." Darren sneaked a hand under her dress. A horn blared out of the car behind them and he groaned when Sheila returned his hand to his lap. Twenty minutes later, they arrived at his house.

"Damn woman." She beamed at him and pulled on the door latch. "Let me get that for you," he said.

Sheila accepted his outstretched hand after he opened her door. She pressed her knees together before swinging her legs out of the car. "I thought chivalry was dead."

"And the only other woman I've seen exit a car like that is my mother," he said. She wrinkled her nose and he hurried to clarify. "I meant we were both raised with old-fashioned habits."

"So opening doors and paying for meals isn't a part of your limited edition dating?"

Darren cocked his head. "Limited edition? Is that something else from TNME book?"

She followed him into the house. "Andrea's term. She says a lot of guys are on their best behavior for the first couple of dates... "

"No, I'll still be opening your doors and putting the toilet seat down a year from now."

SHEILA LOOKED UP SHARPLY. *A YEAR FROM NOW?*

Darren closed the door and turned the deadbolt. "Now, about this dress..." His hands retraced the trail they made along her back when she'd suggested leaving Old Town. This time Darren didn't stop at the small of her back. He fanned light caresses over the curve of her behind before slipping a hand under the dress.

"I've wanted to touch you all day," he said.

A nervous laugh escaped her and Darren lifted his head to meet her eyes. "You *have* been touching me all day," she said. Her lips were red from his constant kisses and Sheila thought the only place he hadn't touched her was the bottom of her feet. The skin crinkled in the corners of his eyes, and they took on an impish glint.

"What?" she said.

"I have been wanting to touch you *here.*" He cupped her bare behind and squeezed. Sheila gasped when he slipped a hand between her legs. "And *here, bellissima, mio.* Would you like me to touch you here?"

Sheila couldn't find her voice so she nodded yes.

"This time, I'm going to go slowly," he said.

Darren reached down and lifted her left leg at the calf. Sheila grabbed his waist for balance.

"Put your foot here." He guided it to the bench atop the shoe rack and ran a finger along the inside of her thigh.

"That tickles," she whispered.

"Is this better?" He drew a finger over her core, once, and Sheila dug her nails into the waistband of his chinos. Her right leg trembled and although she was still wearing the dress, she felt exposed.

"Let's go to bed," she said. *Wow. Was that her voice?* It was low and throaty and—she caught Darren's twinkling eyes—*sexy*. He guided her foot back to the floor before leading her into the bedroom. It was bright from the sun streaming through the sheer curtains. *Oh great, now it's sunny.* He drew the dress up over her head and she thought of asking him for a glass of wine. But her throat tightened when he reached for the clasp at the back of her bra.

"Is this okay, *bellissima*?"

The concern on his face and the tone of his voice made Sheila relax. And she decided, since she was leaving tomorrow, she wouldn't spend their last time together being timid.

"Yes," she said. Sheila laced her fingers around his neck and pulled his head down. He quickly freed her of the bra.

"Oh Sheila," he said. She went for his belt buckle but Darren's hand covered hers. "I want to enjoy you first."

"Can't you 'enjoy me' while you're naked?" Darren raised an eyebrow and dropped his hand. Sheila unbuttoned his shirt before she took care of his belt. She knew her eyes were bulging out of their sockets when Darren's pants fell to the floor because he started to laugh, a deep sound of male satisfaction. "It's so *big*," she said.

"Not obnoxious?"

She winced. "You're not going to let me forget that, are you?" Before he could answer, she grasped his length.

"I—ahhh. Wait."

"You don't want me to touch you?" Sheila said. She slid her hand down his shaft and then back up again.

"*Dio mio*, yes." Darren gripped her forearms. "But I want to take care of you first."

"How about here?" She cupped his twin weights with her other hand and savored the moan he made. His eyes flashed and she realized it was involuntary.

Now that she saw how much pleasure he got from her touch, Sheila felt silly for worrying about being inept. She squeezed and Darren moaned again, sparking a sense of power within her. The feeling was unfamiliar and exciting, and she wanted more of it.

"Sheila..."

The need in his face thrilled her. She kept her hold on his shaft and sank to her knees. If he looked ready to worship her from the feel of her hands on his penis, she guessed he'd melt when she took him in her mouth. She was right.

"Ahhh..."

She closed her mouth around as much of him as she could. His breathing hitched and she marveled at how exciting she found it to pleasure him. Emboldened by his reactions, she focused her attention on his crown.

It was never like this with Rick. Sheila gave her head a little shake, not wanting the past to creep into this moment and Darren yelled again. Her teeth had grazed the ridge of his head and he fisted his hands in her hair.

Sheila gasped. Darren seized her under the arms and threw her onto the bed.

"I said I was going to take it slow this time but you're making a liar out of me." Darren pounced on the bed, gripping each of her legs behind the knees.

"What—" Sheila's question became a cry of pleasure.

"Honey... *dio mio*, you taste like honey." Sheila dug her heels into Darren's shoulders when he dove into her most intimate flesh with his tongue. Darren stopped. "You don't like this?"

"Yes, more."

Darren grinned. "Tell me, 'stop' if you want me to stop, OK?"

"GO."

He snaked his tongue around her opening in a lazy movement and then grazed her swollen nub with his teeth. Sheila cried out and Darren had to clamp his hands onto her thighs to prevent her from shoving him off with her feet.

"*Miele. Dio mio...*"

Darren swept his mouth from side to side before latching onto her clit. He suckled her in a greedy rhythm, feeling on the verge of coming himself when Sheila began panting. She grew louder, and her hips raised off the mattress.

"Come for me," he growled and spared her no quarter. He frantically lapped at her, needing more of her delicious honey down his throat. She cried out and he felt her contractions. When she stopped rocking against his mouth, Darren released her thighs. Sheila's feet fell onto the mattress.

"What's so funny?" he said.

"Your shoulders are red."

He glanced at the oval splotches her heels made above his arm pits. "Are you ready for me, honey?" He positioned himself at her opening.

Sheila put a hand on his shoulder. "We should use a condom."

He suppressed a frown. "Of course." *Why hadn't he thought of a condom?* He rose from the bed and pulled the drawer open on the night stand. *Empty. Maybe there were some in the sock drawer?*

Rifling through the neatly matched pairs, he was ready to dump the thing on the floor when Sheila shifted off the bed. Her arms came around his waist and his cock jerked when her nipple rings pressed into his back. "There might be some in the bathroom. If not, I could go to the store," he said.

Her fingers combed his chest. "You could let me finish what I started," she said. Shudders of excitement followed the southern trail of her soft hands. She clutched his shaft and he was struck by how differently she was reacting to him, compared to this morning.

Darren gripped the sides of the dresser. He felt so torqued he knew he would explode the second Sheila put her sweet mouth on him again. When she tried to step around him, he covered her hand. "I'm so close," he bit out.

"You don't want me to..." her voice trailed off and he heard the doubt in it.

He cursed and spun around. "Only if you want to."

Sheila gave him a coy smile, "I want to," she said. Darren licked his lips. Turning, she pulled him back to the bed. "Lie down."

"*Dio mio*," he murmured. She stood at the foot of the bed, staring down at him. The wonder on her face made him feel ten feet tall. He drank in her naked body too, savoring the view of her lean legs, the flat plane of her stomach, her pert breasts... God he loved her breasts.

The rings hanging from her nipples were uneven; one was flipped up but the other was down and the green jewels sparkled.

Watching her kneel in front of him, his feeling of awe deepened. He lasted longer than he thought he would. The satisfied expression she wore, after he climaxed, let Darren know she'd enjoyed it, too. He pulled Sheila into his arms to hold her before they made a run to the store for round two.

CHAPTER 12

"CALL ME WHEN YOU GET IN?"

"OK," Sheila said. She stood in Darren's driveway with her bag at her feet. Darren's hand tightened on the nape of her neck. His mouth tasted of spearmint when he kissed her goodbye, again.

"Dammit," he said. His cell phone was in his left hand and he swore. "The office," he said.

"Again," she said. "I'll go."

"I want you to stay," he said.

"I'll call you when I get in." They had talked a little, between the many interludes of making love last night, and Darren had asked her to stay another day.

"I leave for New York on Friday," he said.

"OK," Sheila said.

"I'll be back on Monday."

Sheila sagged against Darren when he kissed her for the last time. His length was hard against her belly. The phone continued to ring and Sheila bent to pick up her bag when he answered it.

"Hold on a minute, Doris." Darren put the phone against his chest.

"I'll call you when I get in," Sheila repeated. Darren nodded and brought the phone back to his ear. She descended the driveway and felt his eyes following her movements. Her bag landed in the trunk with a thud, next to a box of books. The tightness in her chest was unexpected when she waved goodbye. Darren's mouth was a grim line when he waved back. He was probably irritated by the conversation with his secretary; his phone *had* been ringing for the past hour.

Sheila shut the car door and took more time than necessary pulling out of the parking space. When she merged onto I40W and passed the sign for the Rio Grande, tears stung her eyes. She wiped at them angrily. An SUV merged on top of her, with inches to spare, and she stomped the brakes. "Pay attention, Sheila," she shouted. *Three days of male attention and she'd already lost her driving edge.*

Her phone chimed and she took her right hand off the steering wheel to retrieve it. A sob welled in her throat. The text message was from Andrea, not Darren. She didn't bother reading it.

The 160 miles it took to get to the Arizona border were a blur. When the gas gauge pinged and she stopped to refuel, she felt drunk. She couldn't shake the image of Darren scowling from the driveway.

Her appointment with Dr. Baldwin couldn't be rescheduled; Dr. Baldwin traveled the globe to visit his patients and her annual meeting in San Diego was non-negotiable. Darren only knew she had an obligation. She wondered, if she had told her lover she was going to see her shrink, what would have been his reaction?

"Umm, Miss?" Sheila jumped at the tapping on her window. She looked out at a sunburned man. "Didn't mean to scare ya. Ya left your gas cap on the roof."

She pulled on the door latch and the man stepped back. "Oh, thank you," Sheila said. She eased into the narrow space between the door and the gas pump. Turning toward the roof, her breath caught on a hitch.

Relax, Sheila, there are plenty of white vans on the road. It doesn't have to be the same white van that was parked on Darren's street.

"You know what? I can put the cap back for ya," the man said.

"Oh." She forced her attention back to the dumpy man. "Thank you, Sir. I'm much obliged."

"You're very welcome. You be careful now, ya hear?"

Sheila nodded and waited until the man started his rusty red truck before she reentered her car. For the next hundred miles, her pulse sped up when she saw an old red truck or a white van.

THURSDAY, JUNE 7TH

"Good Morning," called a male voice.

Sheila smiled at Dr. Baldwin, marveling again at how little he resembled a doctor. He wore a tie-dyed shirt and baggy shorts. And with his disheveled hair, he looked more like a student than a renowned psychiatrist.

"I asked Agatha not to disturb you," she said. "I'm sorry she woke you." Sheila had slept poorly in the hotel and she'd arrived hours before her 10 A.M. appointment. She intended to park her car and walk the grounds, or hike down to the beach, but Dr. Baldwin's assistant, and mother, Agatha Baldwin had spotted her.

"Woke me? No, I was meditating." He stopped a foot from her and extended his hand. "Welcome back, *Ms. Washington.*"

She shook his hand. "It's weird to hear you call me that."

"When will your name change be finalized?"

"In a couple of months, I hope. I wasn't expecting that I'd have to place ads in legal journals to complete the process but my attorney is taking care of it." They walked along the lawn and Sheila stopped to examine a white pole protruding from the ground. She ran her fingers over the words etched into the monument, *May Peace Prevail On Earth.*

"This is new," she said.

"Yes, it's a Peace Pole, a gift from one of our recent graduates, Shen-yee," Dr. Baldwin said.

Sheila nodded, recognizing the name. In general, she avoided news reports, especially the sensationalized versions on television, but it was impossible to *not* hear about the Chinese woman's tragedy. With a shudder, Sheila felt again like her own suffering was a case of a mere hangnail compared to what Shen-yee had been through.

She wrapped her arms around her torso and walked forward until her bare feet were inches from the cliff overhanging the ocean. When she was a resident here, it amused her that a psychiatric treatment facility was perched on a bluff, a seemingly perfect location for a suicide. Back then, she wondered if that wasn't why some families sent their broken relatives here.

Sheila felt like her family, her father, wished she'd never returned from Grand Cayman Island three years ago. The youngest of four and the only daughter, she was the misfit. Her brothers were dutiful, and followed their father's orders, working in the Chase Investment Firm or becoming doctors.

She wanted to become a doctor too but she was expected to marry well, to merge two elite families. The day before the fateful trip with Rick, Grandpa, and Momma she had a horrible argument with her father. What father wouldn't be proud of his daughter's acceptance to Harvard Medical School? Not hers.

Dr. Baldwin's voice pulled her from her dreary thoughts. "A couple of young women will join us for the summer," he said. "They have histories similar to yours and they could benefit from having a graduate to mentor them."

Sheila turned from the slate-colored ocean to peer at the cheery house. It was an extraordinary place to recuperate, with an extraordinary staff. The young women who were coming were lucky, she thought. She was lucky too. She shook her head. "You know I can't do that."

"You can't do what?"

Despite the guilt creeping up, she said, "Stay here; for the summer."

"Why can't you?" Dr. Baldwin said.

"The nightmares will return."

"Have you been experiencing nightmares, Sheila?"

"Not recently. But you know if I—" She stopped and covered her ears against the noise from a helicopter flying offshore.

"You were saying?" he prompted when the noise faded.

She glared at him, suddenly angry. "You know what happens. If I stay in one place too long, the nightmares creep up and I relive *everything*." The patient expression on Dr. Baldwin's face spurred her anger. "What?"

"Are you ready to move past that?"

"Move past *what*?"

"The choice to believe you can't be free from the past," he said.

Her face grew hot and she turned away. The burst of anger embarrassed her because she knew it was misplaced. Dr. Baldwin wasn't her enemy but she resented his suggestion.

Despite her tremendous progress in therapy, Dr. Baldwin hadn't been able to sway Sheila from the belief that one day her enemy, the Butcher, would find her and mete out his revenge.

"You can choose a different belief, Sheila," Dr. Baldwin said. "You can make a new 'agreement,' but you must be willing."

Despite her anger, Sheila smirked, remembering the day she'd met the disheveled doctor. When she was delivered to The Cove, she was catatonic and she weighed 100 pounds soaking wet.

The best treatments her parents could buy yielded no results because she refused to participate. Until Dr. Baldwin. He'd sat on the floor beside her bed and began reading aloud from a book, *The Four Agreements*. Sheila recalled questioning him and her disbelieving look when he'd proclaimed himself a doctor.

Sheila had noticed a copy of *The Four Agreements* on Darren's book

"Ma, Ma. I didn't break anything. I only sprained my ankle."

"Where is she?" Felicity said.

"She who?"

"The woman you were trying to impress with the motorcycle. She should be there taking care of you."

"You should have been a P.I., Ma."

"Well?"

"She's not here. She left town before I had the spill. Sorry I haven't called you back. The medicine's made me groggy."

Felicity pursed her mouth. Darren reacted poorly to pain medication; he'd been that way from a child. If he was taking something for the pain, then it had to be more than a little spill. "Do you have a cast?"

"No, Ma."

"Hmph. I guess you're not coming this weekend, then. Rosie will be disappointed. You're going to miss her opening, again."

"I was going to call soon, I didn't want to wake her."

She looked at the clock. It was 1:30 P.M. in New York. Rose's alarm would be going off in about 10 minutes if she hadn't already hit the snooze.

"She'll have to blow away the crowd with her artwork and secure another showing so I can come to the next opening," Darren said. "I have a trip to Washington coming up in a month. Maybe we can meet up there."

"Will you bring the woman?"

"We met four days ago, Ma."

"When are you going to settle down and give me some grandkids?"

"I'll get right on it."

"Don't be fresh, Darren. You're 37—"

"Rosie's older, why don't you pester her?"

Felicity tried to tease more information from him on the new woman before switching to French. She made a dozen mistakes, using the wrong form of the verb *être*, and she didn't miss that Darren didn't correct her. She hung up then, thinking she'd have to call Stanley to find out about the woman.

THE FRENCH CONVERSATION MADE DARREN THINK OF SHEILA. EVERY-thing made him think of the beauty. He logged into his cellular account online in hopes of finding her number. The motorcycle accident was an embarrassment and an inconvenience. After Sheila left yesterday, he'd decided to take the Norton for a spin but he hadn't made it past the stop sign at the end of his street.

The clutch cable snapped when he'd tried to shift into third gear. The front end had locked and Darren had fallen, spraining his right ankle and busting his cell phone. Since he'd put Sheila's number in his phone minutes before the accident, he didn't have it backed up on the computer.

A neighbor took him to the emergency room where he spent the entire day. Stan was annoyed with Darren when he insisted on buying a new cell phone on the way home from the hospital. The store employ-ees were annoyed too, already in the process of closing, but Darren, lean-ing on his crutches, told them about the accident, and he succeeded in buying a replacement.

Now he was laying in bed, cursing the slow internet connection and hoping to see Sheila's number. She'd left a message late last night, her coy voice telling him she'd arrived safely in San Diego. Although the phone had been on the bedside table, he hadn't heard it ring, and her number hadn't shown on the call log.

He let his head fall back on the headboard and he thought of the morning they'd spent, strolling through the museums in Old Town. Sheila was so easy to be with, peaceful yet intriguing; beautiful yet unas-suming.

Darren, who usually refrained from getting physical in public, couldn't keep his hands off her. He'd found himself kissing her constant-ly and in one of the galleries when they'd rested on a bench, had pulled her onto his lap, his hands roaming her body. He felt like a randy teenager when a security guard shooed them from the room.

Sighing, he adjusted the notebook on his lap. He'd tried to get her to stay another day and pressed her about the nature of the business she had to attend in San Diego. Most women chattered constantly, but not Sheila.

It took some coaxing to get her to admit she had an interview at one of the universities for their anthropology department. Darren immediately launched into a sales pitch for UNM, surprising both himself and Sheila. She teased him, suggesting he switch careers and work in the admissions department of his alma mater.

"C'mon," he growled at the computer. He was sorry they hadn't made firm plans to see each other again.

Shifting the thing off his lap, a glimmer of color caught his eye. Sunlight glinted off a strand of Sheila's hair and his mouth watered to kiss her. He smoothed his hand over the sheet and hoped he could find her phone number.

SHEILA'S PHONE CHIMED AND SHE TOOK A BREATH BEFORE RETRIEVING it from her purse. She could feel Agatha's eyes on her. The phone bore another text message from Andrea. It read, "Haven't heard from u in 2 days missy."

"Thanks for brunch, Mrs. B," Sheila said. She carried her plate to the sink.

"You don't eat enough. You need more protein," Agatha said. "You're too thin, dear. Take some of this with you."

She glanced at Dr. Baldwin and took the container from his mother. The pair were a study in contrasts, but Agatha was the perfect house mother for the traumatized girls who came to the non-traditional facility. A retired R.N., Agatha was the only staff member who lived at The Cove. A full complement of therapists, yoga instructors, and trainers rotated through the facility when patients were in residence.

"Thank you, again," she said to Agatha. She kissed the woman on the cheek and accepted the chicken and rice. It would be a delicious treat for one of the homeless people she often saw holding signs at the freeway exit ramps.

"Will you head north?" Dr. Baldwin asked.

She shook her head. "I'm going to head down to Mission Bay to check on the properties."

"Will you be staying in one of the condos?"

"The management company said they're all rented. I stayed at The Shores last night but I'm not sure where I'm headed next."

She usually shied away from the five-star hotels. At over $300 a night, she could afford the rate for a month straight without blinking. But she feared encountering someone who might recognize her. Or worse, a reporter. The La Jolla Shores Hotel offered some of the best coastal views and she chanced it last night. The massage she'd enjoyed on the balcony of her suite had been worth it.

"Hmph," Agatha said. Sheila looked over her shoulder at the old woman, bent over the sink. "I know where she'll go next."

Sheila's eyes widened and she bent to retrieve her purse. She told Dr. Baldwin about Darren, once they repaired to his office but the door had been closed. *Hadn't it?*

"There are a few weeks before the ladies arrive," Dr. Baldwin said. "I'll look forward to hearing from you before then."

She shook his outstretched hand and left. After the full morning at The Cove, she was uncomfortable with the quiet in her car. She dialed Andrea and started the engine.

"Please pick up," Sheila muttered. She didn't want to be alone with her thoughts, worrying over the possibility of resuming therapy with Dr. Baldwin. She didn't want to wonder about why she hadn't heard from Darren.

Andrea finally answered. "Hey girl," she said. "How did things go with Darren?"

"Good." Sheila said. "Can you talk, or is Raheem there?"

"Raheem, who?"

"Uh-oh, what happened?" Sheila asked.

"Don't ever date a man with kids," Andrea said. "I am so sick of baby mama drama. The kids I can handle," she amended. "But the baby mamas? Uh, anh. I am *so* done."

Sheila listened to her rant for ten minutes, inserting *mmm's* and *what's* where appropriate. She backed Dexter into a parking spot across the street from the condo units she owned; her first real estate purchase.

Her grandfather had brought her here on her 18th birthday and helped her invest part of her trust fund in the properties. Some were year round rentals and others were available by the week. A white van drove past and she gasped.

"What's the matter?" Andrea's voice lost its annoyance.

Sheila watched the Ford disappear around a corner. "I keep seeing white vans everywhere."

"White vans, as in plural vans?" Andrea asked. "Or the *same* white van?"

She let out a grateful breath. Andrea not only listened, she asked the right questions. "I don't know if it's the same one. I saw one down the street from Darren's house and then a few on the road. This one is a Ford."

"Did you get any of the license plate?"

"No."

"Well," Andrea said and Sheila laughed. Momma was full of expressions and *well* was one of her favorites. Growing up, both girls had learned *well* could be a question, an answer, or a statement.

"Well," Sheila said. "I guess that's the end of Raheem, huh?"

"Yes, Lord. I had to give that man his walking papers. You all right,

Sheila?" Andrea's voice softened and Sheila was struck by how much she sounded like Momma.

"Yeah, I mean, yes. I finished up with Dr. B and I'm in Mission Beach now."

"Momma's been dreaming about you," Andrea said.

"Oh," Sheila said uneasily. She used to love hearing about Momma's dreams and visions, at least until her father had threatened to fire Momma because of them. Momma had shocked The Great Michael Chase by laughing in his face at the threat. Sheila would not have believed the story except she'd seen it herself. And although Momma continued to be her nanny until Sheila had gone to college, Momma was less open about what Michael W. Chase had called her witchcraft.

"What has Momma been dreaming?"

"She wouldn't say, she wants you to call her."

"Is she there now?"

"No. She's taking care of paperwork at Safe Haven." Sheila let out a sigh and Andrea continued. "When are you going to see Darren again?"

"Umm..."

"You didn't make plans to see him again?" She fumbled with the door latch. A horn bleated and she recoiled, pulling the door closed again. When the road was clear, Sheila exited the vehicle. "I guess that's a no," Andrea said. "The next question is, why?"

"I don't think he wants to see me again," Sheila said. She recalled his grim expression when she left and the fact that he hadn't returned her phone call either.

"What?" Andrea shouted and Sheila nearly dropped the phone. "Did you sleep with him?"

"Dreya."

"Don't 'Dreya' me. Any man who makes pasta from scratch is gettin' some."

"You're breaking up, I can't hear you," she yelled into the phone. She ran across the street and removed her sandals when she reached the sand.

"Don't pretend your phone is breaking up," Andrea said. "If you use that lame ass excuse on me, I swear I will come to San Diego and kick your skinny butt."

"I'm at the beach. I'll have to tell you about it later."

"Umm hmm. You don't have to tell me the juicy bits now but I do want to know how you left things."

"Does this have to do with Momma's dream?" Sheila asked.

"Quit stalling."

"Okay, okay. Darren looked mad when I left." She dug her toes into the sand.

"Mad? As in rabid?"

"*Angry*, you pain in the ass. I don't know if he was mad—angry—because his secretary kept calling or..."

"Or cuz you didn't swallow?"

"Ohmygawd. You did *not* just say that to me." Sheila's face burned when a couple passing by glanced at her.

Andrea whooped. "Sorry. I know you're too prim and proper for all that." She cleared her throat. "Why would Darren be angry? Did you argue? Was he rushing-you-out-the-door angry?"

"No," Sheila said. "He asked me to stay another day."

"What did you say?"

"Well, I said yes on Monday but when he asked me on Tuesday, I told him I couldn't."

"Wait a minute. Let me get this straight. On Sunday Darren swept you off your pretty pink toenails. He made you dinner on Monday night and asked you to stay till Tuesday. He took the day off to spend with you, and then asked you to stay till Thursday?"

"Um, yes." Andrea's laughter had Sheila scowling at the phone. "Why are you laughing?"

"Please. The man was mad because he didn't want a sweet thing to get away. Did you tell Darren your story about being a vagabond and traveling the country?"

"Yes."

"And he doesn't know why you *had* to go to San Diego?"

"No," Sheila said. She pushed her sunglasses up and pinched the bridge of her nose. She thought of the numerous times Darren had asked her to stay. He mentioned going to New York to visit his family but he hadn't said anything about seeing her in the future.

"Have you talked to Darren since you left Albuquerque?"

Sheila winced. "I called when I got in last night but his phone must have been off because it went straight to voicemail."

"Well," Andrea said.

"Well, what?"

"Are you going to call him again?"

"But I did call him," Sheila protested. "And he hasn't called me back. You always say if you beat a man's phone down—"

"Girl, I know men are tripping over you all the time, they always have. And for the past two years, you haven't given a man the time of day, let alone spent three nights with one. There's got to be something special about Darren that made you say yes to him, right? Don't you want to see him again?"

"Yes but..." Sheila drew in a breath and her words came out in a rush. "But I don't know if I *should* see Darren again. He's close to his family and he asked more than once about mine. I don't want to lie to him but I can't tell him the truth, either. And what can I offer him? What if I do see him again? I don't live in Albuquerque. I don't live in San Diego. I don't live anywhere. I run from ghosts and nightmares. What if he finds out about... what if..."

She couldn't bring herself to voice her deepest fear, not even to her oldest friend. A chill swept over Sheila and she tried to convince herself it was what the locals called *June gloom*.

CHAPTER 14

"FINALLY," DARREN CHEERED WHEN HE WAS ABLE TO LOG INTO HIS CELlular account. He scrolled through the call history and saw an incoming at 12:02 A.M. The number was unavailable. He shoved the computer off his lap, resisting the urge to throw it, and hobbled to the toilet. How long would it be before Sheila called him again? What if she thought he was ignoring her?

"You need to chill, Darren," he said aloud.

"I agree."

"Jesus, Stan, you scared the shit out of me."

Stan affected a comical voice, "Shit? Where shit? Me see no shit." He held up a DVD featuring the robot he'd quoted.

"Whoa, I haven't seen Short Circuit in ages."

"How's the ankle?"

"Hurts."

"Want some Tylenol?" Stan asked.

Darren shook his head. "Did you get the book?"

Stan went back to the living room and withdrew a thick paperback from the bags he'd left at the door. "Since when do you read westerns?" he asked.

"Sheila's reading it. I was curious. A thousand pages?" Darren read over the synopsis and limped back to the bedroom.

"You sure you didn't bump your head on the fall too?" Stan said. "Hey, can we watch the movie in the living room?"

"Why?" Darren said. "The bed is more comfortable than the sofa." He didn't own a TV; they would watch the movie on his laptop.

"You haven't changed the sheets yet."

STAN WATCHED DARREN'S HEAD LOLL BETWEEN HIS SHOULDERS. THE guy had fallen asleep twenty minutes into the movie, ten minutes later than he usually did. He never made it through a movie or a book. D was kidding himself, thinking he'd read a 1,000 pager. The book sat between them on the sofa and he started when it tumbled onto the floor.

Suddenly Darren lurched forward and grabbed his cell phone from the end table. Stan swore to disguise his surprise. The thing had barely gone off. "Hello?"

The conversation was over in less than a minute and Stan gaped in disbelief when Darren told him who'd called. "I thought you liked Marilyn." When D shrugged, Stan put a hand on Casanova's head.

"What're you doing?"

"Checking for a temperature."

"Can I get one of those?" he asked, pointing at Stan's empty. The phone rang again and Darren answered with "Sheila?" His face screwed up at the caller's response.

"Smooth," Stan said. "Who was it this time?"

"Darlene."

"Watching you is better than the movie." Stan chuckled and strode to the kitchen. "Guess you blew that one."

"Doesn't matter," Darren said, drawing on the beer Stan handed him. "'Darren & Darlene' sounded too rhymy anyway."

"What?" Stan pretended to choke on his Sam Adams. "You've become a one-woman man in three days?"

"C'mon Stan, I'm not that bad anymore. I've been on a few dates but I haven't slept with a woman since Zoë and I broke up."

"What about Sophia?"

"Oh, yeah, Sophia."

"Umm hmm."

"Sheila's different," he said. "She's feisty."

Stan lowered the volume on the computer. It sat on the ottoman next to Darren's injured foot. "Ten years different," he said. "Zoë was feisty too and she was local. You don't do long distance relationships, remember? And Sheila's too skinny."

"Twelve. Sheila is twenty-five." He looked at the beer and frowned. "Maybe feisty isn't the right word. She's... complex and she's not skinny; she's slender. She rebuilt a '71 Challenger with her grandfather. Cool, huh?" Stan opened his mouth, shut it, then drew heavily on the beer. "What?"

"Really, D?" His friend scowled at the sarcasm but Stan continued. "How do you know she doesn't have stars in her eyes? Since you won the Gonzales case, you've got your own groupies."

It was Darren's turn to laugh. "You don't know Sheila. She tried to pay for breakfast, lunch, the museum admission—"

"You don't know her either but that's not stopping you from acting like a lovesick pup." He snatched the paperback book from the floor and flung it onto the coffee table.

"Look, I'm probably going to regret telling you this but when Sheila paid for her car repair, she used a *black* credit card."

"No shit?" Stan leaned forward. "It must be her Daddy's. No twenty-five year old could have her own AmEx Centurion."

The phone rang and Darren's voice was hopeful when he answered. "Hello... *Sheila*."

Stan shook his head and went for another beer. From the kitchen he heard Darren telling Sheila about the accident and the busted phone. He put a box of hot wings in the microwave and his own phone rang but he ignored the call. Darren was still grinning stupidly when he returned with the food.

"Ma thought you should be my nursemaid." His eyes were closed and Stan moved the table closer to the sofa and went back to the kitchen for his beer. "Oh Sheila, that would be just what the doctor ordered."

"The doctor ordered you to keep your feet up, not your—"

D gave him the "cut it" signal. "That's Stan, always the comedian. Hang on, let me get a pen so I can write down your number." He began to lower his legs from the ottoman but Stan stopped him and went to the office for a pad and pen.

"You're the man. Thanks." Stan felt the beginnings of a headache when Darren put down the phone and rubbed his hands together. "She's coming back!"

FRIDAY, JUNE 8TH

HERRERA PARKED THE VAN THREE BLOCKS FROM THE OPEN HOUSE. HE was ready to sprint back to the apartment complex on Hornblend Street when the tracking device beeped. He scowled. On his last pass around the block, he'd seen a crowd forming outside the wrought iron gates.

"It's my day off," he growled at the monitor, before hopping out of the van. It took him twenty minutes to find parking in the Pacific Beach neighborhood, which confirmed his suspicions: he had to find a place with assigned parking. For now he was staying with a buddy but the guy's wife was high strung and Herrera was highly motivated to find his own digs.

A dozen people followed the manager inside the small, dark apartment. An argument broke out between two men when one tried to hand over a signed application and deposit, in cash. The manager, a petite woman in her 60's, backed away from the men.

"I don't see what the problem is," the first one said. "I got the money right here. You can check my credit, I don't have kids or pets."

"You can't go throwing money at the lady, thinking you can bribe her." The second man grabbed the manager's arm. "Tell him."

Two middle-aged women gasped.

"I think you should keep your hands to yourself," Herrera said. The man gave him a caustic look. "Assault is a crime punishable with jail time."

"Assault? What are you talking about?"

"Would you like me to call the police ma'am?" Herrera asked.

The manager looked up at Herrera with relief. She didn't get a chance to answer. The man released her and pushed past the watching crowd, to the door.

"Well I guess you'll get the place now," a woman said. She also headed for the door.

"Thank you," the manager said. "Why don't you come to my office for tea?"

An hour later, Herrera left Mrs. Chen's office with the apartment keys. He hadn't been sure he wanted it but she'd been insistent, lowering the rent by $200.

He let out a curse when he checked the tracking device. Vasquez didn't answer his phone. SW was expected to stay in San Diego until July. The transmitter showed her traveling east on the interstate. She was half-way to El Centro. His phone rang and Herrera told Vasquez his suspicion.

"You're going to have to follow the subject," Vasquez said.

He let out a string of his favorite expletives. So much for a day off. *Why hadn't he kept his damned mouth shut?* He could have pretended he turned off the tracking device.

"I saw it too," his boss said. "I was waiting to see how far east the subject would travel before I phoned you. I think I've found your replacement but McKay isn't available for a few more weeks and you're already familiar with where the subject has been in Albuquerque." He rustled some papers. "Maybe the subject has another destination."

"Why don't we upgrade the device so we can listen in to her conversations?" Herrera said.

"The subject," Vasquez said. Herrera wanted to lash out at Mr. Protocol for saying "the subject" so many damned times.

"Look," Herrera said. He turned the key in the ignition. "I signed for an apartment here and I'd rather not get to Albuquerque and have you tell me I'm stationed there."

Vasquez didn't answer immediately and Herrera knew he'd guessed correctly. "It's a possibility," his boss said finally, ending the conversation.

Herrera decided to keep the apartment keys. He'd already told Mrs. Chen he traveled often and who knew what SW would do. After topping off the gas tank, he drove south toward his favorite taco joint but changed his mind and hooked a u-turn.

If he ran into some of his old crew, he couldn't throw 'em a knuckle pound and bounce. Instead he picked up a double-double, and skipped the fries. Two weeks on the road hadn't afforded much time for workouts and he was feeling soft. Herrera had decided that's why Peach had gotten the drop on him.

Peach seemed an unlikely name for such a hard-looking woman. In the Marine Corps, he encountered a few women who were so butch they looked more masculine than some of the younger recruits. Herrera had immediately lumped her with them. But then her face changed when Tom, the old man, had said her kid was sick. *What had he meant when he said the kid had another attack?*

Was Peach married? How had she come by the scar on her neck? The questions mounted, and Herrera acknowledged he was more interested than a third-party observer should be.

SW's signal crossed into Arizona and he thought he might get a chance to ask Peach some of the questions.

CHAPTER 15

SHEILA EJECTED THE BILLIE HOLIDAY CD AND REPLACED IT WITH A new audio book. Cops were scarce on I-40 east and she took advantage, pushing Dexter to almost 20 mph over the speed limit. If she kept up the pace, she would arrive in Albuquerque before 9 PM.

The driver of a black Jetta threw an arm out the window and gestured at a passing semi. A horn bleated from the truck, three short beeps and the Jetta returned them. Sheila clicked her fingernails on the steering wheel and tapped the brake pedal.

She crossed the New Mexico state line and mulled over her return to San Diego. It hadn't been the sweet relief she'd anticipated for months. The highways hadn't been aflame with the fuchsia ice plant she loved. The beach was crowded with tourists and litter. And no one awaited her in San Diego, except the Baldwins. But they were paid to care, well paid. With a sigh, she turned off the audio book.

After talking to Andrea, Sheila vacillated between fear and desire. Both Dr. B and Andrea had encouraged it was time to move on. So she took a chance and redialed Darren's number. The enthusiasm in his voice when she phoned from the beach fueled her desire to see him again. She'd slammed the door on the fearful thoughts and made plans to drive back to Albuquerque.

Darren was sexy, charming, and he wanted her. Sheila wanted him, too. Who knew what would happen beyond this weekend? She was willing to at least see him once more. Passing a sign for the New Mexico Welcome Center, she imagined the welcome she'd get from Darren. The scenario made her increase the setting on the cruise control again.

Several hours later when the grill of her car scraped the dip at the base of Darren's driveway, Sheila did a double take. A pink car seat glowed from the porch.

He has a kid?

The idea upset her and Sheila struggled to determine why. It seemed like vital information he should have disclosed, especially since she'd come back to spend the weekend with him. She didn't know if she wanted to be involved with a man who had a child, in light of Andrea's experiences.

Sheila set the emergency brake with a jerk, glaring at the pink thing beneath the porch light. How old was the girl? What if he had more than one kid? How could he not tell her? She'd talked to him an hour ago to update him on her ETA. Sheila's head fell on the steering wheel.

The front door opened and her head snapped up. The key was still in the ignition and she hadn't quite made up her mind to back out of the driveway, but if Darren had seen her car, it would be cowardly to do so.

"Charlieeeee," called a child's voice. The girl opened the screened door and poked out a curly head, calling for the cat again. "Who are you?" she asked.

Sheila hung onto the car door, straddling the foot board. The little girl had Darren's sun-kissed skin and the loose curls she imagined he'd have if his hair were longer. Her eyes were more of an almond shape than his and they currently were boring into Sheila.

Darren's voice called from the inside, "Did you find him?" Sheila's stomach clenched.

"Someone's here," the girl yelled. She looked about four or five years old and dressed in the same hot pink and greens of her car seat. Sheila couldn't take her eyes off the girl until Darren called her name from the door.

"Sheila."

"Sheila?" the girl repeated. "You don't look like a Sheila. I have a doll named Sheila and she's Black."

Darren opened the screened door. "Hey gorgeous."

"What does gorgeous mean?"

He looked down at the little girl and some of Sheila's anger melted. Her father had never looked at her with such tenderness. "It means really, really, really pretty," he said. "Just like you."

The girl put her little hand on her hip. "Mom says being pretty isn't as important as being smart. Are you smart?"

Sheila found herself closing the car door and laughing with Darren.

"C'mere," he called. She walked toward him and her laughter faded. The child watched closely. Darren framed Sheila's face with his hands and lowered his mouth over hers.

"Ewww, you're kissing."

Darren broke off to say, "Shush," and then he pulled her into an embrace. "Welcome back." She pushed against his torso, some of the anger returning at the "shush." She wanted to question him but not in front of his daughter. "Where's your suitcase?" he asked.

"I'll get it later," she said, mentally adding, *If I stay.*

"Come inside sweetie," Darren said, reaching out for the girl's hand. "Charlie will come home when he's ready."

"Do you think he's at the kitty cat disco?"

"Probably."

"What's your name?" Sheila asked. She bent to remove her heels. At the last rest stop, she'd changed into a sexy, fitted dress and she could feel Darren's eyes roaming over it.

"Joelle Danetta Bustamante. I can spell it too. Do you wanna hear me spell it?"

"Sure," she said. Darren patted the sofa and Joelle ran over and jumped on him, calling out the letters in her name. She got the 'T' and the 'E' mixed up at the end and started over.

He adjusted the girl on his lap and held out his hand for Sheila. She sat next to him, wondering why they had different last names when Joelle leapt from the sofa.

"I can write my name too. You wanna see?"

She nodded and Joelle ran for the office but quickly turned back. "Is it OK if I get some paper from the printer, Uncle D?"

He nodded and lifted Sheila onto his lap. She hoped he missed the wave of relief that washed over her when Joelle called him Uncle D. "Sorry about this," he said. "My cousin called right after you, desperate for a sitter." Joelle returned with paper. "I'll fill you in later."

"It's okay." She molded her lips to his, not holding back this time.

"You're kissing again," Joelle said from the floor.

SATURDAY, JUNE 9TH

HERRERA SLEPT IN THE VAN AGAIN, A FEW BLOCKS FROM ABRUZZO'S house. He checked in with Mr. Protocol and threw the van in gear, to find a Mickey D's. At a stop light he saw an advertisement for the boxing gym and changed directions, surprised at his desire to see Peach again.

It was early and the gym didn't open for another half hour. Herrera parked the van a few blocks away, out of habit, and leaned against a tree across the street. Ten minutes later a truck rolled up with the old man, Tom, behind the wheel. Then a jeep rattled around the corner and Herrera's eyes honed in on the black hair of the female driver.

Peach greeted Tom with a peck on the cheek. Herrera eyed the jeans molded to her ass, the sequined tank top, and the silver earrings dangling from her ears. She smiled at something the man said and Herrera shoved off the tree.

He'd guessed correctly. Peach *was* pretty when she smiled. Herrera waited for them to turn on the lights and flip the "closed" sign before he pushed off the tree with his gym bag.

Tom tried to sell him a membership this time. The door opened and the old man looked up. "You're late, TJ," he snapped.

"S'OK," TJ said. "I know the owner."

"This is your last warning. Don't think I won't fire your ass."

TJ frowned at the old man. "Oh come on Pop, I'm only late ten minutes."

"Pea's got a kid, works two jobs, she's going to school, and she was *still* here early. It don't matter if it's ten minutes or an hour, you're late again, and you're fired."

Herrera found himself nodding and TJ noticed, scowling like he wanted to slug him. Instead the guy lumbered off to the locker room.

"Sorry about that. If you don't wanna membership, the day use fee is $20." Herrera paid the fee and changed in the locker room. He hit the weights in the corner of the main floor. He figured he could enjoy watching Peach for a couple hours before he had to check on SW.

PEACH FELT BAD FOR DUMPING JOELLE ON DARREN. SHE DROVE FASTER than usual, and arrived at her cousin's house ten minutes after leaving the gym.

"Hello?" she called through the open front door. The house was quiet. Darren's reply came from the bathroom. Crayon drawings covered the floor. Peach smiled and wondered if Joelle had used up every piece of paper in the house.

Darren greeted her with a hug. "You got done early?"

"Yeah, it was slow for a Saturday. Thank gawd cuz I've got tons of reading to do. Where's my monkey?"

"Sold her. Got a good price too!" Darren sunk onto the sofa with a grin. "Oh shoot, you want something to drink?" Peach shook her head and he continued. "Sheila took her to the park for a walk."

"Oh. I drove by the park on the way here, I must have missed them." She stood up but Darren waved.

"Hold on, let me call her to see if they're on their way back." He pulled his cell phone from his pocket and spoke briefly. "Joelle wanted to go exploring," he reported. "They're about ten minutes away."

"Which means another twenty. You're a lifesaver, D. I'm sorry to ruin your weekend."

"Don't be silly, you know I love spending time with my goddaughter. How was the catering event last night?"

"Not bad. I wish I could make that kind of money working at the gym. Now, tell me more about this new woman," she said. Darren told the story of how he met Sheila and she rolled her eyes at the part about the serenade. When Joelle came bounding through the front door thirty minutes later, Peach jumped to her feet. "You're not supposed to be running, monkey."

"I'm sorry," Sheila said. "She didn't run far."

Peach gasped. "Liz?"

"No Mom, this is Sheila Washington," Joelle said.

Peach narrowed her eyes, about to argue when Sheila held out a hand. "Nice to meet you, Peach. You have a wonderful daughter."

"You look like someone I knew in high school."

"Isn't it funny how we all have a twin?" Sheila said.

"Uhhh," Darren said. "I shouldn't have taken that medication."

He clutched his stomach and Sheila ran to the kitchen for the garbage can. "Here," she said, thrusting it at him.

"I don't want Joelle to see me hurl," he whispered.

Peach heard him and ushered Joelle to the door. "But I don't wanna go, Mommy. I want to stay with Sheila." She picked up her daughter who wailed and gripped the screen door.

"Cut it out, Joelle," she said and broke the child's hold.

"Darren—" Sheila said.

"Go," he said. "I don't want you to see me hurl either."

Sheila gave him a sympathetic look and followed after Peach. She carried Joelle's car seat to the Jeep. Peach released Joelle and she immediately tackled Sheila's legs.

"We gotta go monkey. Uncle D isn't feeling good." She looked up at the other woman. "He's never done well with pain meds."

"He said so too but Joelle accidently stepped on his foot and—"

"What? He didn't tell me that."

Sheila put her hands up. "Don't tell him I told you. He was being all macho about it but I insisted he take something for the swelling."

Peach shook her head at Joelle.

"It was an accident, Pea," Sheila said.

Peach drew a sharp breath. "What did you call me?" she said. Only her closest friends and family called her Pea.

Sheila pursed her mouth and looked up at the house.

"Liz?" Peach whispered. She hugged the taller woman. "I thought you were dead, Liz."

Sheila shuddered. "Liz *est morte*," she whispered back.

"You're squishing us, Mom!" Joelle protested and Peach stepped back, her face full of questions. It had been a decade since they'd attended French class together but Peach understood *morte* meant dead.

"I met Darren a few days ago," Sheila said. "I don't..."

Peach recognized the conflict on her friend's face. She knew what it was like to run from the past. She clasped Sheila's hand. "I won't tell him."

Sheila brushed at her face with her free hand. "Thanks, Pea."

Joelle swung between the taller woman's legs. "Are you coming home with us, Sheila?"

"Miss Sheila," Peach corrected.

"Not today sweetie," she said, picking up the girl. "Maybe I'll come visit you soon."

"That would be great. We have to catch up," the boxer said. She reached in the jeep to grab a piece of paper and a pen. "How's Andrea? Her son should be about eight now, right?" When she looked up at the tortured expression on Sheila's face, her breath left her.

She squeezed Joelle to her chest, covering the child's ear. "He was still-born."

Peach clapped a hand over her mouth. "Will you call me?" she asked when she recovered her voice.

Sheila nodded and took the paper with Peach's phone number. A flash of color at the house drew her attention and she saw Darren at the door.

"We gotta go kiddo," Peach told Joelle.

"I want to say bye to Uncle D." Sheila carried Joelle up the steps to the house for the girl to kiss Darren's cheek. "Thank you for having me," she said.

"You're welcome. Any time, cutie." Sheila walked Joelle back to the car and lowered her into her car seat.

"Did you say thank you?" Peach asked.

"Yes, Mom."

Peach gave Sheila another hug and hopped in the jeep.

CHAPTER 16

DARREN LED SHEILA TO THE BEDROOM, LAYING ON THE BED FIRST, AND then pulling her on top of him. "Joelle hogged you last night," he said, squeezing her. He had a queen sized bed but he'd slept in the guest room because his little cousin was accustomed to sleeping with her mother.

Joelle traveled while she slept, and three was definitely a crowd with him, Sheila, and the child in his bed. When Sheila tried to leave Joelle in the bed and join him, his little cousin had followed.

"Wait," Sheila said. She stopped his hands from lifting her shirt. "We need to talk about something."

He cocked his head. "What's up, sweetness?"

She braced herself on the bed and twisted out of his embrace. She sat up, crossing her legs. Darren rolled toward her, on his side. "So, on Sunday..." she said, picking at a string on her shirt. "We had unprotected sex and I need to know if..." her voice trailed off again and he let out a sigh.

"Oh," he said, rubbing his thumb over her sweaty palm. "I'm clean. I uh, don't usually have sex without a condom and I've never had any STDs."

"Have you been tested?" She snapped off the string and rolled it between her fingers.

"A few months ago. I have the results on paper if you'd like to see them." Sheila made no answer and he scooted closer, lifting her chin with his finger, forcing her to meet his eyes. "Is there something else?"

She took a breath. "Yes. Look, I know we just met and I'm not asking for a commitment from you or anything, but I'd like to know if you're having sex with anyone else."

Darren found the discomfort on her face made him feel oddly satisfied. "No," he said. "The last relationship I was in ended a few months ago. I'm not into multiple partners."

"I'm not talking threesomes," she said.

He suppressed a laugh. "Our night together on Sunday wasn't the norm for me." At her raised eyebrows, the attorney continued, "I'm serious. I could be asking the same questions of you."

Sheila stiffened. "Why aren't you? Asking the same questions, I mean?"

"Well," he said. "You told me you hadn't been with anyone in a long time and I believe you." He brushed his fingers over her arm. She still looked uncomfortable and Darren dragged himself up into a sitting position against the headboard. He tried to be patient. His efforts lasted thirty seconds. "What's the matter, Sheila?"

"Nothing." She threw a leg over him, resting on his upper thighs. She parted his lips with her tongue and he almost got lost in the delicious feel of her. Darren brought his hands to her face and gently pushed back.

"Tell me."

Conflict marred her face and she finally said, "I'm not on the Pill. I called Planned Parenthood to ask about the Morning After Pill but—"

"You think you could be pregnant?"

She laughed tightly. "I'm not trying to trap you, Darren. I don't want children so you don't have to worry. I—"

"You don't want children?" His voice was incredulous.

She narrowed her eyes and moved off of him. "You want children, don't you?"

"You were amazing with Joelle." Darren reached for the glass of water on the end table, amazed she could read him so clearly. He often joked that dating in his mid-thirties had become as complex as drafting an immigration law capable of passing in both Arizona and New Mexico.

It felt like most of the women were doing the Marisa Tomei impersonation about their biological clocks. Darren never imagined he'd be on *that* end of a conversation. "I'm 37 and I'm Catholic," he said. "I don't believe in abortion, Sheila."

"You don't have to believe in abortion, it's not your body!" She leapt off him and Darren tried to return the glass to the end table but missed. It shattered on the floor, sending glass and water over the narrow space between the bed and the wall.

"Dammit!"

"Stay there," she said. "I'll take care of it." She disappeared briefly and returned wearing his flip flops. Her arms were full of the wastebasket, broom, and a towel.

He tried to help her collect the broken shards but he was barefoot and she repeated the order to stay on the bed. "Be careful. Don't cut yourself." Once Sheila picked up all the visible glass, Darren reached for her hand. "Come here."

"I should go," she said without looking at him.

"I don't want you to go, Sheila." He took the damp towel from her hand and tossed it into the wastebasket. "Please, come here."

She sighed but sat on the edge of the bed. "I'm sorry I brought it up," she said, "but I guess it's for the best. I don't want to waste your time since you're '37 and Catholic.'"

"Sheila, come sit next to me." She shook her head and he scooted down toward her. "I think we would make pretty babies," Darren said. He tugged on the belt loop of her shorts until she leaned into him. Then he laced his arms around her waist. "Don't you?"

She shivered. "God wouldn't be that cruel."

"What do you mean?"

"Never mind." She shook her head and pushed against him. "I'm not pregnant. Let me go."

"What's your favorite color?" he said.

"What?"

"Your favorite color?" Darren said.

"Green, why?"

"That's mine too. Who's your favorite vocalist?"

"Darren—"

"Billie Holiday, right? You were singing along with all the songs the other night. She's my favorite too. And you love muscle cars."

"What does that have to do with anything?"

"We have a lot in common."

Sheila turned to look at him and Darren tried to kiss her. She raised a hand to stop him. "We might have some things in common but not wanting to procreate is a *huge* difference. It's not something you can compromise on, like getting a hamster instead of a dog. I'm not what you're looking for, Darren."

"Why?"

"Why, what?"

"Why don't you want to have children?" he said.

"Why *would* I?"

"Because they're fun and cute and innocent."

"And loud and needy and time-consuming."

"You're young, you'll change your mind."

"No, I won't." She pushed at him again.

"Wait till you get near your thirties."

"Yeah well, you'll be married and working on producing an Abruzzo basketball team for the local Catholic school by then. But I'll tell you what, I'll drop you a post card and let you know how much I'm enjoying my kid-free life."

Darren searched her green eyes, looking for signs of jest but found none. Why did her suggestion he would be married to someone else when he had children irk him so much? A vein on her temple pulsed and he reached out, tracing his index finger over it. He hadn't noticed it before and wondered if it only popped out when she was angry. Sheila's chest rose and fell with rapid breaths and he laid his head there, sighing.

SHEILA STIFFENED. "WHAT ARE YOU DOING?"

"Listening to your heart beat," Darren said. "It's fast." His mouth was right at the V of her shirt and his breath tickled her chest. The sensation was almost too much but she didn't want to move. She wanted to take back the retort and let him kiss her until she was dizzy. But she was afraid Darren was probably going to tell her she was right, she should go.

Sheila was surprised at herself. She couldn't see herself having an abortion; she'd chickened out when the receptionist at Planned Parenthood offered her an appointment for a mere exam. Darren's attitude put her on the defensive.

A minute passed and then several more and her breathing began to slow until it matched Darren's. He was so still against her chest she wondered if he could have fallen asleep. Her side began to ache from the awkward angle and she tried to shift without waking him.

"If you're not pregnant," he said, "then we'll be careful until you get on the Pill. I can wait."

She tensed again. "Wait for what?"

Darren raised his head. He bared his perfect teeth in one of his dazzling smiles but she felt like he was holding a silent debate. "I don't like the scenario you painted of me married to someone else—" he held up a hand when she tried to speak. "And yeah, we just met but I don't want it to end before we really get started."

"What about 'I'm 37 and I'm Catholic'?" She tried to imitate his voice and Darren chuckled.

"Sorry. I got a little carried away." He stroked a hand over her hair. "I always thought I would be a family man by 35 but after things ended with Wendy, I kinda let the dream go..." His lips brushed her mole. "When you said 'Planned Parenthood' and 'Morning After Pill,' I got a little anxious. But it's a moot point if you're not pregnant."

She eyed him, wondering if his *I can wait* statement meant, *I can wait until your period and then all bets are off*. He was after all an attorney. Wasn't he supposed to be good at persuasion?

"Will you lay down with me? Please?" Darren asked.

She hesitated a moment, then kicked off the flip flops, and walked on her knees into his side. He pulled her close, tucking her head into the crook of his neck and squeezing his arms around her. She fit against him perfectly.

"The idea of being with anyone else is repugnant," he said into her hair and threw his leg over hers. "The idea of *you* being with someone else..." he shuddered and squeezed tighter.

She shouldn't like it so much that he was possessive of her when they'd known each other a week. *Less* than a week. Yet Sheila had to agree the idea of him being with another woman made her want to puke.

Wasn't it supposed to be like that at the beginning? Excitement and speculations for the future? It had been like that with Rick but they were both teenagers. If she had more experience with men, maybe she'd know better.

"How was your interview?"

"Huh?"

"Your interview, at USD?"

She tried to remember what she'd planned to tell Darren on the subject. "I'm not ready to go back to school yet," she said finally.

"You should move here," he said.

"Oh yeah?"

"Yeah. Think of all the money you'd save on gas coming to see me." Darren's kiss was rough and claiming. "I don't want you to go back to San Diego," he said. "I want to keep you right *here*."

Darren rose up to his knees, hooked his thumbs under her bra and lifted it over her head, along with her shirt. He tossed the bundle aside and grinned, capturing a breast in each hand. Sheila gasped when he pinched both nipples at the same time. Then he lowered his mouth. His tongue made hot trails, encircling her nipple.

"You like that?" he asked. His breath tickled the moist skin and she shuddered. Pleasure vibrated throughout her nerve endings, and she looked up at him through hooded eyes.

"Umm hmm."

"Where else do you want my mouth?"

Sheila tried to tell him with her eyes, too shy to say it aloud. Darren released her breast and she made a sound of protest before she felt his hands on the button of her shorts. He slid them down her thighs and over her ankles.

"*Non ci credo.*"

"What?"

"I don't believe it," Darren said.

"Don't believe what?" Alarm shot through her body at the bewilderment on his face and she sat up.

"I can't believe how exquisite you are."

"Oh."

He shook his head and she squirmed, uncertain whether the statement was praise. Wanting to take the focus off herself, she stroked her hand over the outline tenting his shorts. Darren hissed.

"You're overdressed." She pulled his shirt up and he helped her get it over his head. She ran her hands over his chest, loving the way his soft hair felt on her fingers. Her hand looked pale sliding over his golden skin.

Sheila tugged the waistband of his shorts over his hips, and bit her lip when his erection sprang free. Darren laughed. His eyes glittered with excitement and she took him in her hand again stroking her thumb over the swollen head.

"Ahhh," he said, sinking back on his haunches and then he let out a different groan, having forgotten the injured ankle.

"I'm not a very good nursemaid." She pushed him down onto his back.

Darren stopped her from inspecting his ankle. "It's fine. You're perfect," he said. "A perfect nursemaid."

"We should put some ice on it—"

He dragged Sheila on top of him and she quickly grew dizzy from his kisses. "*Bellissima*," he murmured against her ear. "*Io te voglio*."

Sheila shuddered, feeling like she could climax from the sound of the sexy Italian words. "That doesn't mean you're going to call me a taxi, does it?"

He chuckled. "It means, *I want you.*"

"Oh good," she said. "More, more Italian!"

He began speaking quickly, in a rush of words she didn't understand. Sheila arched, pressing her breasts into his chest and gasped when Darren flipped her onto her back. He parted her legs, and the word *miele* stood out from the others.

"Honey?" she said. "Does '*miele*' mean honey?"

"*Sì, bellissima.*"

Sheila bucked at his tongue on her most sensitive flesh. Darren groaned, devouring her until an orgasm had her digging her nails into his shoulders. He murmured in Italian and chuckled, but he didn't stop laving her. Sheila was too distracted by his velvety tongue to ask for another translation. She shuddered when he grazed her clit with his teeth, and then suckled the swollen nub into his mouth. The second orgasm slammed into her, making her wonder if it were possible to die from pleasure.

Darren kissed the inside of her thigh before plucking a condom from the end table drawer. He said something else in Italian Sheila guessed meant *turn over* because he took her right leg and used it to roll her over. Then he pulled her onto her knees, pushed them further apart, and pressed her shoulders onto the bed.

He gave a growl of approval when she wiggled her hips from side to side. The head of his penis breeched her opening and Sheila tried to push back on it. Darren held her off with his hands on her hips. "Wait for it," he said.

"Now." Her voice was muffled by the sheet and she turned her head to the side, repeating the demand.

DARREN LET A FEW MORE SECONDS PASS BEFORE HE SEATED HIMSELF into Sheila completely. She moaned and clenched the sheets. When he didn't move, she wiggled again and rose up on her elbows.

"Give it to me."

He kept his hold on her hips, pulling out, and thrusting into her again. He tried to maintain a slow rhythm but then Sheila reached between them. He became unhinged when she squeezed him and he gave over to her demand, driving into her hard. His hips smacked against her ass and Sheila mewed with each of his frantic thrusts. The need for her submission overtook him, and Darren grabbed a fistful of Sheila's hair, using the hold to jerk her up onto her hands. She gasped and craned her neck around. Darren released her hair, feeling a surge of excitement when she gave him a sexy smile.

"Sheila..." he latched onto her mouth, spearing her with his tongue. Then he released some of his weight onto her back. "Stay on your knees," he said. When she continued to sag, he realized he was speaking in Italian again and he translated the order.

Her arms trembled and she dropped her head, panting. Her body rocked forward under his pounding hips. She buckled when he twisted the jewelry on her nipples, and still her submission wasn't enough.

He needed to claim her body so completely she could never be satisfied by any man but him. The urge turned him savage and Darren sunk his teeth into the flesh at the base of her neck.

Sheila screamed and her sheath contracted around his cock. She collapsed and Darren fell with her. He let out a roar of triumph, exploding with the most intense orgasm he'd ever had. When they both finished, Darren pulled out slowly, laying beside his woman.

She reached up to explore her neck. Her hand trembled. "You bit me."

"Sheila—" She rolled over and Darren braced himself but her face was relaxed. "I didn't mean to bite you. Was I too rough? Did I hurt you?"

She shook her head and he let out a breath. "I liked it," she said, nuzzling close and kissing his collar bone.

He tried to keep regret from ruining the afterglow. He hadn't wanted to put on the condom. An image had flashed in his mind, of Sheila laying on her side in his bed, cradling her belly. Pregnant, with his child. Darren had wanted to make it real, to fill her with his seed. He removed the condom and silently cursed his earlier promise to Sheila. Tossing the thing in the direction of the waste basket, he encased her with his arms and legs linked around her body.

The things he'd said to her in Italian, calling her his sexy kitten and promising to worship her body forever, were all things he wished he could tell her in English. He lifted his head and his cock stirred against her hip at the glassy look in her eyes.

Sheila felt so good, tasted so good, smelled so good and Darren thought, *she's wrong*. Sheila was completely wrong about not being the woman he wanted. She was witty and beautiful; strong-willed and independent. Unafraid to meet his temper, yet she was supple and hungry for his passion. Sheila was exactly what he was looking for and she was *his*. She just didn't know it yet.

CHAPTER 17

"Hold up your guard," Peach said.

"My arms hurt," Debbie said.

"Your face is going to hurt if you don't protect it. Arms up." The blonde shook her bangs and started again. "Don't lock your joints," she said. "Jab in and out quickly like this but don't fully extend your arm."

Debbie jabbed and Peach praised her pupil. When Debbie's form slipped again, Peach scanned the gym for help. "Hey, Duke. Give me a hand over here?"

"Sorry Peach, I'm starting my own session."

"Where's TJ?"

"Called in sick, I think," Duke said.

The boxer shook her head. Tommy was going to fire his ass for sure. "Hey stud," she called to the guy who entered the gym. "You wanna give me a hand?"

"You talking to me?" he said and Debbie giggled.

"Yeah, you got a minute?" Peach asked.

"Um Peach, I don't think I'm ready for him," Debbie said.

"No, you're not," she said. The man paused in front of them. "What's your name?"

"Herrera."

"Herrera?" she repeated, rolling the R's. "Okay, Herrera I want you to block me," Peach said and swung at him. Herrera swore and dropped the bag he was holding with his right hand, blocking with his left.

"See how quick it was?" Peach asked the trainee. "We're going to do it again, only I'm going to do what I told you *not* to do." She turned back to Herrera and swung, this time fully extending her jab and dropping her guard. Herrera slipped in an uppercut but stopped before he connected with Peach's jaw.

"Ohhh, I get it," Debbie said.

"Thanks," Peach said to Herrera.

"Muchas gracias," Debbie said.

Peach stifled a groan. The girl was more interested in flirting than boxing and every time she came for a training session, Debbie wore the skimpiest exercise tops Peach had ever seen.

The grant she'd gotten from UNM was a sweet deal, and she could put up with a few airheads. Thankfully, some of the girls in the program were actually interested in boxing, and Peach not only enjoyed those sessions, she would be able to use the data for her thesis.

"Pea, you got a call," Tom shouted.

"That's it for today Debbie; see you next week at the same time." She turned for the front counter and heard Debbie ask Herrera where he was born in Mexico.

"I'm from Puerto Rico," he said. A *Boricua*, she thought, and shivered.

"Peach Nelson," she said into the receiver. She glanced back and saw Debbie skimming a finger over the dragon tattoo covering Herrera's sleeveless shoulder. She found herself wishing the creature would come alive and bite the girl's hand off.

"Hey Pea, it's Sheila."

"Hi," Peach exclaimed and Herrera's head snapped up at her. "I'm so glad you called."

"I meant to call earlier but Darren went back to work today."

"Don't worry about it."

"I'm going back to San Diego soon but I was thinking I could stop by the gym on my way out of town?"

"I get off at 2," she said, looking at the clock. She only had forty-five minutes left.

"Great, I'll see you then," Sheila said.

Peach grinned, excited to see her old friend. She glanced over and saw Debbie chattering at Herrera animatedly but his gaze wasn't on the blonde. Debbie was tall and buxom and Herrera nodded while she spoke. Peach leaned over the counter and set the phone on the lower shelf again.

Most of the customers were regulars, and Peach had pretended to not remember Herrera from last week. But her body started humming when she looked up and saw the *Boricua* striding through the doors.

Debbie said something about showing Herrera her tattoo, in private. Herrera's refusal was polite but loud enough for Peach to hear. She pretended to straighten a stack of brochures on the counter when he moved in her direction.

"Hey," he said. The look he gave her made Peach sure if *she* offered to show Herrera her tattoo in private, there would be no refusal.

"Hey yourself."

"How's your little girl?"

"What?"

"When I was in here last week, you knocked me on my ass, and ran out to check on your kid. Is she okay?"

Peach recovered her voice and raised her chin. "Yeah, she's okay."

"What kind of attack was it?"

"Asthma," she said. "Enjoy your workout." She started toward the locker room.

Herrera caught her hand. "Wait. Is Peach your real name?"

"Duh. Is Herrera your real name?"

He sandwiched her hand between both of his. "Angel. Angel Herre-ra."

"Well, bye Angel Herrera."

"Don't I get a rematch?"

"You want me to knock you on your ass again, in front of all these people? We're busy for a Wednesday. Better you come back on a Friday night when nobody will see you."

"You sure you ain't worried about me knocking you on *your* ass?"

She jerked her hand from his grasp. "Nope."

"Well then come on, mamí," he said, beckoning her with his hands out in front.

Swiping a towel over her forehead and neck, she stepped back. "I don't have time today, but you can see Tommy about my schedule for the rest of the week. Maybe Friday." She spun around and covered her grin with the towel.

SHEILA PASSED THE GYM BECAUSE SHE WAS DRIVING TOO FAST. WHEN she made a u-turn at the end of the street, the boxer was exiting the building.

Peach waved, and crossed to the open window. "There's a little coffee shop a mile or so from here. Do you want to follow me?" Sheila nodded and backed up to allow her to pull out of the parking lot and lead. At the counter, they ordered iced teas, then sat at a table in the back.

"I'm so glad you called," Peach said. "How's Darren's ankle?"

"A little better. He wanted to take the brace off today but Stan and I convinced him to keep it on."

"I feel so bad that Joelle stepped on him." She leaned forward with her elbows on the table. "She's such a klutz."

"She's a sweetie," Sheila said. "And so smart. Bet I know where she gets it."

"Joelle's a great kid although she drives me crazy sometimes. She's so stubborn. I guess you know where it comes from too."

"I remember the time you got into an argument with Mr. Carlson over something in chemistry and he made you stand in front of the class thinking to embarrass you into apologizing." The incident was one of many at the boarding school where she, Peach, and Andrea attended high school.

She laughed with Sheila. "Yeah, he sure learned *his* lesson. That old goat was the one embarrassed when the 45 minutes were up and he had to let me go to the next class."

"You and Andrea," she said. "You two were always causing trouble."

"It's so good to see you, Liz. I mean, Sheila. Sorry," she said. "That must be hard, when people slip up."

"Not really. The only person I keep in touch with from the past is Andrea. It's safer that way."

Peach looked like she wanted to ask something but took a sip of her drink instead. "Where's Andrea? How's Ms. Washington?"

"Momma would have a fit if she heard you calling her *Ms. Washington*." She clucked her tongue the way her nanny used to do. "Anyway, Momma moved back to Nassau a couple years ago and started a safe house for abused women and children. Andrea went with her." The shorter woman flinched and she hurried to clarify her earlier statement. "Pea, I didn't mean I don't want to keep in touch with you."

"No, I know. I..." she hesitated over the question and seemed to change her mind again. "I can't believe you're dating my cousin. You're the last person I expected to run into around here."

"You're telling me. How did *you* end up in Albuquerque? I thought you loved New York."

"Darren didn't tell you?"

She shook her head. "He said you needed a change of scenery."

"Yeah..."

"You don't have to tell me," she said quickly.

"Darren's been good to us," Peach said. Looking down at the paper she'd removed from the straw, she continued. "He invited me and Joelle to stay with him after things ended *badly* with Joey." She shredded the paper with her trembling fingers.

Sheila covered her hands. "I guess we should have gotten margaritas instead of tea for this reunion," she said. Pea withdrew a hand to wipe her face. Sheila peeked at the scar on the Filipina's neck. It hadn't been there in high school. Was it part of the bad ending with Joey?

"Sorry about the waterworks. How's your grandfather? Does he still drive the Corvette?" Sheila's face screwed up and Peach handed her a napkin. "Sorry. Again."

Sheila took a deep breath. "Challenger. The car was a Challenger and he... he was killed in *'The Incident,'* as my father calls it." She hiccuped. "I do have good news though. Andrea opened a little boutique and has her own clothing line."

"Cool. What's it like?"

"Andrea calls her designs 'Shabby Chic.' Wait, I have a picture of one of her dresses. I wore it with Darren last week."

She whistled at the green dress. "Cute but I bet D had a fit." Sheila nodded. "Uh huh," the boxer said. "He's a great guy but he's so old fashioned."

"You mean chauvinistic?"

"Yes, girl. I swear, the only time he and I argued while I was staying with him is when I wore short skirts. Which was damned near every day." The skirt Peach was currently wearing was so short Momma would call it a band aid.

"He's not really a chauvinist," his cousin said, frowning. "He's more... chivalrous. How did *you* end up in Albuquerque?"

"Car broke down," Sheila said, the corners of her mouth pulling into a smile. "Actually I saw a sign for the Rio Grande and decided to take a look." She shook her head. "First Darren, and now you... I'm beginning to feel like it was fate."

PEACH NODDED AND LOOKED UP IN TIME TO SEE ONE OF THE CAFE EM-ployees, a teenager, unscrewing the lid of a silver canister. The girl had neglected to empty the CO_2 fully and white froth exploded, coloring her hair, the walls, and the espresso machine with whipped cream.

Laughing at the mess, she turned back to Sheila and gasped. Her friend was frozen, with a terrified expression on her face, and her hand curled around the plastic drink cup. She was squeezing it so hard the lid had popped off and was hanging askew.

"Sheila?" she whispered. "Hey, Sheila, are you OK?" Waving a hand in front of her immobile face, Peach felt the beginnings of panic cramp-ing her chest. The lid dropped off and the cup trembled in her hand.

"Come back to me, Sheila." Prying the cup free, Peach gently rubbed her friend's fingers. Her terrified expression reminded Peach of Joelle's, in the months after their escape from New York. The shrink Darren had paid for them to see said the mother and daughter were suffering from post-traumatic stress disorder; not uncommon for victims of domestic violence. While Peach had never gone into shock, she had trained with the shrink on how to deal with Joelle's bouts.

With a deep breath, she injected false cheer into her voice. "Hey, do you remember the time we snuck into the cafeteria at midnight and snagged ice cream for a party in the dorm? Everyone thought we were brilliant except for that little twit Mallory who snitched on us and we got 20 hours of community service. Remember?

"Remember how Andrea got her back? The night before homecom-ing, she got into Mallory's room and poured honey all over the snitch's hair while she slept. The boys at the Academy could hear Mallory screaming a mile away."

"The ants," Sheila said.

Peach leaned in. "What?"

"Mallory never got over the ants," she said. "I was in the cafeteria one time when she flipped out over an ant—one ant—on the counter."

"Yeah, I heard about that." She withdrew a hand to swipe a tear.

"Sorry," Sheila mumbled. "That sound…" She got a faraway look in her eyes again and the boxer stood up.

"Let's get out of here," Peach said. Outside, the heat made her feel like she'd been sitting inside a refrigerator. It amused her when people defended the temperatures here by saying, "It's a *dry* heat." Albuquerque wasn't humid like New York but the 100° temps were still suffocating.

"Look Liz. I mean Sheila. Damn. Sorry. I know you don't want to talk about what happened but I was wondering if you do talk to… someone."

"You mean a shrink?" she said and Peach nodded. "Yeah, I've got him on speed dial."

The Filipina gnawed her bottom lip. Her heart ached for Sheila's suffering but she also felt guilty because she wanted to warn her cousin.

Once, when she was staying with Darren, he'd opened up about how awful it had been to watch his ex-fiancée withdraw when something triggered one of her traumatic memories. But Peach had promised Sheila she wouldn't tell him. Should her allegiance be to her old friend, or to her cousin?

The girl with whom she had gone to high school was sassy, like Andrea and herself, which was why the trio gotten along so well. Peach wondered what had *really* happened three years ago; obviously the news she'd heard wasn't accurate. Liz—Sheila was altered. How deeply, she didn't know.

"You're probably wondering what happened," Sheila said. "As much as we hated her back at Prep, I wouldn't wish it on Mallory. I'm sorry if I spooked you in there. The noise sounded a lot like a gun shot." She looked away. "That's only happened to me once in three years and Rick... he was killed by gunshot."

"I'm so sorry, Sheila."

"Not a lot of people know, thanks to 'The Great Michael Chase.' He threw a lot of money at the media to keep the details quiet." She made a sound in her throat, like a cat coughing up a hair ball. "I *hate* him. The only good thing he did was find Dr. Baldwin, although sending me to The Cove was probably Mother's idea." She shook her head. "Anyway, I spent a year recuperating then I took on a new identity. I've been traveling the country ever since."

Peach hugged her and blinked rapidly. In the last year they'd all been at Prep, the three girls had dated guys from Academy: it was Andrea and Anthony; Peach and Juan; Sheila and Rick.

Andrea and Peach were a year ahead of Sheila. When the headmaster learned of Andrea's pregnancy, she was forced to leave before graduation. Peach left too, accepting an early admittance to NYU. She met Joey there, a man who could charm the scales off a snake. Her face burned with shame. She had no room to judge the other woman for her baggage.

"I'd better get going," Sheila said.

Peach squeezed her friend, then dropped her arms. "You said something about San Diego on the phone. Are you living there now?

"No. I've been living out of hotels but I like to spend some time there in the summer. I have those beach rentals, you know. Hey, you and Joelle should come and visit."

"Maybe we will. The poor kid has never seen the ocean."

"Darren said he'd come out in a couple weeks, maybe you guys could come with him."

"I'm sure that's not what my cousin had in mind." She reached into her purse for her keys and cringed when her hand met a glob of whipped cream.

CHAPTER 18

ANDREA WASHINGTON SQUINTED AT THE TINY SCREEN OF THE GPS. "I do not need glasses," she muttered and threw the car into reverse. The device predicted twenty-two minutes of travel time to Mission Bay but an accident on I-5 more than doubled the drive. She silently cursed her mother for insisting she take this trip.

She wanted to see her best friend but Andrea was worried Sheila would freak. The girl didn't do well with surprises, and even if she faked excitement at Andrea's arrival, she wouldn't be happy about the message from Momma.

Over the last year, whenever the Bahamian tried to make plans to visit, her suggestions were always met with sighs and excuses. Then Sheila would stop calling and Andrea knew she'd pushed the limits of whatever rules the younger woman had constructed. Despite what the transient declared about feeling free on the road, Andrea felt Sheila's constant travel was a self-imposed prison of sorts.

Shivering, Andrea left her suitcase in the trunk of the rental car, belatedly worrying her best friend had taken off for Albuquerque again. A month ago, she wouldn't have doubted what Sheila would be doing at 7PM on a Sunday evening.

She rang the doorbell. "Momma dreamt of fish," Andrea said when the door opened.

"Dreya! What in the world are you talking about?" She nearly toppled the shorter woman with her enthusiastic hug.

"Momma dreamt of fish," Andrea repeated.

"If Momma is dreaming of fish, she should go fishing," Sheila said. She ushered her guest inside and closed the door.

"Sheila, you *know* what it means."

"I do?"

"You're pregnant."

"You're crazy. You flew here from the Bahamas to prophecy?"

Andrea looked up at the sound of what must be an elephant tromping down the hall. She recoiled at the appearance of a young woman who glowed with a fake and bake tan.

"Who's at the door—oh hello," the tanned woman said.

"Andrea—Kate, my roommate; Kate—Andrea," Sheila said. "This is my best friend in the whole wide world. She came all the way from the Bermuda Triangle to harass me."

Kate tilted her head to the side and Andrea sized up the roommate. Kate's hair was bleached so blonde it was almost white. The girl couldn't be older than Sheila, yet the roommate appeared to have already sampled the plastic surgeons' smorgasbord. Her breasts and lips were as large as Momma's but she looked about 50 pounds thinner than Momma, and she was at least six inches taller.

"Oh, okay," Kate said. "Sheila, I got a text from Bri, you know the girl whose room you're renting? She's not coming back until August, so let me know if you plan to stay."

"Thanks, Kate. I'll let you know."

"I'm going to get dressed for work," Kate said.

"Would you like tea? We have black or herbal," Sheila said. "Or maybe a glass of wine?"

"Oh you wanna wait until 'Chrissy' is gone?" Andrea said. She followed Sheila into the kitchen, folded her arms, and leaned against the counter.

Sheila pursed her lips and flicked her hair off her shoulders. "You won't believe who I ran into in Albuquerque!"

"What the hell is on your neck?" Andrea said, gripping her shoulders. "Is that a *bite* mark? Girl, what have you gotten yourself into? Is he some kind of wanna-be vampire?"

Sheila shrugged free. "It's not like that, Dreya. Lay off!"

Footsteps echoed in the hall and they looked up in time to see Kate passing the kitchen. "Goodnight Sheila, goodnight Aliya. Nice to meet you." Kate slammed the door and Andrea shook her head.

"Well," Sheila said. Andrea's lips twitched and Sheila reached for her hand. "I don't want to fight with you, Dreya."

Her gaze swept over the bite mark again. "I'm worried about you," she said.

Sheila squeezed her hand. "Don't be. I'm good."

She squeezed back and tried for a lighter topic. "Are you going to live here now?"

"I subleased the room for a month."

"Kinda ironic, you renting a room in a house you own. Does Chrissy know?" Andrea asked.

"No, and stop calling her Chrissy. Kate's harmless. She doesn't ask questions." Andrea huffed and reached for her purse. Sheila grabbed her arm. "Dreya, please. I'm sorry, I... oh hell." She threw her hands up in the air and Andrea almost missed the seat of the chair as her legs gave out. "What do you expect? You show up at my door, all doom and gloom and prophesying. And quit staring at my neck."

She rubbed her eyes vigorously. *Yeah, I definitely need glasses.* The last time she'd seen Sheila in person had been a year prior. She was still too thin but her face had changed, and so had her attitude. "You're back."

"What?" Sheila said.

Andrea cleared her throat and swiped a hand over her eyes. "I missed you, girl. Welcome back."

SHEILA THREW HER ARMS AROUND ANDREA AGAIN. "LET'S CELEBRATE," she said. "Would you like red or white wine?"

"You can't drink."

"I'm *not* pregnant, Dreya. Sheesh."

Andrea put a hand on her hip. "Momma is never wrong. She had the dream *twice*."

"Since when does 'dreaming of fish' mean someone is pregnant?" Sheila demanded. "And if she had the dream twice, does it mean I'll get pregnant *twice* or I'm having twins?" Andrea groaned and she continued. "Momma's wrong. There's a first time for everything." She pulled a glass stopper from a bottle of merlot, and filled a glass.

"So you're telling me you haven't had sex with Darren?"

Sheila turned away. "We've been careful."

Andrea watched Sheila's shoulders turn in, and she took a breath before she spoke again. "Humor me and don't drink the wine."

"I'm NOT pregnant. God wouldn't be that cruel!"

"What do you mean?" Andrea said.

"Nothing. Just, nothing." She tipped the glass to her lips and took a gulp, her eyes blazing. She was furious with Momma for sending Andrea. It couldn't be easy for her best friend to deliver such a message.

"Sheila, you know I love you, girl."

"Yeah, I know," she said. Opening a cupboard next to the sink, she withdrew a glass and filled it with water. "And you know I don't like people bossing me around."

"I probably shouldn't have blurted it out first thing but I'm worried about you. Momma had the dream the night *before* you met Darren and then again three nights ago. I didn't think much of it the first time because you wouldn't so much as look at a man but now..." Andrea's gaze never left the bite marks.

Sheila chugged the water. Turning, she asked, "You've never... had a guy bite you during sex?"

Andrea drew her brows together. "No," she said. "I guess you liked it?"

Sheila's cheeks grew warm and she picked up the wineglass again. "It was incredibly... *hot*." She reached up and fingered the fading bruise. For the past week she'd been careful to wear tops to cover the semi-circular marks. It was warmer today, and she put on a spaghetti strap dress. If Kate had noticed the marks, she kept quiet about it.

"If you say so," Andrea said.

"Let's go sit on the patio," Sheila said. "Or we could go out. Do you want to go out?" Andrea opened her mouth but before she could respond, a ringing sound drew Sheila's attention. She rushed to a laptop on the coffee table and smiled. "That's Darren calling on Skype!"

ANDREA WATCHED SHEILA FLIT TO A MIRROR TO FLUFF HER HAIR, check her teeth, and apply lipgloss before accepting the video call. *Yeah, her old friend was definitely back.* After the murders, she'd stopped wearing makeup, and started wearing the frumpiest clothes sold at the Goodwill.

Now, the Bahamian surveyed the cotton dress Sheila wore with approval. It wasn't something *she* would wear, but it was much more flattering than the muumuu she'd seen her in last year.

Andrea checked her own reflection. Her hair was flat in the back from napping on the plane. She tried to scrunch the curls back to life and fingered the shadows under her eyes, hating how they looked like enormous bruises. *Were the raccoon eyes a result of working late nights at the shop, or the drawn-out break up with Raheem?*

"*Buona sera, bellissima,*" a masculine voice purred.

Andrea's head whipped around, and she steadied herself by gripping the back of the chartreuse love seat. "Hot damn," she murmured.

"I told you," Sheila whispered. The ecstatic smile spreading over her face made Andrea's eyes sting.

Darren spoke in English next. "Someone here wants to say hello to you."

"Hi, Miss Sheila. I miss you. When are you coming to visit me?" Andrea hurried to the sofa, squeezing her hips into the space between the sofa arm and her friend. "Who are you?" a little girl demanded.

The Bahamian leaned forward to examine the child. "I'm Andrea. Who are you?"

"Joelle Danetta Bustamante. I can spell it—"

"Andrea?" Darren's face reappeared. "Wow, it's nice to meet you."

"Nice to meet you too," she said automatically. She examined the similarly shaped faces of the man and the girl and gripped Sheila's thigh.

"Joelle is Darren's cousin," Sheila whispered. To Darren she said, "What are you guys up to tonight? Shouldn't you be in bed already, Miss Bustamante?"

Andrea sat back in relief. Joelle held up numerous drawings of a cat and chattered about someone named Charlie. Darren pulled Joelle onto his lap and nuzzled her neck. The gesture warmed the center of Andrea's chest. Would Sheila and Darren's baby look like Joelle?

Whoa. Did she have that much faith in her mother's predictions? She shook her head, stopping the memory of how Momma had called her up, eight years ago, with dreams of fish.

The expression on Sheila's face had her thinking, *she's falling in love with him!* Andrea was pleased to find the same rapt expression on Darren's face. *Good,* she thought. A baby should be brought into the world with love.

"Mommy," Joelle's squeal made Andrea sit forward again.

"Hey little monkey," a female voice said. Andrea gasped when Sheila clamped down on her leg.

"When did you arrive, Andrea?" Darren asked.

"This afternoon," she said.

"Sheila didn't tell me you were planning to visit. Will I get to meet you in person this weekend?"

"Sorry, no," she said. "I have a big event at the boutique this weekend but I'm sure we'll get to meet each other soon. Maybe you guys could come visit me and Momma in Nassau." Andrea turned to Sheila and whispered, "For the wedding?"

CHAPTER 19

"Let me get this straight," Andrea said. "You're dating Peach Nelson's cousin?"

"Peach Nelson or Peach Bustamante. I'm not sure if she was married to Joelle's dad. Did you know Joey?" Sheila asked.

"No," Andrea said. She shook her head again. "Peach Nelson. This is too weird. I have to call Momma."

"No," Sheila said. Andrea looked up at her sharp tone and smirked. Sheila smoothed a hand over her hair. "It's not that I don't want to talk to Momma," she said. "I, um, think it would be nice if we watched the sunset together."

"Okay," Andrea said. "Do you have a wool coat I can borrow?" She endured Sheila's ribbing at how she'd lost her ability to tolerate temperature changes after living in the Caribbean for only two years. Once they were bundled up and walking along the beach, Andrea said, "C'mon girl, you got to admit this water is cold."

"Yes, but even the Atlantic is cold in June. You're spoiled in the Caribbean."

They walked in silence for a few minutes before Andrea asked, "Are you going to tell Darren?"

"Tell Darren what?"

"About, you know..."

Sheila stopped walking. "Now?"

"Well, I was wondering... would Peach?"

"Pea won't say anything," Sheila said. She resumed walking.

"How do you know?"

"She promised."

"Sheila."

"Dreya."

"She's his cousin."

"And she's my friend," Sheila said. "Our friend. Plus, I saw it in her eyes. She's got secrets too." She shuddered although the air was still and she professed to enjoy the waves on her feet. "Look at those pelicans," she said. "I wish I could fly!"

Andrea followed Sheila's gaze to the dozen birds gliding on an air current above the water's surface. One broke ranks and dove into the ocean. The remaining birds wavered at the break in the slip stream but quickly righted themselves.

"This is where I stood when you told me I should call Darren back," Sheila said. "Did your advice have to do with Momma's dream?"

"No," Andrea said. "It had to do with my feeling." She smiled and took Sheila's hand. "You look happy."

"I feel happy," she said. Andrea turned back to the ocean. "What, Dreya? What is it?"

"I don't want to rain on your parade." The stricken look on Sheila's face made Andrea step closer. "No, no. It's nothing bad... I was wondering about the nightmares."

"Oh," Sheila said. She withdrew her hand and hugged her torso.

"We don't have to talk about it," Andrea said. "Do you want to go back to the house? Get some hot chocolate?"

"Dr. B offered to help me work on the belief behind the nightmares," she said.

"The belief behind the nightmares?"

She pulled Andrea's arm around her shoulders. "It's a long story but the short of it is, he offered to help me get rid of them for good."

"Great. Is that why you took the room with blondy?"

"Kate," she said.

Andrea rolled her eyes. "Sorry, Kate."

With a sigh, Sheila admitted, "Yes."

THEY DIDN'T DISCUSS THE FISH DREAM AGAIN. ANDREA WAS SCHEDuled for a red eye on Wednesday. Sheila declared the rest of the visit argument-free, which, she said precluded any talk of pregnancy. They filled their days with shopping, eating, and laughter.

On Monday they drove to LA's Fashion District where Andrea haggled with vendors in Santee Alley. She purchased enough fabric to fill three suitcases and charmed her way into to a designer trunk show.

The clothes were too heavy for Nassau but the fashionista ordered an entire fall wardrobe for Sheila. "You'll need nice threads if you're going to date Darren, not those rags you've been dragging around in," she said over Sheila's protests. "And you said there would be no more arguing."

Sheila treated them to an overnight visit at a spa in Palm Springs. At lunch on Tuesday a dispute over a glass of white wine ended when the waiter broke the stem of the glass by banging it against the edge of the table.

While Andrea packed on Wednesday, Sheila sifted through her mail and receipts. She'd spent more in the past three days than she usually did in one month on the road. She paid the bills and held out an envelope to Andrea. "Put this in your purse."

"What's inside?"

"A check for Safe Haven."

"Oh girl, you're so sweet. I'll make sure they send you a tax receipt." Sheila waved her off. "Promise me you'll come visit?" Andrea said. She tucked the envelope into her new Balenciaga tote and sat on a suitcase, forcing the zipper closed.

"You know I hate to fly."

"Well, maybe you can work on that fear with Dr. B, too."

"As if my list isn't long enough?"

"I'm glad you're going to do the new program," Andrea said. "My little godchild needs a healthy, nightmare-free Mama."

"You couldn't leave it alone, could you? I thought we had an agreement."

Andrea pursed her mouth. "Well," she said and they both laughed. Sheila walked her out to the car, sighing at streaks of orange on the horizon. "You should see the sunset in Albuquerque. The Sandia Mountains are—What?" Andrea shook her head and hugged Sheila again before getting into the rental car.

When she woke up screaming in the dark hours of Thursday morning, Sheila clutched her abdomen. The nightmare had started with its characteristic violence of threats and gunshots, but she looked different this time. She ran from the Butcher but she was sluggish because of a huge, pregnant belly.

Gasping for air, she chanted, *I am safe, I am safe.* She hit the back light button on the bedside clock. 3:22. She picked up her phone and opened the calendar, counting the days since she and Darren had met. Was it too soon for a pregnancy test? When was her last period? Sheila struggled to remember.

Her phone pinged with a text message from Andrea. "Just landed. Miss u already." She swiped her damp cheeks and reached over to turn on the lamp. Listening for sounds of her roommate; Sheila was relieved when she heard none. The room she was renting was littered with images and figurines of angels. She picked one up from the nightstand and rubbed her thumb over the ceramic wings.

The words she'd blurted to both Darren and Andrea, when they'd discussed pregnancy, returned to her now. *"God wouldn't be that cruel."* She swiped her damp bangs. She wasn't a religious person and she felt annoyed with herself for saying such a thing, for saying it twice.

Everyone from Dr. Baldwin to Andrea had said Rick's and Grandpa's murders were a tragic case of "being in the wrong place, at the wrong time." She never had any moments like the funeral attendees in movies who would lament, *"Why God, why?"* She didn't blame God. She blamed the Butcher. Now, in the yellow light of the lamp, she idly rubbed the figurine.

What would Dr. Baldwin say about this statement? Tomorrow she would start a new therapy program. She'd decided she was *willing* to learn how to be free of the nightmares. She was willing to *try* to have a long-distance relationship with Darren while she temporarily lived in San Diego. But she didn't know if her willingness or more therapy would lessen her fear of the Butcher's threat.

For the past two years, her roaming had been about being safe. She'd told herself avoiding relationships had been about safety too. Any man who got involved with her would also be a target for the Butcher's revenge. But a baby? She shuddered. It would be cruel to bring a baby into her world, when her world was dominated by the fear of being eviscerated by a psychopath.

THURSDAY, JUNE 21ST

DARREN'S CELL BUZZED IN HIS POCKET. HE LEANED BACK IN THE OFFICE chair to pull it out and beamed at the photo and caller I.D. *"Bellissima."*

"Hi. How are you?"

"Your voice has improved my day exponentially. How are you?"

"Not so good."

"What's the matter?" Darren said.

"I have to cancel our rendezvous."

"What? Why?"

Sheila coughed. "If your ticket isn't changeable, I can reimburse you—"

"What? Sheila, what's wrong?"

"I'm not feeling well," she said.

"Are you sick?" he said, then, "Dammit." Darren glared at the phone ringing on his desk. "Sheila, honey, I have to answer this. Let me call you back in a minute, okay?" He pressed the end button on his cell and tried to give his full attention to the client on the other line. Ten minutes later, he was about to redial Sheila when Stan appeared in the doorway of his office.

"Got a minute?" Stan said.

Darren pinched the bridge of his nose. "Is it urgent?"

"What's wrong?"

"Is it urgent?" Darren repeated. "I need to make a phone call."

"Lightfoot's report," he said, waving a folder. "But I can come back in five or ten minutes."

"I'll come down to your office. Shut the door on your way out." Darren ignored Stan's quizzical look and pressed the speed dial button programmed with Sheila's number.

"That was a long minute," she said when she answered.

"I booked a suite at The Grand Hotel for us."

"The Grand?" Sheila said, her voice rising. "In Del Mar?"

"You said your roommate kept erratic hours and I thought it would be nice to have some privacy. I've been looking forward to getting you alone." Sheila drew in a breath and he leaned forward on his desk.

"Is that your work phone again?"

"Yes, but I'm not going to answer it. It's been a hell of a day with the Sanchez case and Stan is waiting for me in his office with what I'm guessing is more bad news. You sound tired. Did Andrea wear you out?"

"No, I—"

"Mr. Abruzzo?"

Darren slammed his hand down on the desk. "Not now, Doris," he barked into the speaker.

His secretary's voice was strained. "I'm sorry, Mr. Abruzzo but Ms. Murphy is holding on line two. She says it's urgent."

"Darren?"

"All right." He removed his finger from the speaker button on the office phone. "I'm sorry gorgeous but the District Attorney is calling. Tell me you want to see me tomorrow."

"I want to see you tomorrow," she said. "But I'm not feeling well—"

"I'm sorry to hear that," Darren said. "Feel better soon." He switched to line two and endured a thirty minute rant from the D.A. Afterward, he found Stan bent over a take-out box of noodles in his office.

"What's up?" Stan asked.

"Janet Murphy is a pain in the ass," Darren said. "You got any more grub?"

Stan pointed at another styrofoam box on the corner of the desk. "One for you right there."

"Sweet. Thanks man." Darren unknotted his tie and draped it over the back of an empty chair. They ate in silence for a minute before Darren's phone beeped with a text message.

"Sheila?" Stan asked.

Darren shook his head. "Marilyn."

"Persistent, that one."

"This is good Pad Thai. Is it from the new place down the street?"

"Yeah," Stan mumbled with a full mouth. "And they deliver."

"Hey, I've been meaning to ask, what's up with you and Liz?"

Stan shrugged. "She's not really my type. Should I wait until you're done eating to tell you what the PI found?"

Darren groaned. "I don't know how we're going to win this." He won his last case, in which Hector Gonzales, a U.S. citizen, had been charged with armed robbery. The crime was committed by a day laborer of the same name and build, as Mr. Gonzales.

It was his first trial as lead chair, and the pressure was mounting for him to win this one, too. The Sanchez case was similar but the details were not unfolding as neatly as the Gonzales case.

Stan pegged him with his blue eyes. "You're going to win it, and you're going to make partner."

Darren pushed the take-out box aside and wiped his mouth. "Okay. Improve my shitty day. What did Lightfoot find?"

"He talked to Sanchez's landlady, Loretta Washington and..." Darren didn't hear the rest. His mind drifted off at the mention of *Washington*. Such a common name. He looked at Stan without seeing him and regretted ending the call with Sheila tersely. He replayed her words in his head, focusing on how she offered to reimburse him for his plane ticket. Was Sheila giving him the brush off? Then it struck him as odd; what did she do for money?

Most of the women he dated recently were happy to let him take care of the expenses, Marilyn in particular. Not Sheila. He remembered the black AMEX card and wondered if Stan was right, about it belonging to her father.

"D."

"What?"

Stan shook his head. "You're not listening to a word I've said. Is there trouble with the new lady love already?"

"I heard you. You said Lightfoot found—what now?" Darren had forwarded his office line to his cell phone and he barked *hello* into the Blackberry.

"I'm sorry to pester you—"

"Hey, Sheila. I didn't know it was you—"

"If you don't want to talk—"

"Hang on a sec," he muted the phone. "I'll be right back," he told Stan. Back in his office, he unmuted the phone. "What's up?"

Sheila cleared her throat. "I know you're crazy busy but I was afraid you got the wrong impression earlier." He sank into his office chair and found a smile spreading on his lips. "Are you still there, Darren?"

"Yes, I'm here."

"So, I was hoping whatever bug I've caught—" she sneezed once, coughed and he heard her put down the phone to sneeze twice more.

"Gesundheit!"

After a few seconds she returned to the phone. "Thanks."

"I'm sorry you're not feeling well. Summer colds are the worst. Are you taking anything?"

"Kate, my roommate, got some homeopathic stuff for me. I'm hoping whatever this is will pass quickly and you can come *next* weekend."

"Next weekend?" His smile grew.

"I feel bad about canceling last minute but you've got the hearing on Tuesday, and I don't want you to catch my germs." She paused and Darren's chest expanded at her concern. "Did the D.A. harass you?"

"How'd you guess?" Sheila sneezed again and he felt some of the tension ease in his shoulders. He hadn't heard the congestion in her voice in their previous conversation. And while he didn't want her to be sick, he was relieved she wasn't giving him lip service.

"I should let you get back to work."

"What are you doing tonight?" he asked.

"Well," she said. "After Momma's baking soda facial—"

"Baking soda facial?"

"You've never heard of it? You boil water, then sprinkle baking soda into the pot and inhale the vapors. It helps clear the congestion."

"Sounds like something my nonna would have done."

"Home remedies are the best," she said and sneezed.

"What are some of Momma's other home remedies?"

"Hmm," Sheila said. "Warm ginger ale for upset stomachs... and vanilla extract for burns."

"I'm familiar with the vanilla extract treatment but warm ginger ale—yeck." Sheila laughed and the sound sent a thrill through him.

"Nonna means grandma?"

"Yes," he said.

"So grandpa would be... nonno?"

"Right again. What did you call your grandfather?"

"Just Grandpa." Her voice was wistful and Darren found himself wishing she would open up about her family. His own family wasn't perfect. They were a bunch of hot heads who argued constantly but loved deeply. Instead he kept it neutral, grateful she'd called back.

"Where did you learn to speak French?" he asked.

"High school." She covered the phone to muffle her coughs. "I was never great but I passed the tests to waive the language requirements for college. How 'bout you? I've been meaning to ask exactly how many languages you speak."

"Only a few fluently: Français, Español, Portuguese. I can get by in German, and I've been flipping through the Japanese dictionary although I might have to actually take a class in that one."

"Only a few? You forgot English, Tagalog, and Italian."

Darren shrugged. "I grew up speaking those."

"Wow," Sheila said. "So you just picked up the others? I guess I shouldn't be surprised, since I know how talented you are with your tongue."

CHAPTER 20

SHEILA SLUNG THE KNITTED SHAWL OVER HER ARM AND HURRIED FROM the baggage carousel to the arrival area again. Another group of people poured through the hallway and she craned her neck in search of Darren.

"Hi, Honey."

Sheila brightened and turned toward the voice. Darren rarely called her by her name, and the, "Hi, honey," sounded familiar and cozy, like they were an old couple, and he was coming home.

"Oh, sorry," she said, backing away. The man stepped around Sheila to embrace a short, plump woman. Sheila blushed and bit her lip, turning away from the couple.

Where was Darren?

Another nightmare had awakened her before sunrise. Dr. Baldwin was patient, talking her through a relaxation exercise over the phone, which had helped for a few hours. Now, in the crowded airport, she felt anxiety closing in on her. The passengers from Darren's flight were retrieving their baggage. He phoned two and a half hours ago, right before boarding the plane.

Had he changed his mind last minute?

They hadn't spoken much since she'd postponed their rendezvous last week. Sheila had spent much of her time at The Cove. Darren worked late hours on the Sanchez case and they played a lot of phone tag. She checked her phone. No signal. She looked around again before walking to the courtesy counter.

The woman behind the desk sat with her head leaning on her hand. "Can I help you?"

"Could you page my—" Sheila stopped, not sure what to call Darren. Boyfriend? Too presumptuous, they barely knew each other a month. Lover? Too intimate. Beau? Friend?

"Miss?" the woman prompted.

"Sorry," Sheila said. She felt a sneeze tickling her nose and turned away from the counter. When she looked back the woman hadn't moved. "Could you page my friend?"

"What's her name?"

"His name is Darren Abruzzo."

She winced when the woman mispronounced Abruzzo. Returning to the arrival area, she switched her weight between her left foot, and then her right.

She'd purchased the new Jimmy Choos at the Fashion Valley Mall yesterday. Sheila wouldn't admit it to Andrea but her friend's recent visit had reawakened her inner shopper. She couldn't resist going into the store and it was even harder still to resist treating herself to the adorable leather, peep-toe sandals.

Now her toes were aching and she hoped she wouldn't have blisters. The automatic doors opened behind her, admitting a gust of wind, and Sheila glanced at the gray sky. Would Darren find San Diego too chilly, too?

A van pulled up to the curb and her shawl slipped from her fingers when she saw the driver's face. He was a young, bearded man, and he was leaning forward, looking directly at Sheila. At the familiar, penetrating eyes, she groaned. *"Oh God, no."*

She carefully watched for white vans over the past few weeks but all the drivers she saw had Hispanic faces. Not unusual in San Diego. But this man was Caucasian. Bile rose in her throat but despite her fear, Sheila moved toward the automatic doors. *It can't be him, he's dead!*

A woman crossed in front of Sheila, breaking her view of the van. She reached out and steadied herself on a cement pillar. It was cool and the texture was rough against her palm. She forced herself to focus on it, to try to stay in the present moment. Still, images from the nightmare—Rick chasing her, his eyes grave and murderous—had the bile lurching up her throat.

I am safe, she said silently. Sheila pressed the heel of her hand against the cement. *I am in San Diego, at the airport, and I am safe.* She forced herself to look out at the van again. The young man was picking up luggage from the curb. She let out a breath, relieved to see the man looked nothing like her dead ex. The van driver was blond and Rick had been a brunette. This man was short and stocky; Rick had been tall and thin.

Sheila shook her head. This was a mistake. Maybe she wasn't ready to date. In the nightmares of the past, Rick wasn't a threatening figure. Last night, however, he was no longer a victim but a coconspirator of the Butcher.

Maybe seeing Darren again, this close to resuming therapy, was a mistake. What if she had another nightmare while they were together? What if—

"Sheila!"

Calling on the poise she learned from Mirabelle Chase, the master of disguise, Sheila dropped her hand from the cement pillar and turned around. She was ready to fake a smile but when she saw Darren pushing an old woman in a wheelchair, she struggled with a frown.

"Honey, come here and meet my new friend."

She moved forward automatically and found a smile.

"Hello, young lady. I'm sorry I kept you from your boyfriend. They were supposed to have a wheelchair ready for me at the gate when we landed, but of course they didn't. Darren, God bless him, offered to wait on the plane with me."

"Mrs. Tejada, Sheila Washington; Sheila meet Mrs. Tejada." Mrs. Tejada wore a scarf on her head but it had slipped midway back to reveal silvery-white hair. Sheila stooped to shake the woman's gnarled hand. She was surprised by the strength of the grip.

"Nice to meet you, Mrs. Tejada."

"Aren't you as pretty as a picture," Mrs. Tejada said. "I thought I might introduce Darren to my granddaughter but I see he's already taken."

Sheila looked up at Darren and smiled when he winked.

"Nanay!"

They all looked up at the young woman who called out. She ran towards the trio, her flip flops slapping loudly against the linoleum. "Nanay," she said again, gripping Mrs. Tejada's hands and kissing her cheeks. She began to apologize for being late and Sheila stepped back, bumping into Darren.

"Oh."

"*Tu m'as manqué.*" Darren said. His hands landed on her hips and Sheila turned to face him. In her new heels, they were almost the same height.

"I missed you, too," she said. Her eyes swept his face, drinking in his handsome features, and landed on his lips. A fit of sneezes sent her digging into her purse. He bent to pick up her shawl.

"You look scrumptious," he said.

She rolled her eyes over the tissue. "Thanks."

"Allergies, huh?" Darren snaked his arm around her waist.

"Ugh," she said. "I wish it was a cold—"

"Thank you for helping my grandmother," the young woman said.

"It was my pleasure." Darren turned to the old woman. "*Dios te bendiga.*"

"*Y tu tambien. Mucho gusto.*"

Sheila waved goodbye. "That was sweet," she said.

Darren shrugged. "I have a soft spot for old ladies. Young ones too." He brushed a hand over her hair. "Are you feeling, okay? When you turned around, you looked like you'd seen a ghost."

She stepped back. "Funny choice of words," she mumbled.

"Where are you going?" Darren said. "I only get you for 48 hours." He trapped her against his body with his hand at the small of her back. Sheila could feel his arousal and her eyes widened.

"I intend to keep you close. Very, very close," he said. Darren slid his tongue between the seam of her lips. He kissed her deeply and Sheila forgot about the ghost. She also forgot she was at the airport. Her tongue dueled with his, urgent and hungry for more. When her hand went searching, Darren broke the kiss.

"Soon, *bellissima*, soon," he said.

"SHEILA, HONEY, ARE YOU OKAY?" DARREN STROKED THE SOFT HAIR AT the base of her neck. His fingers lingered on the faint scar where he'd bitten her.

She lifted her head from his chest. "Better than okay."

Her eyes glistened, and he reached up to capture the tears slipping free. "Are you sure?"

"Yes," she said quietly. "It's just so *intense*. When you're inside of me, the orgasm builds this, this pressure, and then a surge of emotion. It's so intense that I really feel like I'm going to explode and—" she dipped her head.

"And what?" Darren brushed her disheveled hair to the side and captured her face. She smiled up at him shyly. "Won't you tell me?"

She slid off his body, coming to rest on her right side, facing him. He groaned and removed the condom. When he looked up at Sheila again, her eyes were closed and her brows drawn. "Did I hurt you?"

"No." Sheila's eyes flew open and she scooted closer, pressing her lips onto his neck. Darren squeezed her in his arms, and tried to wait. Through the open curtains, the moon shone, high and full. The clouds had dissipated before sunset, and they snuggled in this same spot, watching the sun sink into the ocean. A breeze lifted the sheer curtains, and Sheila shivered.

"Are you cold, sweetness?"

"Not really."

He sat up, keeping Sheila clutched against his body with his left arm and reaching for the sheet with his right. "What's so funny?" Darren asked. He felt, rather than heard her laughter.

She looked up at him from under her lashes. "You weren't joking about keeping me close."

"I always tell the truth," he said. He lowered them back to the mattress. "Now, are you going to finish what you were saying?" The blush creeping over her face piqued his curiosity, and Darren fought the urge to press her further.

"When you're inside me," she whispered finally, "and I'm about to come... sometimes it feels so good it almost hurts. *You're* not hurting me, it's more like the pleasure is so profound, it's almost pain. Like I should stop but if I do, I'll die. Sounds crazy, right?"

Although they'd made love twice already, Darren found himself instantly hard. He rolled Sheila onto her back and caged her with his body. "No baby, it sounds perfect. *Assolutamente perfetto!*" His right hand was tight on the back of her neck, holding her in place to fuse their mouths. His left one went to her breast and he nudged her legs apart with his bent knee.

Sheila gasped for air when he released her mouth, as if resurfacing from a dive. "You're insatiable," she breathed.

"Don't you want more intense pleasure?" Darren rasped, probing her.

Sheila gave his shoulder a playful nudge. "Wait a sec. I need to use the bathroom."

"Hurry back." Darren flopped onto his back. The look Sheila gave him over her shoulder made him want to tackle her and bring her back to the bed. *Had he ever made a woman feel the way Sheila described?* He searched his mind for anyone who made him feel so *insatiable*.

They were inside the Hotel Del Coronado for exactly five seconds when Darren had bunched Sheila's dress around her hips and impaled her against the wall. The second time was urgent too, although they both took their shoes off by then. Sheila had surprised him when she stripped him, pushed him onto the bed, and straddled him.

Darren rubbed a hand across his chest and when he drew it back, one of Sheila's hairs came with it. He lifted the strand between his thumb and forefinger, thinking of the ones she'd shed in his car, on the sofa, even on one of his suit jackets. Each time he'd found one, his body reacted to the thought of her, the least of which was to grin stupidly. Stan was right, Darren admitted. He was gone for that girl.

Twisting the hair around his finger, Darren mused over the miles between them again. How could he convince her to move to Albuquerque? The glowing numbers on the end table clock was an unwelcome reminder of their scant time together. Love on a deadline, he thought grimly. If they lived in the same city, would their connection be so intense?

"You look way too serious for a man freshly sexed." At the sound of Sheila's voice, Darren started to get up from the bed but she met him before his feet reached the floor. "What's on your mind? Are you thinking about the Sanchez case?"

He pulled the covers around them. "No, nothing so mundane. I was thinking about you."

"Oh."

"Don't look so worried," he said with a chuckle. He smoothed his thumb over her forehead. "I was wondering why you chose to rent a place in San Diego."

"Oh," she said again.

"So, why did you? Does this mean you're giving up vagabonding?" He felt Sheila's body tense and he braced himself for her physical retreat. During the time they spent together in Albuquerque, he'd noticed her tendency to pull away when she didn't want to answer a question. After she remained still, he looked down. He wasn't surprised by the shuttered expression on Sheila's face, but he was still disappointed.

"I like to visit San Diego in the summers but it's only temporary. I'll probably go to Alaska next."

"Alaska?" Alarm shot through his veins. "*Alaska?* I thought you didn't like to fly."

"I don't," she said. "I intend to drive there."

He was worried about the 48-hour countdown and Sheila was talking about Alaska?

"When?" he asked. "Wait, you're going to drive *Dexter* to Alaska?"

"No. I might get an SUV and go in August; September, at the latest." Darren suddenly felt like she'd thrown a cinder block onto his chest. Sheila raised her head. "Have you ever been to Alaska?"

"No, have you?"

"Not yet."

Darren withdrew his arms and tried not to wince when Sheila didn't protest. He sat up and snatched a water bottle from the table. He drew on it heavily, then tossed the plastic across the room.

"How long will it take you to drive there?" he asked. Sheila shrugged and Darren wanted to take a mallet to the bedside clock. The glowing numbers invaded his periphery. They seemed to have enlarged to about three feet tall. "Jesus. Why Alaska?"

"Why not?"

The indifference on her face infuriated him. Hadn't she professed to experiencing profound pleasure with him? He interpreted her admission as evidence of something more between them but now he wondered. Was he attributing more substance to it because *he* wanted more? He leapt off the bed, looking around for something to break.

"Darren?"

He looked back at the bed and the startled expression on Sheila's face. How could she speak so casually of traveling thousands of miles away when he was half in love with her? She rose up onto her elbows and the jewels on her nipples sparkled in the faint light.

He seized one of her ankles and yanked her body down the mattress. Sheila gasped but before she could question him, he was between her legs. She clutched his head as he bore down on her, licking, suckling, and nibbling in a frenzy. Her body responded to his attack, quickly growing wet against his mouth.

Sheila writhed and dug her nails into his scalp, trying to thrust her hips upward. Darren tightened his hold on her thighs, pressing them down, not allowing her to move beneath him. He was ruthless because he needed to punish her for torturing him. When her breathing turned to ragged panting, and she quivered on the edge, he flung himself away.

"Darren?" she blinked up at him. Her voice was breathless, her face bewildered, and her legs splayed on the bed.

He locked his joints, resisting the urge to return to her glistening sex. "Fucking Alaska," he roared.

Sheila blew out a frustrated breath. "Can't we talk about Alaska... *after*?" She scissored her legs and he knew she was close, painfully close.

Good, he thought and then blinked at the cruelty. Although he wanted to, he couldn't enjoy feeling cruel. He brought Sheila to the brink and he wanted to leave her there, to leave her feeling as deeply frustrated as he felt.

Staring down at her face, pinched with need, Darren knew Sheila didn't realize how out of his head he was for her. And she wouldn't understand the punishment. If he told her now, like this, Darren feared he'd only succeed in scaring her off.

CHAPTER 21

THE CURTAINS LIFTED ON A BREEZE AGAIN AND DARREN CROSSED TO the balcony. He slammed the sliding door closed and nodded at the satisfying click. The gauzy material fell against the glass door. He seized a panel, poking his finger through a burn hole at the bottom. It gave easily and he took the nylon in both hands, ripping the hole apart.

"What are you doing?" Sheila asked.

Darren heard her shifting on the bed and he looked back. "Stay there."

"Darren—" her voice was annoyed now, her eyes narrowed at the torn curtain.

"If you get off the bed, I'm going to spank you." Sheila lowered a foot to the floor and he yanked the strip free. "Lie back down," he said, moving toward her. Sheila's gaze was on the curtain he'd destroyed. When he took each of her wrists, lifting them in the air, she raised her gaze to his face.

"Remember back at the Frontier, I said I was going to tie you to my bed?" he said. "This one isn't ideal because of the faux headboard," he crossed her wrists and began binding them. "But we'll work it out."

SHEILA'S BREATH LEFT HER BODY IN A SQUEAK WHEN DARREN PUSHED her back onto the bed. It was king-sized so her feet didn't overhang, even though she was now laying crosswise. He kept a tight hold on her wrists, walked around the bed and then hoisted her closer to the edge.

"Yes, I think this'll work," he said.

"What will work? What are you—" she sucked in a breath when he dragged her body to the side and then upwards. Now she was positioned diagonally on the bed, with her hands and head at the corner.

"*Pazienza, bellissima.*" Darren winked and began murmuring in Italian but the sound of her favorite language didn't have its usual affect. She was curious about the binding and a little nervous about his changing moods. Would he tie her feet too? Sheila stretched to the side and watched Darren lift the end of the strip, then purse his mouth. He surveyed the curtain again and she tried to lower her arms.

"Darren, I—" He traced her earlobe with his tongue and the fire in her core started raging again. Sheila pressed her thighs together and hissed.

"Yes, we're going to have to do something about these," he said. She lifted her head to track her lover's movements. His hand landed on top of her bent knees, separating them and pressing her legs back onto the mattress. She meant to ask what he was talking about but her eyes were riveted on his erection. Would she ever get used to it?

"I want you," she whispered.

"What did you say?"

Sheila felt certain Darren had literally caressed every inch of her body in the short time they'd known each other. They'd made love slowly and languidly in Albuquerque. And they'd devoured each other here. She shouldn't be shy about voicing her desire for him but her voice still came out in a whisper when she answered him. "I want you," she said.

"Say it louder," he said. Sheila looked up and shivered. Darren's face held none of its usual playfulness and she struggled to put a name to his current expression. He leaned over her, and her breathing hitched. "Louder, Sheila."

She made her voice louder although his face now loomed inches from hers. "I want you, Darren."

"Are you sure?"

"What?" she tugged at the binding. Then he palmed her wet heat and Sheila's arms went limp.

"I said, *are you sure?*"

Sheila wiggled her hips. "Yes." Darren snorted and withdrew his hand. She was so close and she opened her mouth to tell him so when she noticed the tight set of his lips. "Are you angry with me?" she asked.

"Why would I be angry with you, Sheila?"

The flat tone of his voice and the use of her name, instead of *honey* or one of the other endearments, made Sheila's stomach clench. "Untie me, Darren."

He ignored her and turned away. "I'll give you what you want," he said. "But you're going to have to convince me, first."

"Convince you?" her eyes widened at the sound of the fabric tearing again. "Convince you how? You mean beg?" Sheila waited for an answer but none came. She twitched when he looped the curtain around her left ankle.

She raised her head again, trying to see where he was going to anchor her foot. Her gaze landed on the slick head of his erection and she groaned.

"Is it too tight?" he asked, loosening the ankle binding. Sheila was relieved to see his face soften with the question.

"Darren—"

"Shh." He dragged a finger up the inside of her bound leg, slowly, stopping to circle the underside of her knee. Sheila's leg twitched again, and he paused before continuing up to her thigh. The ticklish sensation grew worse the closer he drew to her aching core.

"Darren!" She dug her free heel into the mattress, trying to raise up into his hand.

"Yes, Sheila?"

"Please, Darren." His finger darted over her swollen nub. "Oh God." Sheila swiveled her hips. If she had the use of her hands, she would have shoved him onto the bed, and ridden him to completion like she had before the pee break, before he'd grown angry. Through the fog of her need, it came to her. *Alaska.* She'd said it unthinkingly, defensively.

"This will be a sufficient blindfold, I think."

"What?" Her hips sank back onto the bed. "What blindfold?" She caught a glimpse of the neck tie before Darren covered her eyes with it. His hand slipped under her head, lifting it to create a knot.

"I'll leave your other leg free. For now."

Sheila's heart began hammering a wild staccato in her chest. She could hear Darren moving about the room. "What are you doing now?" Darren didn't answer. "I didn't mean to—Ack!"

Darren's wicked hahah was close to her right ear and Sheila turned her face. She meant to protest the ice cube encircling her nipple was too cold but then he replaced it with his tongue. The fire between her legs spread up her torso, sparking another inferno in her breast. Sheila yanked at the wrist binding again.

Darren moved to the other side, repeating the torture with the ice and then his tongue. He began murmuring in Italian against her breast and she recognized the word *gattini* immediately. He liked to tease her for sounding like a kitten. Sheila made a growl in her throat, hoping it sounded more like Eartha Kitt in her cat woman role.

"Ah, you like when I caress you with my tongue?"

"Yes, Darren, *please.* I'm on fire." She gulped when he grazed her nipple with his teeth.

"Then you need more of this." The ice cube touched down on her sternum and Sheila tried to squirm away. Darren made a trail down to her navel, blowing on the wet line. "Better?"

"How can you be so cruel, teasing me like this?" she whimpered.

Darren ripped the blindfold off and she yelped at his livid face, inches from hers.

"No, you're being cruel," he said. "How can you talk of going to Alaska when I'm falling in love with you?"

Sheila gasped. She thought she was in agony from sexual frustration but Darren's face bore the emotion in the truest sense. Her eyes stung when he moved off the bed and jerked her wrists free from their anchor. Darren crossed to the doors, and dropped his head onto the glass.

The sound of her heartbeat was loud in her ears. Slowly, Sheila sat up. She felt dizzy and her shoulders ached when she reached for the binding on her ankle. Her fingers shook and slipped off the fabric repeatedly. Then it was impossible to see because of the onslaught of tears.

He was falling in love with her? Sheila's throat tightened and she brought her bound hands up to wipe at her eyes. Darren remained immobile against the door, his hands flat on the glass, and his head turned away from her.

Was she really surprised? Everything he said and did was over the top, according to Andrea's assessment. She'd told her best friend about the multiple bouquets of flowers he'd sent, the airline tickets he purchased for her to fly to Albuquerque, the five star hotel he booked last week. Andrea had warned that men didn't do such things in the name of casual sex.

Sheila studied his taut body and wished she could rewind the clock. She opened her mouth to tell him she wasn't set on Alaska but the words got stuck. She couldn't promise Darren anything. "I'm sorry," she murmured.

He lifted his head but didn't look at her. "I tell you I'm in love with you and your response is '*I'm sorry*'." Darren shook his head. "I guess you're leaving now."

She flinched at the hollow sound of his voice. Was he telling her to leave? Of course he was. She'd insulted him. Why would he want her to stay? The burst of pain in her chest made her look down to be sure she was intact.

"I guess I should get those off you," Darren said. He bent to free her ankle. Sheila's breathing hitched when his fingers brushed her skin, unwinding the torn fabric. The wrist binding was twisted but he worked at it quickly. Too soon, her hands were free. Darren stabbed his legs into a pair of jeans.

"Where are you going?" she asked.

He paused with one arm in a shirt sleeve. "I'm going to request a clean room. I can't sleep in that bed."

Sheila recoiled from the disgusted look on his face and examined the bed. Strands of her hair clung to the pillows and rumpled sheets. The abandoned ice cube sat beside her thigh, darkening the sheet as it melted. Another spot discolored the sheet, in the center of the bed where they'd made love. She stared at it, feeling dirty.

"Well, what are you waiting for? A farewell fuck? You want me to finish getting you off before you run away to enchant the next man?"

"Don't you *dare* talk to me like that!" Anger flooded her face and she lunged at him. Her hand flew out, landing with a crack on Darren's cheek. She drew back to strike him again but he captured her forearm.

"Don't hit me." He gave her a rough shake and she was too pissed to be scared by the edge of danger in his eyes. "Ever."

"And don't you talk to me like I'm some cheap whore. You have no idea what I've been through." She tried to wrench free of his grasp and Darren grabbed her other arm.

"I would if you told me," he said. "You don't have to shut me out, Sheila. I want all of you—"

"You can't handle all of me."

"Are you saying I'm weak?" His fingers tightened on her arms.

"Darren…" The anger drained from her face, and her tone turned bleak. "If only it were a matter of physical strength. But it's not. You're looking for a wife and a mother for your children and I'm not," she swallowed. "I can't—"

"We can get through it together, whatever is haunting you from your past."

"Is that what you told Wendy?"

CHAPTER 22

"Wendy? What does Wendy have to do with us?"

Sheila tried to yank her arms free. "Let me go."

"Dammit woman." Darren backed her against the wall and pinned her with his knee between her naked legs. She moaned and fisted his shirt. "Now tell me you want me to let you go," he barked. He pressed his thigh against her sex and jerked her forward.

"Darren wait. You asked me to be honest with you," she said. "My past is..." she flattened her hands on his shirt and shook her head. "I can't... if we keep on like this we'll only end up with broken hearts."

The logical part of his brain urged him to back off. It was making the connection between Sheila's behavior and his ex-fiancée's. His heart couldn't survive loving another woman who refused to face her past, who refused to heal.

But staring into Sheila's anguished face, Darren sensed a difference in her, a mettle Wendy lacked. "I have a suggestion," he said. "What if you come back to Albuquerque with me and we'll find someone to work with you there?"

She slackened against him. "You mean a, a therapist?"

He nodded. "One of my college buddies is a psychiatrist and he could probably recommend—" he stopped when she looked away. "What?"

"I have a therapist, here," she said. "I didn't want to tell you because..."

her voice trailed off and he palmed her cheek. Sighing, she leaned into his hand. She kept her eyes closed when she spoke. "Because it seemed like more *TMI*." Her eyes fluttered open briefly. "I've been in therapy in the past and it helps but I still get these awful nightmares and I *have* to be on the move... It's, it's complicated, Darren."

He let out a breath he didn't know he was holding. Sheila looked nervous when she reopened her eyes. He brought his other hand up to her cheek, clasping her face gently. "My parents were about the same age as we are when they met," he said.

"Ma wouldn't give Pop the time of day 'cause she said he was too old; there were fifteen years between them. Pop kept after her though, showing up at her job with cannoli or hand picked daisies until she finally went on a date with him. They were married a year to the day, after they met." Darren stroked her cheek with his thumb.

"Pop told me not to be afraid to fight for the woman I want, and as God is my witness, I want *you*, Sheila. We have an amazing connection and you make me feel so, so *alive*.

"I know you're scared of what's developing between us but I'm asking you to let me love you. Are you willing to do that, honey?" He stopped the tears slipping from her eyes with his lips. "I won't push you to tell me about your past. You can tell me when you're ready and we can focus on the now, on enjoying every second of every minute we get to spend together."

"Darren—"

Brushing his lips over Sheila's, he continued. "Listen, *bellissima*. Ma used to tease that Pop would die from a heart attack because he refused to change his eating habits. But a hit and run stole him from his bride. We don't know how much time is promised to each of us. Let's not spend ours fighting."

"LET ME DOWN," SHEILA CROAKED. DARREN WITHDREW HIS HANDS from her face and slowly lowered his leg. "I'm not running away," she cleared her throat and brought a trembling hand up to wipe her face. He plucked a tissue from the box on the desk and gave it to her. Mopping her cheeks, she sank onto the corner of the mattress. She tried to remember the ten tapping points Dr. Baldwin had taught her but it was impossible to focus with Darren hovering.

"What you said was... beautiful. Beautiful, but overwhelming and I can't think straight." He unearthed emotions within her she thought she buried and others she didn't know she had. Sheila stared at her stinging palm. "I can't believe I hit you. I, I need a minute."

Darren's voice was strained when he responded. "You want me to leave?"

Sheila stood and faced him. "No, I'll do it in the bathroom."

"Do what in the bathroom? You're not taking drugs, are you?"

"No, nothing like that. I barely take Tylenol when I'm on my period." She gave him a weak smile. "My doctor taught me this tapping thing... it's supposed to be calming but it's embarrassing. I can't do it in front of you."

"If it helps, you don't have to hide—" he stopped and she looked up. "Go ahead, sweetness. I'll wait for you."

Sheila moved through the EFT exercise clumsily. She'd only learned it two days ago and although Darren wasn't watching her, she knew he was waiting for her and wondering what she was doing.

Tapping the ten acupressure points was supposed to help move her through bouts of anxiety. It helped a little when she'd done it under Dr. B's instruction, but now she couldn't concentrate and she blew out a frustrated sigh. Then she laughed dryly at the irony.

Darren was standing by the balcony when she emerged from the bathroom in a towel. "Better?" he asked. His face was guarded and she knelt in front of her suitcase.

"I think a walk on the beach would do me good." She pulled out a pair of jeans and a sweater, dressing quickly. Darren's mouth was a grim line when she slipped into her flip flops and looked up at him. "You don't want to come?"

"May I?"

She nodded. "I'm sorry I hit you. I promise to behave and keep my hands to myself."

"I'm sorry I provoked you," he said. "I guess we both have to work on our tempers, huh?" Laughter laced his words and she let out a relieved sigh.

"Do you have a sweater? It'll be chilly" she said.

He nodded and his smile made the ache between her thighs flare. She watched him nimbly closing the buttons on his shirt and briefly reconsidered the walk.

Outside, Darren laced their fingers and he led her to the beach. The moon illuminated the sandy mountains and valleys made by footsteps and she watched the play of light on her feet. They walked north before she angled them closer to the water.

"This is the best medicine," she said. "Listen to those waves." Sheila tucked her hands into the pockets of her sweater. Closing her eyes, she turned her face into the cool breeze. "Did you know there are huge kelp gardens off the San Diego coast? Mmmm, I love that smell..." She took several deep breaths. Darren didn't respond to her rambling and she turned a questioning look on him. "Are you all right?"

"I feel like an intruder," he said quietly. "This is obviously special to you."

"You're not an intruder. You're special to me too," she said. He beamed at her and Sheila stepped into his embrace. "I can't promise you anything, Darren," she winced at how that sounded like the guy's line. "But I'm willing to try to... be present with you, when we're together."

Darren traced the pattern of moonlight bisecting her upturned face with his fingertips. "You're so different from Wendy. I see you struggling with your fear, and sometimes I hear you cry out in your sleep." She gasped but he touched his index finger to her lips and continued. "But you're working on it, and I respect you for trying. Wendy wouldn't. She'd withdraw or run away and she refused to acknowledge how her pain overshadowed her life. *Our* lives."

Sheila cringed. "Don't put me on so high a pedestal, Darren. You're the first man since..." She turned her gaze to the waves. Her voice was small when she continued. "And I still run away."

His warm fingers caressed her cheek. "You didn't run away. And you didn't shut me out."

"Yeah, but if I don't feel safe my knee-jerk reaction is to bolt," she said.

"Do you feel safe with me, honey?"

Sheila turned her face back to his and nodded. "You make me feel... a lot of things." Her heart fluttered at the love shining in his eyes. She wanted her desire for Darren to be greater than her fears. Right now it was. Sinking to her knees, she tugged him down with her.

SUNDAY, JULY 1ST

"See you on Friday?" Darren asked.

"Yes."

An announcement called out from the overhead speakers. "This is the last boarding opportunity for flight 363 to Albuquerque."

Sheila sighed against her lover's mouth. Darren had used his charms to get her a gate pass and now he was the last passenger at the gate.

He picked up his bag. "I'll call you when I get in."

"A bientôt," she said.

"Je t'adore," he said. Her heart did jumping jacks at the sentiment. *I adore you too,* she thought. Darren handed over his boarding pass and gave Sheila one last, heated look before descending the boarding ramp.

Sheila spent Monday through Wednesday nights at The Cove. Dr. Baldwin was wrong about her being a mentor for the new patients. Kyra, a petite girl with wildly curly hair, walked around in a daze with eyes always on the verge of spilling water.

LaTonya reminded Sheila of a Tasmanian devil and she tried to stay out of the stout woman's path. Most of the time, Sheila sat in the kitchen chatting with Agatha, or the other therapists she hadn't seen in the last year.

"I have a new assignment for you," Dr. Baldwin told her on Wednesday afternoon. Sheila didn't look up from the afghan she'd pulled off the back of his office sofa. She picked at the fuzzy beads with her thumb and forefinger.

"Sheila?" he called.

"Hmm?"

"In addition to the hypnotherapy CD, and the EFT, I'd like you to try programming yourself for good dreams," Dr. Baldwin said.

She looked up. "Programming myself, how?"

Dr. Baldwin twirled a pen between his fingers. "If you are *willing*, before you go to sleep, tell yourself what to dream about." At her blank face he continued. "You're going to plant the intention. You can say to yourself, I am going to sleep peacefully and wake up feeling refreshed."

"Or I'm going to wake up with the answer for world peace?"

Dr. Baldwin chuckled. "Sure, why not?"

"I'll give it a try," Sheila said.

"Would you like to discuss the nightmare you had last night?"

"They're all the same…" she said. Dr. Baldwin watched her closely and Sheila lowered her eyes. One of her hands went to her abdomen. It was flat now, but in the dream last night, it was swollen, with fish. She stifled a tremor and wondered what Dr. B would say if she told him.

He broke the weighted silence. "I guess we'll see you after you return from Albuquerque, since you're not staying for the BBQ tonight."

"Okay," she said lamely.

"Happy Independence Day, Sheila."

Sheila pushed open her bedroom door with the toe of her new Ferragamo's. She held shopping bags full of sassy outfits and sexy lingerie for her visit with Darren. Some of the contents toppled out when she dropped them on the bed. She almost missed the large rectangular box beneath the bags.

"What's this?" she mused aloud. The box was too small to hold the clothing she and Andrea had ordered at the trunk show. Sheila didn't recognize the return address.

In the kitchen, she hunted through the drawers for a razor or scissors but found none. She finally used a steak knife to cut through the packing tape. She sifted through the packing peanuts and the smell of new vinyl overwhelmed her. Sheila read the message on the gift receipt and shook her head in amusement. It was almost midnight in Albuquerque but Darren picked up his cell phone on the first ring.

"I received the package you sent," she said.

"Oh good. I was worried he wouldn't get there before you departed."

"Why did you send me an inflatable man?"

"He's your new, approved traveling companion." Darren continued over her laughter, "I worry about you driving by yourself. I wish you would use the plane tickets I bought."

"You should be worried about me passing out from trying to blow up this thing. Sixty inches tall; it'll take me all night," Sheila said.

"Not if you take Freddy to the gas station."

"Yeah right. I am *not* taking this thing to the gas station. I'll look like a total pervert. Someone will think it's a sex toy."

When their laughter faded, Darren asked, "How was your appointment today, sweetness?"

Sheila set the doll on the floor and laid on the bed. Then she got up to rearrange the shopping bags. Finally she said, "Riveting. How was the deposition?"

"I think we're turning a corner. It's looking like we might have a chance to win this thing. Hang on." Sheila heard Darren issuing directions and an answering female voice. "Sorry."

"You're still at work?"

"Yes," Darren said. "I'm trying to get out of here but there's still a couple of clerks in the library."

"Female clerks?"

"One of them is a woman, yes."

She sat up. "I hope she looks like a troll."

"Don't worry honey, she's happily married. And according to Stan, I'm as 'hopeless as a penny with a hole in it.'"

"I love that song," Sheila said.

"Me too. Shall I sing it to you?"

"Yes," she said and nestled into the pillow. She heard the click of his office door before Darren began to sing the Dionne Ferris song in his smooth alto voice. Sheila closed her eyes, deciding she'd program herself to dream about her hopeless lover.

CHAPTER 23

WEDNESDAY, JULY 11TH

"So NOW WE WAIT?"

"Yes," Herrera said.

"Why are we shadowing the guy if there's a transmitter in his vehicle?"

Herrera looked at his replacement, Sean McKay. "Because the boss said so."

McKay shifted in the passenger seat of the van. "Seems like a waste of resources to have both of us sittin' here while the lawyer has tea."

"*Tea?* Look man, Vasquez has a system. He doesn't make up shit." Herrera said. He actually agreed with McKay but he was fed up with the guy's yammering. The Boricua was also fed up with Vasquez for insisting he spend the day showing the Scot around when the guy was as overqualified for the job as he was.

"Ooch. There's a saucy lass," McKay said.

"You need to get laid," Herrera grumbled.

"Get a look at the legs on this girl," McKay said and thumped on Herrera's arm. "I bet she's got an arse you could bounce a quarter offa."

"Arse?" Herrera mocked. He followed McKay's pointer finger. "Fuck."

McKay slapped his palm against his thick leg. "Didn't I tell ya?"

"That girl wouldn't give you the time of day," he snapped. *That girl wouldn't give him the time of day either. Not since—*

McKay cocked his head. "You know her?"

He leaned onto the steering wheel. "Yeah. She works at the boxing gym where I been going. I heard from the owner's son she don't date white dudes."

"I'm not white," McKay said. "I'm Scottish." He winked and slipped from the van. Before Herrera could protest, the long-haired pain in the ass was sauntering across the street.

"What the hell is he doing?" He white knuckled the steering wheel when McKay sidled up to Peach and she smiled at him. Joelle clung to her mother's leg, and hid her face in Peach's skirt when McKay stooped in front of her.

Peach swept her hair over one shoulder. God, he wanted to get his hands in her hair; he wanted to get his hands on her arse—

"How does she know *him*?" He hadn't noticed Abruzzo arrive but suddenly the guy was there, hugging Peach. McKay waved to Peach and Joelle and took off down the street.

Herrera picked up the closest thing, an empty Rockstar can, and squeezed it until the aluminum bit into his palm. He couldn't pursue Peach if she knew Abruzzo. He snorted.

Who was he kidding? A month had passed since he'd gotten a brief taste of her in the locker room. The following night, he'd tried to complete their unfinished business at Peach's apartment when she hadn't shown at his hotel. But Joelle had been there, sick with a fever.

McKay opened the door, stopping Herrera from remembering the night he'd met the little girl. "That was strictly against protocol," he snapped.

"I didn't know she was related to the subject's boyfriend. Ya could have told me."

"Related? Related how?"

"Second cousins, thrice removed."

Herrera twisted in his seat. McKay grinned broadly and Herrera's anger threatened to get the better of him. "Don't fuck with me, man. Is Peach his cousin?"

"You dinna know?" McKay said and Herrera cracked his knuckles. The idiot actually laughed. "Ooch. See my methods do yield results."

"What did you say to her?"

"Relax. I complimented *Peach* and her pretty girl. Joelle is the one who told me they were meeting a cousin for lunch. Then the cousin pops his head out, looking for 'em." McKay lowered the backrest and folded his arms behind his head. "Peach," he said. "I bet she tastes like peaches."

"We haven't seen you in a while," Peach said.

"I'm sorry. I've been falling down on my godfather duties, haven't I?" Darren picked up Joelle and kissed her cheek. "How's my girl?"

Joelle giggled and tightened her grip on Darren's neck. "Mom has a boyfriend," she whispered loudly.

"She does?" Darren shifted the child onto his hip.

The hostess interrupted. "Your table is ready, if you'll follow me." Darren gestured for Peach to go first.

"Who is your Mom's boyfriend?" Darren asked.

"I don't have a boyfriend," Peach hissed.

"Here you are," the hostess said. She placed three menus on the table. "What a beautiful little girl. She looks just like her—"

"Cousin," Peach interjected.

"Cousin," the hostess said, her eyes brightening. "Susan will be your server and she'll be with you in a minute."

"Thank you," Darren said. "Come on little monkey, sit down." He chose this restaurant because it was near work but he now realized Joelle was the only child present. She tried to sling the strap of her little

"Maybe we can call and invite her to our party," Darren said.

"Yay! I like Auntie Sheila. She's smart and pretty *and* she let me run after the soccer ball and I didn't even get asthma." Darren heard Peach shifting in her seat and looked up.

"Stop swinging your feet, Joelle," Peach said.

"Joelle could spend the weekend with me... and you could see your *angel*."

"He's not my boyfriend," Peach said. She straightened the knife beside her plate. "And you don't have to keep her this weekend."

"I want to. It's been a while and even if you *don't* have a boyfriend who's enchanted your daughter with Spanish serenades, you deserve a weekend off."

"How are things going with Sheila?"

Darren pursed his mouth. He wanted to push Peach on the subject of the man but he decided to let it go. For now. "Good, I think," he said.

"Good, you think?"

"I wish she lived closer," he said. *Like next door.* "We have a great time when we're together but the weekends go by too quickly. She's not much of a phone person. And she's pretty private."

"Hmm," Peach said. She busied her mouth with the straw, drawing deeply on the bubbly water.

"I saw her briefly last weekend," Darren continued. "She was wearing another scandalous dress her best friend made." Peach snorted and covered her mouth. "Are you okay?"

"Yep," she said. "Actually, I'm going to take Joelle to the bathroom to wash hands. C'mon monkey."

"I don't have to go pee."

"You need to wash your hands before lunch. Now, come with me." Peach tapped her foot while she waited for her daughter to climb down from the chair. She felt like the child was being deliberately slow, and she almost threatened to deny her chocolate milk. Instead, Peach scooped

Joelle into her arms.

The restrooms were adjacent to the entrance and Peach spotted the hostess hurrying toward their table. She knew the girl would use the opportunity to pass Darren her digits. Would Darren take them? Would he call the girl? Peach didn't know the answer. She opened the door to the ladies room and pursed her mouth.

Darren had always been a flirt, although he toned it down around Joelle. Today was the first time the three cousins had gone out since he'd met Sheila. Peach wondered if Darren was refraining from flirting with the restaurant staff because of his goddaughter or because of Sheila.

Last month, she'd been thrilled to chat with Sheila and Andrea online. Andrea had teased Sheila relentlessly about Darren. Sheila's reactions made Peach think she was falling for Darren. Peach's conversations with Andrea offline had confirmed her suspicions. It had only been a month since her cousin had met her old high school friend but—

Joelle interrupted her musings. "Mommy, will you cover it?"

"What baby?"

"The automatic potty!"

"Don't shout, Joelle." The little girl waited to sit on the toilet until Peach covered the sensor with her hand. Joelle scooted off the seat quickly and covered her ears until the flushing stopped.

Peach knelt beside her and helped Joelle pull up the nylon tights she'd insisted on wearing. It didn't matter to the four year old that it was ninety-seven degrees outside. Joelle had insisted on wearing a fancy dress, tights, and her patent leather shoes for her *date* with Uncle D.

At the sink, she looked at her own reflection in the mirror and fingered the pearlized buttons on her tank top. She also dressed up, in one of her longest, knee-length skirts.

Her cousin's comment on Andrea's designs had her smiling to herself. Dreya had forced Sheila to model dresses through the Skype connection and Peach was looking forward to wearing the ones she'd ordered.

"I'm hungry," Joelle said. Peach shut off the spigot with a paper towel and clamped a hand on Joelle's shoulder when she tried to sprint back to the table.

She shook her head when Darren stood. "You should have been named Dominic, after your father."

"Believe it or not, little cousin, some women like chivalry."

"I have a hard time imagining Li—I mean Sheila likes it."

"Why?"

"She seems like a modern girl." She pretended to be engrossed in smoothing her napkin over her lap. When she looked up again, Darren was smiling.

"She is modern but *she* has some old fashioned habits too. She's so, so..." Darren focused on a point in the distance. When he met her eyes again, she was surprised to feel a prick of envy at the reverence shining in his face.

"She's sublime."

CHAPTER 24

"WHAT'S UP WITH THE HAIR?" STAN ASKED. HE GLANCED BACK AT THE clock; one more minute till game.

"Growing it out," Darren panted. His hair was beginning to curl under, though at the moment, it was frizzy from the vigorous racquet-ball match. "Sheila saw a picture of it when it was long, back in my Jiu-Jitsu days."

Stan caught the ball with a backhand. He was down a point, even with Darren coming off the ankle injury. "She coming out here this weekend?" he asked.

"No, I might fly out there. Why?"

"I was thinking we could go camping," Stan said. Darren dove and caught the ball, slamming into the wall with his shoulder. "Nice," Stan said. "Good game, old man."

Darren swung the racquet at him, and Stan ducked.

Stan cracked a towel at Darren and he dodged by an inch. "What about camping?"

"I don't know."

"You've seen that girl every weekend since you met," Stan said.

"It hasn't been every weekend." Darren plopped down on the bench and removed his sneakers.

Stan teased him for spending more time fussing over his hair than he did in the shower. Darren endured the ribbing, which Stan kept up until they scarfed burritos from the taco cart outside their office building. Once inside, Darren's secretary informed him of a delivery awaiting him in his office. She was smiling slyly and Darren turned to question Stan over what joke he pulled, but Stan had been accosted by Philip Morris. He opened the door slowly.

"Surprise!"

"Hey gorgeous." Darren met Sheila at the side of the desk. "I thought you were getting work done on Dexter?" She reached for him and he held up a hand. "I've got onion breath."

"Onion breath? I drove 800 miles to see you and you've got 'onion breath'?" He made a show of removing a tin of mints from his desk and offered her some.

"Are you saying I need one too?"

Darren looked her over. She wore jeans although it was easily 100°. "How did you get here?"

Sheila took his hand and led him to the window. "That's my new ride," she pointed at a silver motorcycle in the parking lot.

"Nice. Wait, you rode that from San Diego?"

"It's no Gold Wing but—"

"I was referring to the heat. What kind of bike is it?" Darren tried to make out the emblem. "BMW?"

"Yes, an F800ST. I thought we could ride up to the crest together. If you can handle the heat."

He gave her ass a swat and wondered again about how she was financing her vagabond lifestyle. The last time she was in town, he'd stripped her of a La Perla baby doll. The lingerie came with $300 tag; he knew because he'd shopped for something similar for her online.

"I haven't replaced the clutch cable yet—" the phone rang and Darren made a face before he picked it up. Sheila examined his framed awards and degrees on the wall and he tracked the way her ass shifted in the tight fitting jeans.

"What are the chances you've got a cocktail dress in your saddle bags?" She turned toward him with a puzzled expression. "I have the fundraiser tonight."

"Oh, right. I forgot. I'm sorry. I'll get out of your way."

"No, I want you to come. Oh good, Stan's here," Darren said at the appearance of his best friend. "I was going to call you. You're off the hook for tonight." He opened a desk drawer, picked up a set of keys, and held them out to Sheila. "Take the Challenger. Get something red or green. The theme is a play on chili/ Christmas in July."

"Red or green?" she asked.

"On second thought," Darren said. "I'll walk you out."

Sheila never came to Darren's office and she suspected he didn't want to kiss her at work. As soon as the elevator doors closed, Darren snaked an arm around her waist. "I like your hair—" she moaned when he trapped her face between his hands. His mouth was spicy from the mint and she leaned into his body, hungry for more of him.

"If I hadn't just returned from racquet ball and lunch with Stan, I'd take you home." They reached the ground floor and he pulled back before the doors opened.

She took her purse and toiletries from the motorcycle's luggage and put them in the trunk of Darren's car, along with her riding gear. He ran down the itinerary for the evening and she was sorry she forgot about the fundraiser. "I don't need to meet the governor of New Mexico. You should go with Stan. I could visit Joelle—"

"Don't be silly. You're a much better-looking date than Stan." Darren winked and opened the car door. "I'll see you at 5."

Sheila pulled out of the parking lot and turned onto Central Avenue. At the red light, she mused over how Darren hadn't actually *asked* if she wanted to go to the event. He gave her orders for what kind of clothing to buy and a time to pick him up. She stared out the open window, annoyance overriding her excitement at seeing him.

A series of beeps erupted behind her. "Green light," yelled the driver.

She drove through the intersection, then pulled over. She cranked the dial for the AC and angled the vents in her direction. Where was she supposed to shop for a cocktail dress in this dusty city? She pulled out her phone and searched the map app for nearby boutiques. It was unlikely she'd find Halston or Balenciaga here. Damned Albuquerque.

The trustafarian shook her head. Six weeks ago, she'd driven into Albuquerque wearing a thrift store dress... and she'd met an incredibly sexy man. Before Darren, before Albuquerque, the landscape of her life was monochromatic; monotonous.

Sheila leaned against the steering wheel and looked past the hood of the Challenger, past the sprawling buildings, to the Sandia Mountains in the distance. She smiled at the ribbons of deep red threading the rock face. Darren, with his unrestrained passion, had weaved color and excitement back into her life.

The air conditioning finally grew cold. She shivered and called up the directions for the mall, hoping it had a Neiman Marcus. It didn't.

Shelving her frustration, she flipped through the racks at Macy's. The red and green offerings were scanty; even fewer in her size. She overheard a girl in one of the fitting rooms mention a resale boutique and decided to give it a last try. The resale shop was tiny and Sheila nearly skipped it but she had pulled up right in front and the cashier waved through the window.

"Welcome to Fabulous Finds. I'm Lorna," The cashier said." Can I help you find something?" Sheila told her about the event and Lorna steered her to the cocktail dresses in the back. "We've pretty much sold out of our fabulous red and green last week but we might have a few things."

She took the only options to the fitting room. She was loosening a glittery green dress from its hanger when Lorna called over the curtain. "This one doesn't fit the color scheme but it's your size and I bet you'd look fabulous in it."

Sheila wondered if Lorna was required to say fabulous in every sentence. She poked her head out the curtain and took the azure, chiffon halter dress to be polite.

"Wow," Lorna said when Sheila pivoted in front of the 3-way mirror. "You look like a freaking supermodel, like that woman, what's her name?"

Sheila smiled at her reflection. The sales girl had been right. The dress fit perfectly.

"I have the perfect shoes. Size 8 or 9?"

"Nine," she said. Lorna returned with a pair of silver stilettos. They were flashier than what Sheila would have chosen. But she had less than two hours to shower and style her hair.

"I'll take them both," she said and whipped out her credit card. Once she'd changed and signed the receipt, Lorna beamed at her.

"Have a fabulous time," she said.

Before Sheila stopped chuckling, her phone rang. "How'd the shopping go?" Darren asked.

"Fabulous," she said. "I'm heading back to your place to shower and dress now."

"You haven't showered yet? Well, I guess I'll have Stan drop me off and you can meet me there."

"I don't want to show up by myself—"

"Gotta go baby, see you soon."

Sheila huffed and tossed the phone onto the passenger seat. When she toweled off thirty minutes later, and searched the bathroom cabinets, her annoyance piqued. Her lover didn't have a hair dryer. She didn't have hair pins. Or nail polish or any of the tools to get ready for a semi-formal evening.

Darren didn't answer his cell when she called back to tell him to take Stan. Sheila sat on the edge of the bed to do the EFT tapping points before she slipped into the dress.

When she pulled up to the hotel hosting the event, she spotted a couple entering the building and feared the blue chiffon was a big mistake. The man wore a suit with a double-breasted vest featuring a chili pepper print. The woman wore a red dress, exactly like the one Sheila bought from Macy's, and chili pepper earrings. Another man walked up wearing a Santa hat; his date wore a Santa dress.

A valet attendant opened her door. "Good... eve...*ning*," he said.

Sheila looked up at his heavily accented voice. Was it Irish? The pale-skinned man was tall and bearded. She swallowed a shaky breath and gathered her wallet from the passenger seat.

The wallet didn't match her outfit but she hadn't thought to buy a purse, or jewelry. En route, she'd stopped at a drug store to purchase pins for her hair, brushing the damp mess into a chignon. Her throat was bare and but at least she had her usual diamond stud earrings.

A BMW idled in front of the Challenger. Sheila cringed when the attendant beside it whistled at her legs emerging from Darren's car. She accepted the hand of the valet holding her door and stood up.

"Wow," he said, his eyes were fixed on her cleavage. She half expected him to offer the valet claim ticket to her breasts. He looked vaguely familiar. Before she could process where from, a man whistled behind them. The valet ducked into the Challenger, revving the engine and waved for her to pass in front.

Feigning composure, Sheila held up her head and strode into the building. She couldn't spot Darren in the mass of red and green inside the banquet hall. Resisting the urge to touch her hair, she smiled at the women whose stares were the opposite of the men's.

"All that beauty in one woman ought to be illegal," said a man behind her. He drew out the word illegal into four syllables. Sheila turned to face the speaker. He was not a slim man nor was he tall. His line of sight was level with her breasts and he continued, addressing them. "In fact, when I'm Senator, I intend to make it law."

"Now Mr. Johnson, that's no way to compliment a lady," another man said.

Sheila looked to the left and smiled in relief. "Kevin."

"Tell me Miss Washington, have you been dreaming of our last dance together?" Kevin said.

She laughed lightly. "Do you think you can help me, Kevin? I can't find my date."

"Don't tell me it's that rascal Abruzzo?" Kevin said.

"Sheila." Darren said her name at the same time he placed a cold hand between her shoulder blades. She flinched and turned to face him. The hard set of his mouth made her smile falter.

"I was looking for you," she said.

The attorney's jaw ticked. "You didn't get very far," he said. "Montgomery, Mr. Johnson, would you excuse us?" Using his hold on her back, Darren steered her from the entrance and into an empty conference room. He shut the door quietly and drained the whiskey glass he'd been carrying.

He gathered a fistful of the dress skirt and Sheila's heart sped up. For a brief moment she thought she'd misread the anger on his face but then he spoke. "This. Is. Blue." His voice was harsh and he tugged on the dress as he punched out each word. She craned her neck around him and whipped her head back and forth. "What are you doing?" he snapped.

"Looking to see who you're talking to!"

"Sheila, I told you to buy a *red* dress or a *green* dress. Not a *blue* dress." He let go of the skirt and she glanced at the crinkle marks where he'd been holding it. She resisted smoothing them out.

"Excuse me? Maybe you could go back out there and find the real

Darren Abruzzo. I don't believe I know you."

"This isn't a game! This is an important event for me. The most influential people in New Mexico are here tonight. Do you see anyone else wearing blue?"

"This dress fit better than anything red or green," she said. A tightness seized her throat and she shook off the tears threatening to shame her. "I thought the color of the dress wasn't as important as my company. Obviously, you'd rather be with someone who can follow orders." She snatched the door knob, pulling the door open but Darren barred her way.

"Where are you going?" he asked.

"Get out of my way."

"Ohh, sneaking off for a little hanky panky?" a voice called from the hallway.

Darren flashed his teeth and she turned her head from the door, not wanting to see the man who'd spoken.

"Stay," he said.

"You jackass. If you think I'm going to stay after the way you just talked to me, you must be suffering from split personality disorder."

"You're even more beautiful when you're angry," Darren said. He kissed her quickly, and covered her hand on the door knob. His body shielded her from view and he used his other hand to tweak one of her nipples.

Sheila moaned despite her anger. "You're still an ass," she said when he released her mouth.

"I'm sorry," he said. She gritted her teeth and pulled on the door when he said nothing more but it was blocked by his foot. "Do you have any idea how absolutely stunning you are, Sheila? Do you have any idea how crazy I am about you?"

"You're crazy, all right."

Darren's left hand still covered hers on the doorknob. He encircled her waist with his right and tugged her against him. "I was in the middle of a discussion with Senator Guthrie when he held up a hand to point out the woman in blue who walked in with *Kevin Montgomery*."

"I came in *alone* you arrogant ass—because you wouldn't wait for me—and that sleaze ball Johnson was ready to grope me. Kevin stopped him." She jerked on the door. "Get off me!"

"Sheila." He tried to kiss her again but she turned her face. "Honey, I'm sorry. Kevin always tries to steal my women and... my jealous streak got the better of me. *Bellissima mio, per favore*. Stay."

She narrowed her eyes. "I don't belong to you."

"Would it be so bad to be mine?" he asked. Before she could answer, Darren captured the back of her neck and took her mouth roughly. His whiskey-laced tongue speared her mouth again. He didn't have to muscle her from the door because her body responded to him without her permission.

She released the knob and kissed him back, meeting the demanding thrusts of his tongue. Darren's hand left her neck to press her shoulders against the wall. Then it dipped under her dress.

"You're so hot," he said against her cheek. "And wet. *Dio aiutami*. I could take you right now." He nudged her trembling thighs further apart.

"You can't win an argument with sex, Darren." She raised her hands to his chest to push him away.

He angled his mouth over her ear. "Oh no, kitten? You want me to stop?"

Her breath came in short pants. "No, I mean yes," she said. It was hard to focus with his fingers caressing her sex. She had to fight to keep from arching into him like a cat.

He chuckled and withdrew his fingers. "We'll finish this later."

He led her back to the banquet hall and she wanted to crawl under a table when she glimpsed her reflection in the mirror behind the bar. Most of her lipstick had transferred to Darren and the blush in her cheeks wasn't courtesy of M.A.C.

The cocktail hour was over and the room quieted when the emcee took the podium. Darren's dinner seat was at a round table in center of the room. Sheila sat next to him, reluctantly. She couldn't concentrate on the speech Johnson gave on the importance of saving the Rio Grande because a memory of her mother invaded her thoughts.

She was only eleven when she started menstruating. Before she knew what sex was, Mirabelle Chase was lecturing her on its power. "Withhold sex, it's your ultimate power over men," Mother had ordered.

Sheila pushed away the untouched dinner plate. She ignored Darren's questioning look and escaped to the restroom. When she looked in the mirror, Sheila felt a stab of panic at the scowling image of her mother. She blinked and Mirabelle was gone, leaving the young woman staring at her bewildered reflection.

What am I doing here, she thought bleakly. How had she escaped her dominating father only to take up with a man so much like him? *No.* Sheila shook her head; she could never fall in love with a man like Michael W. Chase.

Darren was leagues apart from the man who ran his family like one of his conglomerates. Darren was a good man, kind and passionate; not ruthless and cold. The crazy chemistry between them made him impulsive and jealous.

Wait—she was in love with him?

Mirabelle hovered at the edge of her thoughts and Sheila wished she had a relationship with her mother like the one Andrea had with Momma. What would it be like to have a mother who was a friend and confidant? Before she could contemplate the answers or lose herself in pity, Sheila heard the click of heels approaching the bathroom and she ducked into a stall.

The door opened, admitting the sound of applause. It was muted with the closing door, giving way to two female voices. "...is a over-cooked ham."

"You're right, Marilyn. He should go back to Alabama where he came from."

"Did you get a look at the twig hanging on Darren's arm when he sat down?" Marilyn said.

"No wonder he hasn't returned your calls. D'ya think she bought those boobs?"

Sheila caught herself from gasping and looked down at her breasts. The halter dress was very fitted but her breasts weren't *that* big. She thought she might break off the flush handle when she shoved it with her foot. She forced herself to walk calmly to the available sink, the one in the middle.

The woman on the left was a platinum blonde and she held a tube of lipstick in her hand, forgotten. Sheila recognized her as the slinky red dress who'd accompanied the chili pepper-vested man. The woman on the right wore a green, tiered ruffle dress.

Sheila washed her hands, dried them, and retouched her lipstick. She selected several hundred dollar bills from her wallet and fanned them on the counter next to the blonde, the one whom she thought had called her a twig.

"Buy yourself some class, sweetheart," she said.

CHAPTER 25

Darren loosened the chili pepper tie. Sheila's scent lingered on his hand and his lids fluttered. *Damn, she was addictive.*

The whiskey buzz made him feel warm and relaxed. He didn't usually drink hard liquor but Senator Guthrie had insisted on sharing a bottle at the beginning of the cocktail hour. Guthrie was a good man, and Darren was lucky to be groomed by the best. And he had the hottest woman in town, the hottest woman in California, coming to Albuquerque to see *him*.

The evening had almost been ruined but Sheila was young and he easily persuaded her to stay. Standing with a group of city council members, he watched the direction of the ladies' room.

"Great event huh, Abruzzo? Where's the after party?"

"At your place," Darren said reflexively. He caught a flash of blue heading toward the exit.

"Where did you find that beauty, Abruzzo? Does she have any younger sisters?" The men chortled and he lost sight of Sheila. Ten minutes passed before he could extricate himself from the group. He found her outside.

"If you go to Alaska in August, it rains about 50% of the time," Montgomery said. "So you probably don't want to drive the motorcycle up there."

"There you are," Darren said. Sheila didn't acknowledge him. She waved at a valet and Darren turned to watch his car approach.

"Enjoy your ride, Sheila," Montgomery said and Darren scowled at him.

"Thanks, Kevin," she said. Sheila stepped off the curb and tipped the valet.

"I'll drive," Darren said.

"No you won't," she said. "You've been drinking."

"I can drive myself home," he said too loudly.

"You might drive yourself home," she said. "But you won't drive with me."

"Everything okay, miss?" the valet asked.

Darren leered at the imposing red-headed man and dropped into the passenger seat. "What were you doing talking to Montgomery?" he demanded. He slammed the passenger door.

"Who?" she asked.

"Don't play coy. You planned to meet Kevin here."

"Darren, I don't think I like you when you've been drinking."

He leaned toward her. "How does it look when my date starts and ends an event talking to another man?"

Sheila stomped the gas pedal and hooked a sharp left onto Central Avenue. Darren lowered the window for fresh air but the breeze was too hot. He fumbled with the controls for the air conditioning, and turned the vents toward his face.

She hit the dip at the base of his driveway too fast and he flung open the car door, lurching to the pampas grass. He didn't immediately toss his dinner but he lingered on all fours because it felt like a serious possibility.

"What are you doing?" His voice sounded too loud in his ears. How could she ignore him when he was feeling so woozy? "Sheila," he called and stumbled into the house.

"I guess I *am* young and dumb," she said, finally appearing in front of him.

"What are you talking about?"

"You think you're the only one with feelings Darren Abruzzo? Get out of my way."

Darren felt like he'd missed something and drew himself up to full height. "What are you talking about?" he repeated.

"I'm talking about the blondes, and the brunettes, and the raven-haired women, Darren. I say hello to the only other man in town whose name I know, and you fly into a jealous rage. Meanwhile I can't go to the damned bathroom without tripping over a woman you've slept with."

Darren tried to work out what Sheila was saying. She wasn't wearing the blue dress he'd planned to take off of her. He'd been looking forward to finishing what he'd started in the conference room but she'd changed into jeans and a t-shirt, and she was carrying her helmet.

"Where are you going?" he asked thickly.

"To a hotel."

"A hotel?" he said. "Why?"

"Because right now I don't like you very much."

Darren stumbled forward and caught his balance on the arm of the sofa. Sheila was crazy about him. She'd driven from San Diego, in 100° temps, on a motorcycle, to spend the weekend with him. He looked up to make the point but she was gone.

ONCE SHEILA WAS A FEW BLOCKS AWAY, SHE CALLED A TAXI. SHE IN-tended to go to her motorcycle, which was parked at Darren's office. By the time the taxi arrived, she was sobbing on the curb.

"You okay, Miss?" the driver asked.

Sheila climbed inside and slammed the door. "Just peachy."

"You ain't running away from home or nothing, are ya?"

"I'm a long way from home, Mr. Harris."

Mr. Harris craned his neck to peer into the back seat. Sheila pointed to the license taped to the divider with his name on it. "Where to?" he asked.

"The closest hotel," Sheila said. She was too worked up to ride anywhere tonight, let alone back to San Diego. But she'd be gone before Darren slept off his hangover.

FRIDAY, JULY 20TH

ALTHOUGH SHE HADN'T BEEN DRINKING, SHEILA AWOKE WITH A HANG-over. Andrea called it a crying hangover, when you baptized your pillow with tears and woke up looking like you'd lost a fight. She was tempted to call her best friend and pour out her heart but she might mention the damned fish dream again.

It was almost 10 A.M., much later than when she usually awoke. Twenty minutes later, after cabbing it to Darren's office building, she was stunned to find a clamp on the front wheel of her motorcycle.

"He's out looking for you, annoying the hotel employees all over town," a male voice said.

Sheila tented her eyes and found Stan watching her from the shadow of the only tree in the parking lot. "Then you did this?"

"Yeah."

"Why? You don't even like me."

"Because you're what he wants," Stan said. "For now."

Sheila glared at him. "Well, let's get this over with."

"You'll stay?"

"I'll talk to him. I won't promise to stay."

"Fair enough," Stan said. He phoned Darren and Sheila could hear his whooping. She watched Stan's face tighten and she hugged her arms around her waist. "He's on his way."

"Now call the tow company."

"Not until he gets here," Stan said.

She balled her hands into fists. "You want Darren to know you put a boot on my bike?" Stan grimaced and made the call. Within minutes, a tow truck turned the corner and the large driver ambled over to them.

"Don't I know you?" he said. Sheila rolled her eyes and he continued. "From the river, a few weeks ago, right? We gotta stop meeting like this." Sheila cringed when he winked and she turned away from both men.

Stan was sullen when he paid the man in cash, and he ignored Sheila until Darren zoomed into the parking lot. Before Darren leapt from the car, Stan was half-way to the office building.

"Oh Sheila, I'm so sorry," Darren said. He tried to hug her but she put the motorcycle between them.

"About which part, Darren? For insisting I show up to your event alone and then acting like a jealous prick? Or for arguing with me about driving drunk?"

Darren pulled up short. "Sheila."

"Forget about the sad puppy-dog-eyed trick. Your wing man only bought you thirty seconds. Bye bye." She shoved her helmet onto her head, put the key in the ignition, and climbed on the motorcycle. Darren made no move to stop her and she peeled out of the parking lot, burning the rear tire.

She opened up the throttle, pushing the bike to the red line before shifting. When she passed a gas station, she made a u-turn. She'd gas up and head west. At the pump, a wicked thought came to her.

Why not do what Darren accused her of? She pulled Kevin's crumpled business card from her bag. His voice mail picked up and Sheila hesitated, then left a message. She bought a pack of gum, popped in her earplugs and stomped back to the motorcycle.

The cell phone vibrated in her pocket and Sheila felt stupid for hoping it was Darren. It wasn't. "You called," Kevin chirped.

"I'm headed out to the crest," she said. "You up for a ride?"

"Sorry beautiful. I've got a meeting here shortly and I didn't ride the hog to work. What about tomorrow?"

"Maybe next time," she said.

"Hey, Sheila?"

"Yeah?"

"I'd like to believe you called because you prefer blonds, and you've dumped Darren. But, on the off chance you're mad at him, do yourself a favor. Don't ride the crest now. It's a pretty technical road and you don't want to ride it if you're upset."

Sheila bit down on her lip. "OK," was all she could manage before she hung up.

When she passed a sign for the Santa Ana Pueblo, she let out a curse. Kevin was right, she was too distracted; she had taken route 25 north when she meant to take 40 west. At the next exit, she got off the freeway and sat on a bench outside a convenience store, weighing her helmet in her hands. Another motorcycle pulled up beside her and she watched the rider sizing up her bike.

"Nice ride," he said. She gave him a quick nod and turned her head away. His neon yellow jacket had her swearing again. She'd been so ticked last night, she'd left her own riding gear in Darren's trunk.

"You lost?" a gruff voice demanded. Sheila sighed at the police officer staring down at her and shook her head. "Which way you headed?"

Why couldn't men leave her alone? She wanted to lash out at the uniformed man but getting flagged with an 800 mile ride ahead of her was not what she needed.

"West," she said, rising from the bench.

"I wouldn't advise that," he said. Sheila looked more closely at the cop. There seemed to be only concern in the middle-aged man's face. "I heard a report of an 18-wheeler jumping the divider and 40's gonna be closed for a while."

"Thanks for the tip," she said. He nodded and continued into the store. Sheila tried to put on her helmet but her shades bit into the bridge of her nose. She yanked them off, then slid the helmet over her face, and fastened the strap. She wasn't going back to Albuquerque and since she was halfway to Santa Fe, she would check out the Georgia O'Keefe museum there. Then she would put New Mexico behind her for good.

Stanley Sheffield wondered if he did the wrong thing in preventing Sheila from leaving. From the office lobby, he watched the girl peeling out of the parking lot. Darren marched back to the Challenger, looking like he was going to chase her, but then he slammed the car door and stalked into the office building. The guy was still sullen when Stan dropped by his office at lunch to raise the subject of camping again.

"It's supposed to rain tonight," Darren said.

Rain had never prevented them before. Did his friend think the girl was going to come back? From what Darren told him of his drunken blunder, and the pissed expression on Sheila's face, Stan was guessing it was over. At least he hoped it was.

"What about sushi?" Stan asked. "We haven't been to Uki's since April."

"I don't know," Darren said. "Maybe." He answered the phone and Stan returned to his own office, skipping lunch and accomplishing nothing more than shuffling the paper stacks on his desk.

At 4:30, the dejected man popped his head into Stan's office. "Let's do Uki's. I'll pack a bag and we can spend the weekend up there."

"Sounds like a plan," Stan said. His friend's suggestion lacked enthusiasm but Stan offered to drive. An hour later, they cruised north in his Volvo. "You wanna talk about it?"

"Nothing to talk about. I blew it."

Stan let a few more minutes pass. "I've got points at the Hilton. We could walk to Uki's from there."

"I haven't felt that crazy jealousy since Wendy and I swear, when I saw Sheila talking to Montgomery, I blew it."

"Well, Kevin *did* try to steal Wendy," Stan said. He swerved around a piece of shredded tire. "You'll find another one, D you always do."

"This girl is different." Darren said and the driver snorted. "I know what you're thinking and it's not just the sex. I mean the sex is great and her body is pure poetry but it's more than physical."

"Pure poetry?"

Darren turned his back to the passenger window. "Haven't you ever felt drugged out on a girl—on someone?" Stan opened his mouth but Darren spoke over him. "Sheila is not only sit-forward-in-your-chair beautiful, she's smart and more well-read than you, even. And she's got this, this something about her I can't figure out. She's totally altar materi-al and I fucking blew it."

"Wait a minute, D. The girl didn't even give you a chance to defend yourself." He took his eyes from the road and saw his friend's jaw tick. "Didn't you tell me she doesn't want to have kids? And she's estranged from her family? And what about those nightmares? You wanna marry a girl who wakes up screaming another man's name?"

"That's only happened a couple of times," Darren said. "I think she witnessed her boyfriend's murder."

"You think? You mean she hasn't explained it yet? C'mon, D. You don't need somebody with all that baggage. You don't need anoth-er Wendy."

Darren let out a deflated breath and shifted in his seat. The driver waited a minute before turning on an old Metallica CD. For the rest of the drive, he mulled over a plan to make Darren forget about Sheila.

When he spotted a silver motorcycle parked in front of the hotel, Stan stomped the brakes. Darren regarded him questioningly and when

Stan glanced again, he let out a breath. The bike wasn't a BMW. The girl was probably half way to San Diego by now, he assured himself.

Two receptionists worked at the check in counter and both were busy with customers. Stan wondered if they'd be able to get a room. He nudged Darren. "I think the red-head is digging you," he stage whispered. "She keeps looking over here."

Darren didn't look at the red-head and Stan followed his gaze across the lobby, to the atrium and pool. "Told ya it would rain," D mumbled. "And I'm staying away from women for a while. Too much drama."

They watched the rainfall dot the surface of the water and scatter the people lounging around the pool.

"We have one room left," a receptionist said, drawing Stan's attention. "But it only has a king-sized bed."

"That's fine," he said. To himself, he thought, *that's perfect.*

"Sheila!" Darren sprinted across the lobby and Stan balled his hands into fists.

A twelve foot glass pane separated the atrium from the lobby. The girl didn't look up when Darren burst through the door but Stan saw the surprise on Sheila's face when her former lover blocked her from grabbing a towel. He scooped her into an embrace and swung her around. Without stopping to put her down, he planted one on her mouth.

"Aww, how romantic," the receptionists said. Guests who had been on their way to the elevator also stopped to watch. Stan thought he might hurl at the collective cooing. Instead he picked up his keys from the counter and the jingling brought the receptionist's attention back to him. "Oh, I'm sorry, sir. Here's your room key. Do you need one or two?"

Stan was about to tell her to forget it. He didn't want to stay in the room by himself if Darren was going to end up with Sheila but a quick glance at the pool area caused him to hesitate. Sheila wasn't reciprocating Darren's excitement. She pushed him away and strode through the lobby, still dripping. Darren's entire front was discolored from the wet embrace and he slipped on one of her footprints.

"Better leave a key here for Romeo," Stan told the receptionist. "I'm not sure he can win that argument."

CHAPTER 26

STAN TOOK THEIR OVERNIGHT BAGS TO ROOM 421 AND WAITED. AN hour passed with no word from Darren. He phoned downstairs to ask for Sheila's room number. The operator couldn't find her in the system and Stan wondered if she'd checked out already. If so, where was Darren? He turned on the TV and flipped through the channels without interest. One of the wireless ads gave him an idea and Stan logged into the GPS feature on his phone. In May, he arrived late to a concert at one of the reservations. He and Darren had opted into the GPS family locator feature to find each other.

"Yes," he said triumphantly. It was still enabled.

At first Stan didn't think it would work. The dots showed he and Darren were at the same location but he fiddled with the zoom and left the room to move between the numerous hotel floors. Stan walked past a couple on the second floor and their curious glance made him feel silly. What would he do if he found Sheila's room?

If Darren hadn't returned by now, it was because they were going at it. Stan turned on his heel and spotted a couple groping each other by the elevator. He turned back to the other direction and headed for the stairs. At the end of the hall, across from the stairwell, Darren's voice stopped him.

The voice was gruff, tickling the hairs on the back of Stan's neck.

He told himself he didn't want to hear what was going on in there but his knees locked and wouldn't work with his feet to move him to the stairs. His ears tweaked at a feminine whimper followed by a deeper, husky groan.

Darren's voice grew louder, more insistent. "Mine." Sheila's response was muffled. D growled again, "Mine."

At the sound of a smack, Stan gripped the door jamb. He imagined his best friend behind the girl, slapping her ass and driving himself into her. Stan's face wasn't the only thing growing warm when he heard another smack.

The elevator chimed, startling the eavesdropper. His phone slipped from his fingers and clanged to the floor. He scooped it up and ducked into the stairwell.

Thirty minutes later, he was surprised to find he wasn't alone in the hotel room. Nervousness knifed his stomach and Stan wondered if Darren heard him taking his release in the shower.

"Get dressed so we can go eat. I'm starving," D said. Stan rubbed a towel over his chest, and tilted his head. "What?" Darren asked.

"What do you mean 'what'? What happened?"

"I apologized and we made up." He stepped out of his pants and loosened the two buttons holding his shirt together.

Stan wanted to ask what happened to, *I'm taking a break from the drama.* Instead he flipped the towel over his back. "You don't look too happy—Jesus, Darren." Diagonal welts slanted across his shoulder blades. Some were still bleeding.

"I'm tempted to pick another fight with her for the makeup sex," D said.

"That's gonna leave a mark. Or eight."

He shrugged and pulled on a pair of dry jeans. "Sheila said so too but I think it'll be all right. What better scars could a guy hope for?"

Stan tossed the damp towel onto the bed. "Where is she?"

"Downstairs, in her room," Darren said. He shrugged into a clean shirt and faced Stan. "Get some clothes on, man. I want you to go get her."

"What?"

"She wouldn't agree to come to dinner. Didn't want to be a third wheel and ruin our guy time." Stan stared at him blankly. "If *you* invite her she'll come."

"Great, so I get to be the third wheel."

SHEILA SMIRKED AT THE RAPPING ON THE DOOR. SHE'D EXPECTED Darren to come back by her room after he changed but she still hadn't dressed. When she saw Stan looking down at her sullenly, she tightened the robe around her throat and poked her head out the door in search of Darren.

"He sent me to collect you," Stan said. "Get dressed so we can go eat."

Sheila folded her arms across her chest.

Stan blew out a breath. "You like sushi, right?"

"Yeah."

"Darren wants us both to go to dinner with him and Darren wants sushi. So put on a happy face and let's go." Sheila glared at him. She was ready to tell him where to go and how to get there when he drew a hand over his damp hair. "Look. All day, I've put up with Darren dragging his ass and sulking about how he screwed up with you. He wants to make it up to you but he doesn't want me left behind. So we'll go, eat some appetizers, and I'll bug out early. You two can continue making up without a third wheel."

"Fine," Sheila said. "I'll meet you downstairs in fifteen minutes."

"No. I'm to 'come down with you or not come at all.'"

Sheila peered at the martyred expression on Stan's face. "All right then. I'll get dressed."

The first time he'd stood in front of Sheila's hotel room, Stan hadn't noticed the window. He stared outside now, not seeing the tourists strolling along the street. He was remembering the time he'd kissed his best friend.

It was their last night at UNM. Darren was trashed and Stan, who rarely drank back then, was feeling good with two PBRs in him. They remained roommates since freshman year and Stan had practically carried Darren from frat row back to their apartment. He stripped the puke stained clothes and muscled D into bed. After four years of living together, he'd seen the guy naked often. Darren changed in front of Stan without thought or awareness of how it made his roommate blush.

Stan had kept his feelings hidden, fearing rejection or the loss of their friendship. But the next day they were graduating and he was leaving for Penn. Stan watched his best friend snore. The guy was passed out on his side but Stan reached down to stroke Darren between the legs and he rolled to his back. He looked up to see if D had woken but he was slack-jawed, eyes closed.

Darren did wake when Stan kissed him. It was a quick one. Darren's mouth was sour and Stan was nervous. D stared up at him in the darkness for the briefest moment before turning on his side and lapsing back into sleep. Stan never knew if his friend was aware of the kiss and he'd never gotten up his nerve to ask.

Stan's breath fogged the window. They remained close friends after graduation, despite the miles between them. But then Darren met Wendy and it seemed to Stan he missed his opportunity.

When a job opened up at the firm last year, Stan moved back to Albuquerque. Darren dated often but never kept a woman for more than six months. It had been less than two since he met Sheila. Now Stan regretted not confessing everything when D had raised the subject of Stan's *persuasion*.

Stan looked up from the window to find Sheila watching him.

They stared at each other for a minute and the girl broke the gaze with a "hmph."

Darren looked relieved when Sheila and Stan stepped off the elevator together. "My two favorite people in the whole world. Hey Stan, I have a surprise for you," he stage whispered. "She might not be your type but the red-head, Melody, was checking *you* out. I invited her to dinner so you don't have to be a third wheel."

HERRERA PROWLED THE NEARLY EMPTY APARTMENT. HE STOPPED IN front of the card table and stared down at the article and the photos on his laptop. He snatched up his business cell and hit the only number programmed in speed dial.

"This had better be good," Vasquez barked. Music blared in the background.

A woman's voice called, "*¡Vuelve, papí!*"

"*Déjame en paz,*" Vasquez shouted. Herrera jerked the phone away from his ear. *Leave me alone.* He'd heard those same words from his woman. No, not *his* woman. He sought her photo on the computer screen.

For the past week, he'd been researching Peach Nelson. He told himself he was following orders and learning all he could about Abruzzo's and SW's connections. What he discovered about Peach, and how she'd come by the neck scar infuriated him.

The female with Vasquez screamed and Herrera brought the phone back to his ear. "What the hell was that?" he asked. He tensed at the scuffling in the background and strained to make out a second male voice.

"This had better be good," Vasquez repeated.

Herrera peered at the phone to be sure he dialed the right number. "What's going on over there? You been drinking, man?" he asked. Vasquez was an ass, and they never spent any time together off the clock.

But the employee couldn't imagine his boss hitting a woman.

Vasquez knew about Herrera's past, and his intolerance for abusive men. The guy had used the knowledge to persuade Herrera into extending his contract for this job. McKay was supposed to be his replacement. Now the Scot followed SW when she was in Albuquerque; the Boricua trailed her when she was in San Diego.

"Either tell me what the fuck you want, or get off the phone," Vasquez said. "I got company."

Herrera let out a curse of his own. He should call back tomorrow after the guy sobered up. He never heard Mr. Protocol curse.

"I don't think McKay is the right man for the job," the employee lied.

"What? Why?" his boss said. The music quieted and the other male voice spoke in the background. Feminine laughter followed.

"I've been looking at McKay's reports and something is off. I think I should stick with the subject—"

"You been bitching about getting back to San Diego for three months but now you're there and the target is—"

"The target?" Herrera said. "What target?"

"I said the *subject*. You're the best man I've got and if she's gonna get snatched, it will be in San Diego—"

"If she's going to get snatched then I should be wherever she is, since I'm your best man," Herrera said.

"Since when do you give a fuck?" Vasquez said.

The photograph McKay had taken of Peach entering Abruzzo's house glowed on the laptop. Herrera snapped the thing closed. "I don't trust McKay," he said tightly. Vasquez howled in laughter. The sound was off and it made his shoulders tighten. "Yo man, where you at? Here or Albuquerque?"

"None of your fucking business. Keep your ass in San Diego until I say otherwise!" he said and ended the call.

Herrera tossed the phone onto the table. He only wanted to keep

McKay from moving in on Peach. His counterpart had gotten a membership to the boxing gym and enjoyed goading him daily. It irked Herrera, not knowing if Peach reciprocated the Scot's interest. Now, however, the Boricua's gut told him something was seriously wrong with his boss.

Herrera didn't know Mr. Protocol before he took this gig. Vasquez interviewed him on the recommendation of a mutual acquaintance, Benson, in April.

The Marine just finished a contract, a lame ass job, working security for a senator in D.C. According to Vasquez, SW's rich daddy wanted her followed because of a stalker ex-boyfriend. Herrera dismissed the story as bunk after trailing SW for a week; six weeks before he followed SW to Albuquerque.

When McKay signed on, Vasquez persuaded Herrera to stay, too. The alleged ex-boyfriend was allegedly pissed about SW replacing him. Right. The pay was good, and since he didn't have anything else lined up in San Diego, Herrera hadn't questioned the weak story.

Who was the gringo with Vasquez? Herrera was sure he heard Vasquez say target. Why had he *really* been hired to follow SW? He picked up his phone. It was time to find out.

CHAPTER 27

SHEILA AWOKE WITH A START. SHE SCRAMBLED OUT OF BED TO CROUCH over the hotel toilet.

Darren followed. "What's wrong, honey?"

"Sick. Go—" Darren ignored her request and gathered her hair away from the bowl. "I don't want you to see me like this."

"It will take more than vomit to scare me away, sweetness." He insisted on carrying her back to bed after she brushed her teeth. Then he phoned Stan. "You and Melody go on to breakfast without us."

Sheila could imagine Stan's annoyance at having to go to breakfast with Melody but she didn't have the strength to feel sympathy for the redhead. Her empty stomach churned and her entire body ached.

At checkout time, Darren tried to book the room for another day but it wasn't available. A knock sounded on the door, interrupting their debate over the motorcycle.

Stan and Melody entered. "You guys are arguing again?" Stan said.

"I don't think she should ride the motorcycle home if she can't stand up without dry heaving," Darren said.

"I'm fine," Sheila said, then bolted to the toilet.

"I've got a truck," Melody said. "You could borrow it and haul the motorcycle in the back."

"That's a great idea," Darren said. Sheila emerged from the bathroom in time to catch the scowl on Stan's face.

Two days later, she was still miserable.

"Let me take you to the doctor," Darren urged. He pressed a mug of ginger tea into her hands.

"It's just the flu." She sniffed the tea. "This smells funky."

"Are you sure you're not pregnant?"

"From two nights ago?"

"Sheila." He brushed the hair off her forehead. "Honey, it's been six weeks..."

"Ugh." She was already hot from a fever and she hoped her face wasn't turning any redder. "My cycle isn't regular but I had some spotting last week." She gave him the mug and sank onto her side. "Besides, I don't think fever, chills, body aches, and diarrhea are symptoms of pregnancy."

He put the mug on the bedside table. "I have to leave for D.C. tomorrow but I don't want to leave you like this. I wish I could cancel the trip. I'll ask Stan to come look in on you."

"No," she said and rolled over to face him. "Don't bug Stan. I'll be fine. I bet this is the worst of it and I'll be feeling better by the time you leave."

Darren slid down on the bed and pulled Sheila against his chest. "Ma and Rosie are coming down from New York on Saturday. They want to meet you."

"Mmm," she said, and closed her eyes. He scratched little circles over her back. "That feels nice."

"I know, *gattini*." Sheila pinched him and his chest vibrated with laughter. "I'll be gone a week, and home for a couple of days but then I have to go to Vegas for a bachelor party."

"Mmm," she said again and yawned.

"Will you meet me in Vegas?"

Sheila opened her eyes. "You're not supposed to invite your girl-friend to a bachelor party." *Girlfriend.* She liked calling herself his girl-friend. They'd settled that in Santa Fe.

Darren's eyes smoldered. "Who cares about the party? I want to be with you. All the time. Every day." He pressed a quick kiss on her lips. "You could just stay, you know."

"Stay?"

"Yes, stay here." He threw a leg over hers. "In Albuquerque, with me."

Her heart took off at a sprint. "You mean move in... with you?"

"I probably should've waited until you're feeling better to ask. I just—" he squeezed her and took a deep breath. "Your lease is up soon, right?"

"It's only been six weeks..." Sheila said.

"I know but I was sick out of my head on Friday when I thought I'd lost you. I want to wake up with you, *bellissima*, every day. I want to come home to you, lounge on the sofa and read books together. You make me feel..." His chest swelled against hers. "Being with you, Sheila, is like being *home*."

"You don't read books, you sleep on them," she said playfully. "Have you even made it past chapter two of *Lonesome Dove*?"

Could she move in with Darren? She'd been heartsick on Friday too, unable to withhold forgiveness when he groveled at her hotel room door. Her boyfriend's arrogance and possessiveness drove her crazy but she was far from perfect. He made her feel cherished. Alive.

He chuckled and squeezed her again. "See how well you know me?" Darren said. He leaned back to grin at her. "*Ti amo.* I love your sense of adventure, your delicious body, your tenacity—"

"Now you're lying," Sheila laughed. "You don't love my stubbornness."

"I didn't say 'stubborn,' I said, 'tenacious.' Everyone knows feisty women never get boring."

"Darren..."

He put a finger on her lips. "You don't have to answer now."

WEDNESDAY, JULY 25TH

STAN KNOCKED ON THE DOOR TWICE BEFORE INSERTING HIS KEY IN THE lock. "Hello?" He heard an answering rustle in the bedroom. "Charlie? Hey cat, are you itching to go out yet?"

"Charlie is hiding in the office," Sheila said. "He and I have an understanding to stay out of each other's way."

Stan straightened from untying his sneakers. "I didn't think you were still here."

"Then why did you knock first?"

He shrugged. "Darren asked me to come by and look in on you. I called and when you didn't answer, I figured you left already." Sheila stared at him intently and he dropped a stack of mail onto the coffee table. "You look like you're feeling better."

"Yes, I am."

"When are you leaving?" he said and Sheila raised her eyebrows. "I'm supposed to take care of the cat after you leave."

"Right," she said.

"Darren asked you to move in with him." He nodded when she wrinkled her forehead. "You're surprised he told me?" Sheila didn't answer and Stan shrugged again. "He shares everything with me."

"Funny." She crossed her arms. "You don't share *everything* with him."

He narrowed his eyes. "I looked for you in Penn's alumni records but I didn't see a listing for 'Sheila Washington.'"

"And your point is?"

"I went to Penn, for law, but I don't think *you* did."

Sheila tilted her head and smiled. "You're threatened by me."

Stan's fingers tightened on the door knob and Sheila's smile turned smug. "You're hiding something," he said. "I'm going to find out—"

"Auntie Sheila!" Joelle called behind him. Stan spun around at the sound of the child's voice. "Hi, Mr. Sheffield," she said.

Auntie Sheila? He opened the screened door. "Hi, Joelle, how are—" Joelle stepped around him and threw her arms around Sheila's legs.

"Auntie Sheila! I missed you."

"What are you doing here, Stan?" Peach asked.

"Just stopping by to say farewell to Sheila," Stan said.

"I have a new purse. Look at my new purse," Joelle chanted.

Peach stepped around Stan and dropped her purse onto the sofa. "Farewell? I thought you weren't leaving till tomorrow?"

"Stan has his own ideas," Sheila said. She knelt in front of Joelle and widened her eyes at the purse. "Ohh, sparkly."

"Let me know when you're gone so I can check on the cat," Stan said.

Sheila pulled Joelle against her chest with her right hand and flipped off Stan with the left.

PEACH BARKED OUT A LAUGH. JOELLE, STILL CLINGING TO SHEILA, turned around to regard Peach. "What's so funny, Mom?"

"Your Aunt Sheila." Peach looked back at the sound of the screen door banging shut.

"Will you draw a picture with me, Auntie Sheila?"

Sheila brushed a hand over Joelle's wily hair. "Sure baby. Go get the crayons and paper."

"Shoes first," Peach said.

Joelle stepped out of her sandals and ran into the office. "Charlie," she called. "Where are you Charlie?"

The Filipina removed her heels and shut the storm door. "What did we walk in on?"

"Oh Pea." Sheila crossed to the sofa and flopped onto the left cushion.

"I think I'm in trouble."

"What? How?" Peach tugged her skirt down before sitting next to Sheila.

Her words came out in a rush. "Darren asked me to move in with him and he told Stan and Stan is snooping around—you know Stan is gay, right?"

"Yeah. But wait, Darren asked you to move in with him?"

"Yes."

Peach sank back on the sofa. "Whoa," she said. "He told me after Wendy, he'd never live with a woman until he was married."

"Oh shit." Sheila dropped her head into her hands.

"Ooh, I heard that!" Joelle said. "You said the S-word."

"Joelle."

"Whoops," Sheila said. She lifted her head. "I'm busted."

"Why don't you go get a treat for Charlie," Peach said. "See if there's some in the pantry."

"Charlieeee. Treat," Joelle said. She dropped the box of crayons and skipped around the corner to the kitchen.

"Inside voice monkey, jeez," Peach said.

Sheila scrambled onto the sofa when the cat galloped through the living room. In the kitchen, Joelle shook the treat pouch and the cat yowled.

The taller woman shuddered and the movement drew Peach's attention back to her. "I guess he'll have to find a new home," she said, trying to keep from laughing. "Still afraid of cats, huh?"

Sheila cradled her knees. "You'd be scared of cats too if one bit you on the cheek when you were only two. And I didn't say yes to moving in with Darren."

"Yet."

She shook her head. "I really like Darren but things are going too fast. And now Stan is digging into my past..."

"You haven't told him yet?" Peach asked and Sheila grimaced. The boxer scooted closer, clasping Sheila's hand. "Oh honey, you gotta tell him. You won't scare him off. Actually, I think he's kind of a magnet for girls with crappy pasts."

Sheila lowered her feet to the floor. "What do you mean?"

"I think Darren's got White Knight syndrome," Peach said with a shrug. "He's gone through a few girlfriends in the two and a half years I've been here. Some of them were cool, too. He never invited any of them to move in with him. And he never gushed about them like he does with you."

"Yeah, but those women were probably local, right?" Sheila said.

"Yeah, they were local. But here's my point: the only other woman he was serious with, that he lived with, was Wendy. She was molested by her dad…"

"That's awful," Sheila said.

Peach nodded. "I never met Wendy but from what I know about their relationship, Darren tried really hard to help her get over it. He even took a semester off from grad school when their relationship started to fall apart.

"Then there's me. I mean, not that we were romantically involved," she wrinkled her nose. "That came out wrong. Our moms are twin sisters. I didn't really know Darren growing up. His folks moved around a lot because of Uncle Dom's engineering job. When our families got together, Darren always hung out with my older brother and sister. But when Darren found out about me and Joey—"

Peach broke off and fingered the scar on her throat. She leaned back on the sofa and peeked in the kitchen. After confirming Joelle was still distracted with the cat, she continued in a whisper. "Darren literally flew in and rescued us. He brought me and Joelle here to start over and took care of us until I could get back on my feet. So if you're worried about Darren freaking out about your messy past, don't."

"But you're family." Sheila lowered her voice to a whisper too. "His reaction to me witnessing the murders isn't the only thing I'm worried about. Don't you think he'll be mad I didn't tell him about my... family?"

"You mean that you're a millionaire?" Peach said. "Yeah, right. What a hardship, to fall in love with a millionaire."

"I don't know, Pea. I got a taste of his temper last week—"

"And I bet you gave him a taste of your temper, too," Peach said. She squeezed Sheila's hand. "That's why you're good for him. Darren needs a woman who'll stand up to him."

"I don't know—"

Joelle skipped back into the living room. "Can we color now, Aunt Sheila?"

CHAPTER 28

"The nightmares have changed," Sheila said.

"Changed how?" Dr. Baldwin asked.

"Instead of a straight replay of the murders, or the B-Butcher catching me, the players are... different."

"Give me an example," he said.

Sheila pulled the afghan from the sofa, into her lap. She didn't tell him about the pregnant dream. "On my way back from Albuquerque on Friday, I stopped at a motel outside of Phoenix. I probably could've made it back here but I was sleepy and then Kate called to say she was 'entertaining.' I took a quick shower—the water wasn't very hot—and it seemed like as soon as I got in the bed, the dream started." She gave Dr. B a guilty look. "I forgot to plant the intention for a *good* dream."

He nodded and she dug her fingers into the knitted blanket.

"I was running from the—*him*. He shot me in the leg and I fell onto my side. When he stood over me and said, 'I told you, you'd pay,' his face was wrong. It was Stan's."

"Darren's best friend?" Dr. Baldwin said.

She nodded. "'Darren's mine,' Stan said, but it was the Butcher's voice. Then Darren burst into the alley, followed by a guy covered in tattoos.

The gun went off, and I had the weirdest feeling when I woke up..."

"The weirdest feeling?"

She unknotted her fingers and smoothed the blanket. "I wanted to call my mother."

"Your mother, or Momma?"

"Mother," Sheila said. "Pretty ridiculous, huh?"

"Did you call her?"

"No. I mean, what would I say? 'Hi, Mother. I know I was a total bitch the last time I saw you, but I just had a bad dream. Can you check under my bed?'"

Sheila felt the smile in his voice when Dr. B responded. "You feel like you were a bitch to her in April?"

She shrugged. "I was pretty mad—angry. She's been calling a lot, asking if we can meet but I can't handle her right now. Darren is pushing for me to meet *his* mother. And," she drew in a breath, "he asked me to move in with him."

"How do you feel about that?"

"Like I've got to come clean with him before Stan digs up my past." Dr. Baldwin tilted his head and Sheila explained the threat from Stan and her suspicions about his crush on Darren.

"You're worried about Darren rejecting you?"

"Peach said he wouldn't—I stayed with her and Joelle a couple of nights—but I don't know. I think he'll be mad I didn't tell him from the start. What do I do?"

"What do you think you should do?"

"Oh, don't give me that crap," Sheila said. The blanket fell onto the floor when she stood up and crossed to the window.

She considered her recent conversation with Darren. He gushed about his family visit and his excitement over introducing her to his mother and sister was palpable. He kept his promise not to pry into her past, or ask about her family, but what about his mother? Felicity

Abruzzo would ask questions.

"I think you already know what to do," Dr. Baldwin said. "How does Momma put it? 'Grown folks already have their minds made up when they ask for advice.'"

SATURDAY, AUGUST 4TH

"Good morning, honey. How's the drive coming?"

"Hmm."

"Are you still in bed?" Darren asked.

"No, well yes. I'm not in San Diego though. I'm here."

"Here? Here where?"

"Las Vegas, silly." Sheila yawned and stretched onto her back. "I got in late last night—"

"If you got in last night, why didn't you call me?"

"I wasn't invited to the bachelor party, remember?" She yawned again and glanced at the clock. "Kate had an impromptu party and I wasn't feeling the vibe so I decided to come here. What are you doing up so early? I thought you'd all be sleeping off hang-overs."

"Sheil-la, I thought you agreed not to drive at night."

She sat up. "Dar-ren," she said, mocking his tone. "I've driven across the U.S. twice. I can handle a five hour trip—"

"*Dio aiutami*—"

"Hold that rant," she said. "I'm going to the bathroom." She left the phone on the bed. When she returned, she blanched at the loud music in the background. "Where are you?"

"At the pool. Why don't you get dressed and come have a mimosa with us?"

"I need a shower and I haven't eaten..."

"C'mon, Sheila. The guys are leaving soon and I want you to meet them. I'll order some food for you."

If she had stuck to the plan and arrived in the late afternoon, she would have avoided meeting his frat buddies until the wedding in three weeks. Raj, the groom-to-be, had also attended Penn for grad school. Sheila worried that Stan would be listening closely if their alma mater came up in conversation.

"We don't have to stay long," Darren said loudly, over Lady Gaga. "But I would like it if you'd come meet my friends."

"All right," she said finally. Rifling through her suitcase, she pulled out her Speedo. Sheila cringed and redressed in the clothes she'd worn on the drive last night.

When she arrived at the doors opening to the pool of the Venetian, she stopped short. All the women were clad in barely-there bikinis. She wore cut-offs and a wrinkled tank top.

"Excuse us," a haughty voice said.

Sheila stepped back to allow a quartet of women to pass, and her mouth fell open. One of them had on a high-waisted thong, and she heard whistles from a group of men at the far end of the pool.

Her eyes narrowed when she saw her boyfriend among them. He looked up when a dark skinned guy nudged him in the ribs but Darren's gaze didn't linger. Sheila's did.

She drank in his tanned body. Most of the men around the pool, and in his bachelor party, wore knee-length board shorts. The black Lycra briefs hugging Darren's narrow hips and his delicious rump weren't the only thing holding her attention.

His hair was longer, and the muscles in his abdomen flexed when he brushed the curls off his forehead. It had only been a few weeks since they'd last seen each other but he'd obviously been working out. He was lean to begin with but now he had the cut abs and obliques of an underwear model.

Darren brought a champagne flute to his lips and she found herself envying the glass. It reflected sparkles onto his chest. Her nails cut into her palm when the bikini quartet sauntered up to the bachelor party.

Sheila turned around and headed back to one of the boutiques off the lobby. She'd be damned if she followed those girls wearing scrubs.

DARREN PICKED UP HIS PHONE AGAIN. WHAT COULD SHE BE DOING FOR thirty minutes? "Honey, where are you?"

"Hey D, check out the rack on the chick in the purple," Raj said.

"I'm the chick in the purple," Sheila said.

Darren followed Raj's outstretched hand and slapped him in the back of the head. "That's my woman," he said at the same time he ended the call. He waved at Sheila. She smiled and his cock waved too. "*Non ci credo*," he murmured.

His woman wove through the crowd lining the pool and Darren thought he heard his phone groan from him squeezing it too hard. Or maybe it was one of the saps ogling her. Why hadn't he realized she'd come to the pool in a bikini?

He was hypnotized by the sway of her hips, transfixed by the semi-circular outlines of her nipple jewelry. They were apparent through the triangle of fabric, even at a distance. His mouth watered in anticipation.

Her breasts were suddenly jostled to the side and the attorney lurched forward. *Oh hell no.* Some muscle head was about to lose his arms. The guy had purposefully bumped into Sheila, caught her from falling, and now he was faking an apology.

"D looks like he needs to cool off," Raj said. "Don't you think so, Bo?"

Darren darted to the side but he wasn't quick enough. Raj caught his arm and spun him sideways, into the pool. He resurfaced next to one of his Reef sandals.

Sheila crouched at the ladder. "Are you okay?" she asked when he swam over to her.

"Yeah but I don't know about my phone," he said. She took the Blackberry from him and he climbed the ladder. "Ouch."

"What's the matter?"

"Damned ankle." He tried to put his full weight on it and grimaced. "Must have twisted it going in."

"Put your arm around me," Sheila said. "That's right, now, sit down over here." She guided him to a cabana.

"This one's taken," a woman said. "Oh no, you're bleeding."

"I am?" Darren sank onto the cushion and leaned forward to examine the jagged cut on his toe. "Raj you piece of—" he broke off at the look on Sheila's face. "Are you all right, honey?"

"I don't uh, do so well with uh, blood."

"Sheila!" Her body folded and Darren caught her. He braced himself to pull her up onto the chaise and pain skewered his ankle.

"Everybody step back, I'm a doctor," Raj said.

"You're an idiot," Darren snapped. "Go sit down before you hurt somebody else. Bo, help me get her onto the cushion, will you?"

"Sure thing, D." Bo caught Sheila's legs and swept them up. Darren cradled her head in his lap.

"Let me through," a gruff voice demanded. He looked up at the approaching lifeguard. "Who's bleeding?"

Sheila let out a whimper and he clasped her tighter. "I scraped my foot. She fainted at the blood."

"Okay people, show's over," Bo said. He spread his arms and waved the crowd off. "If y'all don't back off, we're gonna have to start charging admission."

"The wound looks superficial. I'm going to check her pulse and call for the paramedics," the lifeguard said.

"No ambulance," she croaked.

"Take it easy, miss."

"You might want to stay where you are, sweetness. I'm still bleeding."

She groaned and squeezed her eyes tightly.

"Does your head hurt, miss?" the lifeguard asked.

"Yes, I mean no. I'm just a little dehydrated. And hungry," she said. Sheila turned her head to look up at Darren. "Are you okay?"

"No. I nearly died when that meathead pawed you. I swear woman, you'll be the death of me," Darren said. Sheila gasped and he flinched from the lifeguard swabbing ointment on his toe.

"It's just a scrape but you'll want to ice this ankle. I called for a wheel-chair to take you inside." Darren began to protest but when he tried to stand up again, the throbbing forced him to shelve his pride.

SHEILA LEFT THE WHEELCHAIR IN THE HALLWAY AND PUT THE DO NOT DISTURB sign on the door knob. She ducked into the bathroom and found Darren, naked on the bed. "Aren't you presumptuous," she said.

"I need sexual healing." Darren held his hand out and tried to tug her onto the bed.

"Hang on a sec. I need to tell you something." He sat up and cupped her breasts. "Easy," she said. "They're kind of sensitive right now."

"What do you need to tell me? Are you on your period?"

"No."

"Did you see a doctor?" He tugged the string tied at the back of her neck and freed her breasts.

"A doctor? For what?"

"To get on the Pill," he said around her nipple. In a smooth move, he tugged her down onto the bed and removed the bikini top without re-leasing her breast.

"I don't remember agreeing," she sucked in a breath, "to that."

"But we talked about it." He slipped a hand beneath her and captured the bikini bottoms.

Sheila raised her head and saw the rest of her swim suit sailing toward the desk. "*You* suggested it. *I* don't want the side effects or the extra hormones in my body. Besides I don't feel a difference with the condoms."

Darren's mouth made a popping sound when he released her nipple. "I do."

"Right. It's all about you and your pleasure. Meanwhile I have to be the responsible one. Are we in the 21st century or what?"

"Sheila, you know that's not true. C'mon sweetness, can't we have one night without an argument?" Darren tweaked her jewelry with one hand and moved the other between her legs.

She sat up and swung her legs to the side, annoyed with him for sidetracking the conversation. She needed to get the secrets off her chest before she lost her nerve, or one of his frat boys came knocking on the door.

"If there were a birth control pill for men, I'd gladly take it."

"There is an option for you," she said. "You could get snipped."

He cupped himself. "Ouch," he said. Sheila turned away and plucked a robe from her suitcase. "Hey, hey, what's with the robe?" He pulled her down, on top of him before she could slip into the silk garment.

His erection was hot against her stomach and she hid her laughter with a cough. "You do realize that even *if* I agreed to get on the Pill, we'd still have to use a backup for at least two months?"

Darren claimed her mouth while he simultaneously rolled her onto her back. He dusted kisses over her breasts, down her abdomen, pausing only when he reached her thighs.

"Oh yeah?" he said, and she lifted her head at the thickness in his voice. She couldn't see his eyes because they were hidden by the curtain of curls hanging from his head. But she saw his pink tongue snake out of his mouth and tickle her tender flesh.

"Yeah," she hissed. Her head fell back and she fisted her hands around his locks. "Yeah."

"You're so hot... *molto caldo*." Darren teased her with little flicks of his tongue. She felt the orgasm building quickly and the pressure was more intense than usual.

"Don't stop," she said.

Darren chuckled, a deep sound of male satisfaction. "Don't worry, baby, I'm just getting started. He nipped her and she bucked against his mouth. Another chuckle, then, "Where are the condoms?"

Sheila looked up through hooded lids. "What?"

"You don't have any condoms?"

Her brows knit together. "You always have them."

"My things are in the other room."

"Oh." She saw his mouth turn up in a wry smile and she waited for him to throw her own words back at her.

"There's always the rhythm method," he said. Her eyes went big but Darren didn't see them. He dipped his head again, and she screamed when he dove into her with his tongue. His hands held her thighs tightly, keeping her from clamping them around his head. Sheila grabbed one of the pillows and covered her moans with it.

"Don't." He ripped the pillow from her face and flung it away. "Don't ever hide from me. I want to hear exactly how much you enjoy *me* giving *you* pleasure." His face was inches from hers and for a few seconds, Sheila was lost staring into the striated pattern of his irises.

Darren's pupils narrowed slightly, then widened, and the impish light in his eyes faded. He shifted his weight and brought his right hand up to her cheek. His fingers feathered over her skin and his tenderness melted her.

She'd never been looked at with such adoration and Sheila fought the ridiculous urge to ask what he was staring at. Her heart swelled with love and it tumbled out of her mouth. "I love you," she said.

"Ah, *bellissima, mio. Ti amo, anche.*"

Gone was the tenderness. Darren crushed her mouth in a kiss that punctuated his declaration. Her tongue met his, stroke for stroke and she gave herself over to the earthquake of emotion rocking her from the inside out. She finally said it! It had been there for weeks, perched on her tongue but she kept the admission from leaping into the open. Now she shook with joy and relief.

She loved this sexy, passionate man, and she suddenly needed him inside of her. She needed to *really* make love to him. Palming his delicious rump, she urged him between her legs. He broke the kiss to regard her questioningly.

"Rhythm method," she breathed. Darren gifted her with one of his dazzling smiles and buried his length inside her slick heat. Sheila linked her legs around his waist and squeezed her arms around his back. "I love you," she said again.

CHAPTER 29

"I LOVE YOU, TOO," DARREN SAID AND FLEXED HIS COCK. SHEILA GAVE him a seductive smile and squeezed him back. With a grin of his own, he rose to his knees, closed a hand around one of her calves, and pushed her leg toward the headboard. The position sank the tip of his penis against her spot and she cried out, demanding more. He plunged again and again, reveling in the way she chanted his name. He could feel the excitement building within her soft walls like a storm.

She seized his forearms. "I'm going to," she cried out and contracted around him. Darren ground his teeth but her pleasure tipped off his orgasm and he tried to pull out.

"Sheila!" Darren's eyes widened and he gripped her hips, trying again to withdraw. He glanced between them and his eyes confirmed what he felt; they were fused together. Her labia were engorged and they'd clamped down on him, locking Darren inside.

"I can't—ahhh!" Darren threw his head back and yelled. Sheila's sheath contracted, milking him until he collapsed on top of her, panting. "Wow."

"Yeah."

"So much for the rhythm method," he said. "Has this ever happened before?"

"You would know if it had." She wiggled her hips, trying to dislodge him and Darren sucked in a breath.

"Easy sweetness. I think we have to wait until some of the blood goes back to your head." She slapped his ass and he beamed. Darren pressed a kiss to her chin before resting his head on her chest. "Wow," he said again. He half expected a popping sound to mark her body releasing him but it was only a gentle softening.

"I think you're trying to get me pregnant," she said, rolling to her side.

Darren gathered her against his body, pulling the covers over them. "Hey now, *you're* the one who clamped down on *me*."

Sheila gave him a jab with her elbow at the amusement in his voice. "I could go for a nap but I'm afraid your friends will come looking for you."

"You can sleep, honey. They don't know which room we're in."

She yawned and he stroked the hair from her forehead. "Stan will hunt you down."

"Stan's not here," he said.

"What?" she lifted head her head and peeped over her shoulder. "He wasn't invited to play?"

"He was never tight with Raj, Bo, and Larry."

"Hmm," she said, lowering her head. "Raj seems, what's the word?"

"Handsome?"

"Asinine. Tell me the others aren't like him." She felt Darren wince.

"No, they're cool. Raj used to be cool, too."

"Why's he getting married if he's still chasing tail?" Darren sighed and she hurried to apologize. "It's none of my business—"

"He doesn't want to get married but he's doing it to please his parents. They're old school, still living in Calcutta and they chose a wife for him."

"Poor woman," she said with another yawn. Her mind began to drift and Darren's breath tickled the back of her neck.

"Hey, Sheila, what did you want to tell me?"

Her stomach flipped. "Nothing," she said. "Nothing."

SATURDAY, AUGUST 18TH

"HONEY, WHAT WOULD YOU LIKE FOR BREAKFAST?"

Sheila rolled onto her belly. "Five more minutes."

"It's already ten o'clock. My stomach has been growling for hours."

"Go ahead and eat, then." She yawned and let her lids droop shut again.

Darren traced the length of her spine with his fingertip. "We're meeting Peach and Joelle at the pool in an hour."

Her skin pebbled and she squirmed to the side. "Okay," she said and yawned again. "How 'bout eggs and bacon."

He propped his head on his hand. "Bacon? Since when do you eat bacon?"

"I saw some in the fridge last night. It sounds good."

"When you were standing with the door open and devouring the entire bag of carrots?"

She stretched onto her back. "Where are you going?"

"I'll be right back." He kissed her mole and she rolled back onto her stomach. "Hurry up cuz I gotta go too." She heard the door on the cabinet below the sink bang shut and smiled. He tickled the bend of her knee and Sheila raised her head from the pillow. "You're insatiable—" The color drained from her face at the box he held. It wasn't condoms.

Darren lifted her feet, placing them in his lap after he sat on the edge of the bed. He set the box beside his leg and rubbed a hand up her calf. "Your breasts are more sensitive than usual. You've been sleeping late every day this week, and eating more than usual too."

Sheila twisted onto her side and the box slid over the sheet, landing lightly against her abdomen. "When did you buy it?"

"After the conversation we had in Vegas," he said. "If you don't want to get on the Pill, then there are other alternatives. I made an appointment for you to discuss them with the best OB-GYN in town." He pressed a kiss to her bent knee. "But let's be sure you're not pregnant first."

She willed her hand to raise itself from Darren's bed and lift the box. It would be their bed if she said yes to his invitation to move in. He asked again last night. She'd eluded the question with a kiss. Her hand moved in slow motion. The words, *"Results 5 days before your missed period,"* seemed to glow on the box.

"All right," she said finally.

"I'll get started on the bacon," he said.

"All right." His hand fell on her shoulder when she moved toward the bathroom and she jumped, dropping the pregnancy test.

Darren retrieved it. "I love you," he said.

Sheila took a long shower. Then she dressed and brushed out her hair. Finally, she peed on the stick and washed out the tub.

She stared down at the pregnancy test and imagined another path opening up in her life. What if Dr. Baldwin was right and the Butcher never came after her? It *had* been three years and he was in jail. She'd been doing well with the finger tapping therapy. She still felt silly doing it but it worked to calm her when she awoke in a sweat. And Darren didn't laugh when she did it. What if she could have a life with him? What if... Her heart raced and she peeked at the stick again.

She thought of the morning when she told him about calling Planned Parenthood and how he'd flipped. If she showed Darren the test results, with a line in the second window, there would be no going back to her life on the road.

Who was she kidding, *if* she were pregnant? Momma had dreamt about it. And she hadn't had a period in two months. How long would she have kept lying to herself before Darren insisted on a test? A blue line appeared on the stick. She checked the second test and gripped the sides of the sink to keep from sinking to the floor.

"I'm going to have a baby," she whispered. Gathering both sticks in one hand and, heart galloping with hope, she flung open the bathroom door. Padding down the hall, she inhaled the smell of bacon.

"Well, Mr. Abruzzo you're—" Sheila stopped short when she reached the living room.

Darren stood by the window and he held a stack of papers in his hands. His face was a mask of anger, and warning bells in her head had Sheila slipping the sticks into her back pocket. Stan sat on the sofa, and when he smiled, she thought she might get sick.

"Hello, Liz," Stan said.

Looking over at Darren, the path she'd imagined disappeared.

"You lied to me," he said.

"Could we discuss this alone?" she asked. Stan leaned back on the sofa and crossed his feet on the coffee table.

"What's to discuss?" Darren said. "This file says everything. You're an heir to the Chase fortune. You were engaged to marry Cornelius Fitzgerald shortly before you met me. And he's been searching for you for the past six months."

"That's not true, Darren. I never—"

"Stop lying! It's here, it's all right here." Darren flung the papers at her and she ducked. "How long were you going to keep it up, Sheila? Or should I call you *Elizabeth*?"

She stooped to pick up the closest picture and her face leeched of color. "These aren't real."

"It's your picture, with your fiancé. Here's the announcement." He shoved another paper at her. "Are you going to stand there and lie to my face?"

"Darren, please. Haven't you ever heard of Photoshop? Someone has gone to a lot of trouble—"

"Is this photoshopped, Elizabeth?" He shoved something else at her and Sheila took it reflexively. It was one of the name change announcements. She had the ridiculous thought, if Darren were a cartoon character, steam would be coming out of his ears.

"That's how I found you out," Stan said. "In a legal journal, of all places."

Sheila ignored him. "I can explain, Darren. I know I haven't been entirely honest with you but—"

"No, but the lies have been so sweet, haven't they? How could you make love to me when you're engaged to another man?"

"I'm not. If you'll let me explain—"

"I can't believe I thought I was in love with you!" Darren spat. Sheila felt her heart break when she reached out and he recoiled. "Don't touch me."

Sheila dropped her hand and turned her face so he wouldn't see the tears. Her purse lay on the floor by the shoe rack and she stooped to pick it up. She reached for the handle on the screen door.

What about her toiletries? She shook her head. She must be crazy for thinking of the toiletries and her bag of clothes in the bedroom. Her life was falling apart again, and she was thinking about toiletries.

"Your fiancé will be here to collect you shortly," Stan said smugly.

Sheila had the sudden urge to take the pregnancy tests from her pocket and stab him with them. She wiped her cheeks and leered at him instead.

"I've met Cornelius Fitzgerald exactly twice," she said. She was surprised her voice didn't tremble. "The first time I was probably fifteen. The second time was when my oh-so-helpful father announced he arranged for Neil to marry me.

"Neil needs a beard, you know about that, don't you Stan? A 'cover,' someone who'll support the appearance that he's *straight*. Neither of them asked me what I thought or what I wanted. Although *you* won't believe it, I declined. But since he's on his way over here, I'll be sure to introduce you, Stan. You're a much better match for him."

She kicked the screen door open. Where were her keys? Thank God she hadn't ridden the motorcycle.

"Sheila," Darren yelled. She took off running for Dexter.

"Miss Washington?"

She ignored both voices. "Get off me," she spat when Darren's hand fell onto her shoulder.

"I wouldn't do that if I were you," the other voice said.

Unable to resist turning, Sheila narrowed her eyes at the man. "You," she said. It was the tattooed guy from her dream. She stared at him for a heartbeat and her mind recalled him in a white van, outside Peach's apartment building. He was shorter than Darren but the height difference didn't stop him from gripping her lover around the neck and throwing him off with one hand.

The tattooed man stepped toward her. "You need to come with me."

"Fuck you!" Her fingers closed around the key in her purse, and she jerked open the car door.

"You're not safe on your own," he said. "The Butcher is after you and you need to come with me—"

Sheila didn't know if her knees gave out or if she'd been lowering herself into the car of her own volition. She dropped into the seat and managed to get the key into the ignition before one of the men grasped her arm. They talked over each other and she pounded on the horn with her free fist.

"Get. Away. From. Me."

Neither of the men moved.

"You have to come with me," tattooed man said.

"Sheila, you're too upset to drive," Darren pleaded.

Ignoring them both, she threw the car into reverse and didn't stop when it crunched into the vehicle behind her. The men were forced to jump back and her door swung shut. She shifted into first gear and gunned it.

"God help me," Darren muttered. Sheila's car barreled up the street. It didn't heed the four way stop.

"You asshole," the shorter man said. "If she ends up wrapped around a fucking tree, you'll be pissing red for the rest of your sorry life." He sprinted away and Darren shot after him.

"Who are you? And who's this Butcher—" The man threw an upper left hook, landing Darren on his ass. The attorney shook his head and caught the guy's ankle, toppling him. A horn bleated and he spared a glance at the approaching tires.

"What the hell is going on here?" Peach asked through the window.

Darren's captive jumped up and wrenched open the door of a van. "Move the car, Peach!"

"Angel, what are you doing?"

Darren reached for Angel again. "Move the car, Peach. Sheila's in trouble and I'm—"

"Don't move the car, Peach. Call 911," Darren ordered. He could hear Joelle crying and Angel took advantage of his distraction, shoving off Darren's hold. He jumped into the van and started it up.

"Who bashed up my car?" someone shouted.

Darren looked up at his neighbor, Jose, and pointed to the van. "Don't let him get away!"

"Where do you think you're goin'?" Jose jerked the door open and staggered back under the force of a fist to his jaw.

"Angel?" Peach ran up to the melee and Darren stopped her with a hand on her shoulder.

"What the hell is going on, Darren?" She ducked from his grasp and his neighbors echoed his cousin's concern. He glanced at their startled faces, then back at the man Jose tackled. The sun glinted off a piece of plastic on the ground. He stooped to pick it up.

"*Dio aiutami!*" He ran his fingers over the splintered pregnancy test. What was the result? He tried to recall Sheila's face when she had emerged from the bathroom. What came to him was red, the color of his rage at the contents of the envelope. The envelope Stan had brought.

CHAPTER 30

SCREAMS RENT THE AIR. EVERYONE TURNED TOWARD THE VAN.

"What is that?" Jose said. He was trying to plant Angel's face into the asphalt with his sneaker.

"Feed from the transmitter." Herrera said. "Let me up."

A masculine voice spoke from the van, "Get out of the car."

"*Madre de Dios*," Herrera said.

"What?" Darren said.

"Vasquez."

"Who is Vasquez?"

"My boss," Herrera spit out.

Sheila's scream pierced the air again and Darren nearly ripped the van door off its hinges. "We have to go, *now*!"

The sounds of struggle were muffled but Vasquez's voice was clear. "If you don't cut the shit, and get out of the car, I'll send someone to kill your boyfriend."

SHEILA HADN'T MEANT TO TURN ONTO THE NARROW STREET BUT BEFORE she could reverse Dexter, she was rear-ended. Her head throbbed from smacking into the steering wheel and she was startled when the driver door opened. Then she was yanked from the car by her arm.

Vertigo threw her body into a spin and she tried to focus on the man's face but he ushered her ahead of him, jabbing at her with what she guessed was a gun. She caught a glimpse of a woman, across the street, with a phone aimed at them. Sheila wanted to warn the woman, to tell her to run but her mouth felt like it was full of cotton balls.

A hand between her shoulder blades pushed her into an open van. It was black. She caught herself with her palms, saving her head from slamming onto the uncovered floor.

"Get your goddamned legs in there and move over to that bar."

She banged her right knee and cried out, not from the knee pain, but from the man's hand shoving on her butt. Then he cuffed her wrists to a vertical bar. She was confused when he left the door open and jogged off.

Seconds later, Sheila twisted away from feminine cries approaching the van. She soon saw it was the woman with the phone, flailing at her attacker. Her body slammed headfirst against the side of the vehicle and Sheila screeched. The kidnapper shoved the woman inside.

The engine roared to life and Sheila brought her knees up to her chest, curling as closely to the bar as she could. Dr. Baldwin's voice came to her, *I am safe*, and she couldn't laugh at the affirmation.

She was definitely *not* safe. All those assurances the Butcher would never seek her out... This man had to be one of the Butcher's. She was going to die. Today.

"Leah, go get my handcuffs and then take the little girl inside the house," Jose said, nodding at Joelle in the Jeep.

Herrera struggled to get up. "No. You need me."

"That's what your 400 pound cell mate is going to be telling you down at County. Assaulting a police officer is a felony," Jose said.

"I didn't know you were a cop. Look, I ain't the bad guy. I work for Michael Chase."

"You're lying."

"I don't think he is, Darren," Peach said. "I met him at the same time Sheila showed up in town."

"He's your Angel? How could you let him near Joelle?" Darren said. Peach gasped and stepped back. He knelt beside the man on the ground and jerked his head up by his hair. "You said you work for the guy who snatched Sheila."

"He was my boss but not anymore—" Jose's wife returned with the cuffs and Herrera cursed when they were tightened on his wrists. "I can explain," he said. The cop guided him to his feet and Herrera scanned the faces of the gathered crowd.

"The boys are on their way," Leah said.

"Good," Jose said.

Herrera watched Peach return to her car. "I don't want the girl to see me like this," he said.

"Like the lying criminal you are? Don't worry, you'll never get near my goddaughter again."

"Call him," Herrera said. "Call Michael Chase." His eyes narrowed on a thin man pushing his way through the crowd.

"You don't look up Michael Chase in the White Pages," Darren said.

"I got his number in my phone. And Peach knows how to reach him," Herrera said. The thin man was getting closer. "Peach can call Andrea and Andrea—"

"All this is getting us nowhere," Darren bellowed. "We have to find Sheila."

"I know where to find her," a new voice said.

Darren spun around. "Who are you?"

It was the thin man. He held out a hand. "Neil Fitzgerald."

"You lying sack of shit—" Darren lunged at the sallow-cheeked man but Stan caught him. "Get off of me, Stan. This is all your fault."

Darren swung at his best friend and Peach pressed Joelle into Leah's arms. She ran over and almost took one in her left cheek when she tried to pry Darren off Stan.

"No," Herrera yelled.

"Get a grip, D. Sheila needs you." She stared into her cousin's crazed eyes and repeated herself.

"How do you know where to find Sheila," Jose asked wearily.

Fitzgerald cleared his throat. "I was already on my way here when I received a call telling me if I ever wanted to see my fiancée again, I had to bring these two men to a specific address."

Jose stepped toward Fitzgerald. "What about a ransom request?"

"No," Fitzgerald said. "The man ordered me to bring Darren Abruzzo and Stanley Sheffield."

"Where?" Jose asked.

"To the Butcher," Herrera said.

"The Butcher?" Darren and Stan said together.

"You don't know about the Butcher?" Herrera shook his head. "Unfuckingbelievable."

"Who is the Butcher?" Darren's voice was hysterical and Peach tightened her hold on him.

"You don't know *the* Butcher, Nigel deBoer?"

"You mean the sick sonofabitch who bombed those churches in South Africa a few years back?" Jose said.

Darren's legs buckled. "What would a terrorist want with my Sheila?"

"You're a fucking idiot and you don't deserve her," Herrera said.

"Just tell me."

"Sheila and her boyfriend were getting freaky in an alley when they overheard deBoer offing an employee. The boyfriend got it in the back and Sheila's grandfather took down the shooter, the Butcher's younger brother."

"And the Butcher wants revenge on Sheila..." Darren made a strangled sound and sagged against Peach.

THE SOUND OF FALLING WATER JERKED HER AWAKE. SHEILA COULDN'T see and it took several seconds for her to realize something covered her aching head. A cloth? A bag? It smelled musty and she quickly forgot the smell when she heard *his* voice. The voice had haunted her for three years. She only heard it once but she'd never forgotten it.

"You've done well."

"I got the photographer, too."

"Good. We'll wait until the others arrive. Then, the party begins. Then, I get my revenge."

A conversation followed in Spanish and Sheila cursed herself for never learning the language. Who were the others? How was he going to mete out his revenge? *Please don't let it be Darren!*

He would never know he was going to be a father; she would never make him a father because she was going to die. She would pay for breaking her isolation and an innocent person would pay too. The sob broke through the barrier of her lips and Sheila retched when an answering cackle filled the air.

"ESCUCHA ME," HERRERA SAID. "PLEASE PEACH, LISTEN. THIS IS A MIS-take. You've got to believe me." The whir of police sirens grew louder.

"Tell it to your attorney," Jose said. Herrera was now cuffed to the banister at the base of a staircase. Jose stood in front of him. Peach lingered behind the cop.

Herrera tried to look around the cop's legs at Peach. "I know you're mad at me but I can help. I didn't want to say it in front of him but I recognized Fitzgerald's voice."

"What?" she said.

"Two weeks ago, I called Vasquez and he was all worked up. I heard a woman in the background and... Fitzgerald's voice too."

"How can you be sure it was the same voice?" Jose said.

"I'm sure. I'm a Marine and I worked in Intelligence—"

"He's lying," Jose said.

The sirens got louder and Herrera knew he didn't have time to give her the full story. "Peach, listen to me. Vasquez doesn't know I'm here but McKay does. Do you remember the Scottish dude who hit on you when you had lunch with Darren? He works with me. You've got to call him."

Peach narrowed her eyes. "Sean? Sean works with you?"

Herrera didn't like the way she said Sean's name but this was no time for jealousy. "Yes, call Sean. He can track Vasquez's location—"

"He's lying," Jose repeated.

"What if he's not?" she said.

"I'm not," Herrera thundered up at the cop. "If that girl dies, her blood is going to be on your hands too."

"Give me his phone," Peach said.

The cop stiffened. "APD can't—"

"You're not even on duty. And you allowed those three men to leave *without* APD. If Sheila dies, if my cousin—" her voice broke and she put her hand out, palm up. "I saw you take it from his pocket. Give me Angel's phone."

GETTING INTO THE CAR WITH FITZGERALD WAS A MISTAKE, HE KNEW, but Darren didn't have any other choice. A mile from his house, two vans sandwiched in Fitzgerald's sedan, and masked men separated them from Stan.

Darren took no satisfaction from the startled expression on Fitzgerald's face when he was also handled roughly by the goons. It was probably part of the show. However, when they arrived at a warehouse twenty minutes later and they were both tied at the wrists, Fitzgerald protested in a high voice. "This wasn't part of the agreement," he said.

The attorney looked around the dark interior for Sheila but all he saw was the approaching form of a man.

"Right this way, gentlemen." He gestured for them to follow and Fitzgerald sped up to fall in step with the man. "I've done my part, now what about—"

The answering voice was smooth and reassuring. "Not yet, Cornelius. You haven't done your part yet." He snapped and overhead lights flooded the space. Darren ducked his head, blinking rapidly. "Now we begin."

Darren tried to move toward Sheila's shrieking before he could focus on her location. Her siren was cut off abruptly and he groaned at the scene before him. Sheila, on a stage illuminated by dozens of lights, was being held under water by a thick man. Her head was lifted from the barrel by her hair and Darren gasped with her.

"No—" his protest was scarcely out of his mouth when a hand shoved her back under the water. He moved toward her but something solid connected with his ribs, knocking him onto his side.

Sheila clawed the arm of the brute drowning her. Again, her head was pulled from the water. Her body spasmed with coughs. Darren's own throat gurgled when his girlfriend was dunked again. He watched with impotent rage.

"P-Please," Fitzgerald said. "Untie me." Darren's head jerked in the direction of another cry. Was it Stan? "Oh God," the traitor cried.

Darren looked back to the stage. Sheila's arms flailed and water sloshed over the sides of the whiskey barrel. The bastard holding her had moved to the opposite side, out of her reach.

"Finish it," the man said. Not a man. The Butcher.

The earth buckled beneath Darren. Hands lifted her by the waist and she was held upside down, her feet skyward. Her dress fell into the water, revealing white panties and a tattoo on her right thigh.

Darren felt a surge of relief; the woman wasn't Sheila. It was quickly chased by horror when the thrashing body stilled.

CHAPTER 31

SHEILA COVERED HER EARS BUT THE SOUNDS PENETRATED HER HANDS. From the echoing in the room, she guessed the screams came from speakers but she still couldn't see. When she'd tried to remove the bag on her head, someone had smacked her hands.

Her head snapped up at the sound of the door banging against the wall, followed by footsteps. Panic knifed her chest when the cover was removed and she stared into the coldest blue eyes she'd ever seen.

Three years ago, she'd only glimpsed him from afar, a shadow. The Butcher was no longer a disembodied voice.

"I've waited a long time for this. Are you ready?" A hand landed on top of her head, fisted around her hair, and forced her to nod, yes. "Bring them," he said.

Sheila's head was forced toward the door. She watched two men pass through it.

"No, no more," Neil wailed. "I can't watch anymore."

"Watching's over, Cornelius. Now it's your turn," the Butcher said.

Sheila didn't rub her aching scalp when her hair was released. She did scoot away from the Butcher when he pulled a switchblade from his pocket. The ropes fell from Neil's wrists and she swallowed when he cried out.

"Take it."

"No."

"Don't you want your revenge, Cornelius?"

"Yes."

"Then shoot her."

"I ca-can't." Neil said.

"Where is the bravado you showed three months ago when you came to me after my prison brake? You told me Michael Chase promised to restore your fortune if you married his crazy daughter. But she refused you and he gave you nothing for the embarrassment. Now you can punish her and get the money you deserve. Shoot her."

"P-Please—"

The Butcher's tone hardened. "Either you shoot her, or I'll shoot you."

"But you promised me the mm-money. You didn't say anything about me pulling the—"

Sheila lurched from the sound of the gunshot. Neil crumpled to the floor, and his head made a *thump* when it hit the cement slab. Something warm and wet tickled the inside of her leg. *It could be sweat*, she told herself.

The Butcher cackled. "This is better than I'd planned." He said something in another language and Sheila kept her eyes on the ground. Heavy footfalls approached the direction of Neil's body, and she squeezed her eyes shut against the scraping sound that followed. When she looked around cautiously, she saw a long, red smudge from where Neil had been dragged out of the room.

Her fear was so strong she thought she could smell it coating her body. It was a nasty metallic like the inside of a can. *Could the Butcher smell it?* He kept inhaling deeply as if he could, as if smelling something he liked a lot. Sheila surreptitiously sniffed her hand.

"I can smell your fear." He cackled again when she jumped.

Over his laughter, she heard someone panting. Sheila glanced toward the noise. Darren. How had he gotten here? With Neil? Sweat darkened his shirt, and she watched his chest rise and fall with his rapid breaths.

Nervously, she raised her eyes to his and gasped. His wild eyes were fixed on her. The Butcher's foot rose up and kicked Darren in the ribs, toppling him onto his side. "No," she cried out.

"Get up, you piece of shite."

Darren grunted and rocked his shoulders to the side, trying to right his body. His gaze never left her. The Butcher looked over his shoulder and called, "Bring in the faggot." Stan was led into the room by the man who'd kidnapped her. "Now get out," the killer snapped and the door banged shut again. He shoved Stan at Sheila, and she yelped when he landed at her feet.

"Sheila—"

Darren got another kick before the Butcher sauntered over to Stan. He snatched the bag off of Stan's head and Sheila yelped again at his bruised face.

"I spent three years refining my plan on how to punish you. I always planned to do it myself but I think it would be more entertaining for you to do it, Stanley." He yanked Stan up by his hair, forcing the battered man onto his knees. Sheila tried to scoot away but the wall was at her back. More warmth flowed out of her when she moved. She doubled over at the horrible cramping in her abdomen.

"Shoot her."

Darren yelled and the Butcher fired a shot in his direction. Sheila clamped her hands over her ears. *No no no.*

"I'm going to put this gun in your faggot hands and you're going to shoot her."

Stan's answering voice was hoarse. "I can't see."

No no no. Dr. Baldwin had been wrong. She wished she hadn't been right. She wouldn't get to tell him, "I told you so."

"You don't have to see. Pull the fucking trigger, or I'll shoot your boyfriend."

"Don't do it, Stan."

Another shot fired and Sheila began rocking back and forth.

No no nonononono.

"Shut up!"

No no nonononononononononono.

"I said shut up." Pain exploded in her neck and Sheila's eyes opened without her permission. The Butcher slammed her against the wall, and suddenly the face of her dead boyfriend loomed in front of her.

"Rick," she squeaked.

"What the fuck did you call me?" The Butcher loosened his grip on her neck and she gulped for air.

"I'm so sorry. We'll be together now, Rick, just like you wanted." Her voice was a weak rasp. "I should have died with you."

"You're damned right you should have died with Rick. Bobby should be alive, not you!" His fist crashed into her cheek, knocking Sheila's head back into the wall again. Fireworks exploded in her head, a kaleidoscope of pain and stars.

Gravity tugged Sheila's body back to the floor when he released her neck. She didn't have the strength to look away from the blood staining her shorts. She watched her hand move in slow motion and flatten itself in the sticky, red mess. Her baby's blood. Her blood. They were both dying.

A shadow moved in front of her. "Just like you, Rick."

"Look at me you, you bitch! I'm the Butcher and I want you to know who I am when I send you to hell."

A thunk echoed in her head and she heard someone whimper. Rick held out his hand but it was fading, and the shadow was growing bigger.

"Come with me, Liz," Rick said. She reached out with her bloody hands, and Rick led her away.

Her skin felt clammy and she pushed away his roaming hand. "They'll come looking for us."

"No they won't. They're probably making out too," Rick said.

She was too annoyed to laugh at the suggestion. Grandpa and Momma? Ridiculous. He leaned into her neck and she tried to duck away.

"Rick, stop. I want to go back to the hotel."

"You don't like the beard, do you?" She didn't like the beard. Instead of answering, she started back to the mouth of the alley. "C'mon, Liz. I thought you liked exploring."

"Not dark alleys near the loading docks. I wonder what happened to Momma and Grandpa."

Momma had instigated the trip. She was considering moving back to Nassau, and Grandpa had offered to escort Andrea, Liz, and Momma. Andrea changed her mind last minute, and Rick had leapt at the opportunity to take her place.

"What about a skinny dip?"

Liz lifted the bangs sticking to her head. "I want a shower." He grabbed her hand and dragged her back into the shadows. "Rick, I think we should go back."

"Gramps and Momma have been hogging you," he said. He slipped his hands under her shirt and she sighed. He misinterpreted her response, grinning, and leaning down to kiss her. At 6'4, Rick had pro basketball ambitions *and* the talent to pursue them, but his father had insisted on a medical career.

Dominant fathers was a trait they had in common. Liz had been drawn to the shy, beautiful boy, and they'd become fast friends. They both matured in their almost decade of friendship, losing their virginity together but she felt she'd outgrown him.

"Let's get married, Lizzie. Let's do it tomorrow."

"Rick..."

"I know it's not the ideal place to propose but—"

Liz pulled his mouth down to hers. She kissed him for two reasons. She didn't want him to get on his knee and ask, and she needed time to compose her refusal. Again, Rick misinterpreted her. He'd pressed her back against a door and trapped her face between his long fingers.

"Liz, I love you so much. I want to be with you forever!"

"I hear something." Rick tried to silence her but she stopped him with her hand. "I think someone is in there," she whispered. She used her thumb to gesture behind them to the building. A gunshot rang out and she screamed.

Rick grabbed her hand and jerked her forward. The door behind them opened and she screamed again.

"Liz?"

"Grandpa?" She stopped to look back, and saw a man burst from the building.

Rick pulled her forward, and she resisted because her grandfather was behind them, charging toward the shooter.

"We have to—"

"Run Liz!"

The sound of boots pounding the cement in pursuit made her obey the command. She ducked low when she heard a shot and then left, down another street. Lights glowed at the end of this one.

"Run Liz!"

"I'm going to get you, you little—" an explosion drowned out her attacker's voice and she ran several feet before taking a chance and looking back.

The hefty man fell and took someone down with him. "Grandpa!" Fear rooted her feet to the ground and she whipped her head around frantically. *Where was Rick?*

"Get out of here—"

The attacker threw an elbow into her grandfather's face and the old man lost his grip on the gun. She screamed again when the second shot rang out.

"You'll pay for this!"

"Police! Get your hands in the air!"

Liz's eyes were the only thing moving. Her hands stayed at her sides, while her eyes moved between the three men lying on the ground. Grandpa lay on his back, the shooter too, a foot away.

Rick was the furthest from her but suddenly a flurry of lights appeared behind her, illuminating the blood. Blood on Grandpa, seeping from his chest, onto the ground. Blood on the shooter. Blood on Rick's beard, his forehead, around his lifeless eyes which were cast in her direction.

"I said, get your hands in the air!" Someone nudged her in the back, and she fell onto her knees. "Go after the other man."

"What a mess," someone else said. "Miss, are you hurt? Have you been injured?" A sweaty, brown face appeared in front of hers but Liz didn't see it. "Miss? Oh, I think she's going to faint."

DARREN COULDN'T AFFORD TO WAIT ANOTHER SECOND. THE BASTARD was intent on squeezing the life out of Sheila and she wasn't fighting. Lunging forward, he swung his bound hands over the killer's head, looping them around his neck. Darren jerked upwards, under the chin.

The Butcher twisted as they fell backwards, landing with his shoulder in Darren's rib cage. His breath left him in a grunt, and before he could react, the Butcher swung with his left fist. The blow connected with Darren's nose in a painful crunch.

"The gun," Darren panted.

"I can't see," Stan said.

Darren scrambled to keep his hold around the killer's neck, and took another hit to the nose. Still on his back, he raised his hips and swung his legs up, trying to lock them around the man's torso. He cursed when the killer twisted his left arm free and braced it on the cement floor.

"No you don't," Darren huffed. Nearly two decades had passed since he'd studied Jiu-Jitsu but he was glad the training rushed back to him now. He threw his right leg around the Butcher's neck.

Instead of throwing another fist to Darren's nose, the murderer clamped his right hand on Darren's throat. The attorney quickly linked his left leg over his right ankle, ignoring the burst of pain in the joint and locked the hold.

Sheila whimpered and the sound was as sharp as any knife in his chest. With a roar, he lifted his bound hands from the head and yanked the Butcher's hand from his throat. He pulled the arm across his body, and squeezed his thighs, cutting off the carotid arteries. The Butcher went limp. Darren's previously injured ankle burned but he squeezed for several more seconds. The Butcher made no sound when Darren un-hooked his feet.

"Help me Stan," he said, panting. "She's bleeding. Did he shoot her? Oh God get this piece of shit off me!" Darren didn't know how long the bastard would be unconscious. He bucked his hips to try to throw off the body. Panic made him thrash when he felt something on his shoulder.

"It's me, D. It's Stan."

"Get on the other side. God, he weighs a ton. Lift his shoulder, help me roll him off." The body was crushing his chest. He needed to get to his woman and Stan was moving too slowly. "Sheila!"

"Don't shout. His goons will come in here."

"She's bleeding Stan. *Dio aiutami*, hurry up." He felt Stan's hands creeping in search of the immobilized man's shoulder. "Lower, now lift." Darren grunted and shoved his forearms against the heavy chest. They rolled the bastard onto his back. Finally free, he scurried to Sheila. She lay slumped on her left side. When Darren saw where the blood emanat-ed, he started to pray.

"Look for a pulse," Stan croaked.

"Her pulse is—I can't find it."

"Don't move her," Stan ordered and Darren looked back at him. Both of his eyes were swollen from the beating and he was holding one lid open with his fingers. "I can see her chest moving. Check the bastard to see if he has a cell phone." Darren gaped at him and Stan continued. "Do it, D."

He forced himself to pat the killer's pockets. "There's no phone."

"Empty them, Darren. Make sure."

Darren shelved his disgust and dug out the contents. "Thank God." He flipped it open and dialed 911.

"Shoot her now or I'll do it!" Darren whipped around to gape at Stan. "It's been too quiet," Stan hissed.

"What's the nature of your emergency?"

"Can you track this phone?" Darren asked. "We've been kidnapped and we're in a warehouse. Sheila is hemorrhaging and there are armed men and—"

"Sir, I need you to calm down. I can't understand you," the dispatcher said.

"Don't tell me to calm down. My girlfriend is bleeding to death! You need to send the paramedics immediately."

"Do you know where you are?"

"If she dies because of your incompetency I will—"

"Give me the phone, D."

He handed the thing to Stan and knelt beside Sheila. He brushed his fingers over her cheek and the muscle ticked. "Can you hear me, honey?" She liked it when he called her honey.

Why had she been addressing the murderer as Rick? Was she hallucinating? Was Sheila wishing for her first love? She wouldn't look at him at the end. Even when he'd sneaked over, to pull the killer off her, she'd looked past him. What if her mind had snapped?

"Lie down," Stan hissed at the same time Darren heard the door creak. The Butcher groaned and Darren echoed the sound, flattening his body. He hoped the bastard would be out longer from the triangle choke. Where was the gun? He raised his head.

"I've still got it," Stan whispered.

"Peach says she's going to kick your arse if you die," a voice called out. Darren heard Stan's exhale. He tried to push off the floor and the heel of his palm slid on Sheila's blood. "I'm Sean McKay, and I'm going to come in now." The barrel of a gun preceded McKay's body and the pale faced man nodded at them. "Are you injured?"

"Sheila needs an ambulance!"

"There's one on the way," he said.

The Butcher groaned again and rolled to his side. Darren was stunned when a red pattern bloomed on the killer's chest. He slumped to the floor and Darren looked back at McKay. He hadn't heard the shot because the gun McKay held was fitted with a silencer. The fury in the shooter's face had Darren scooting closer to Sheila.

CHAPTER 32

THE FAMILIAR SOUND OF DARREN'S SNORING PENETRATED SHEILA'S sleep-fogged brain. She tried to smile, grateful she'd awoken from another of her graphic nightmares, but the ache in her cheeks made her wonder. She turned her head and the feeling of a thousand needles speared the right side of her skull. She pressed her lips against the gasp, not wanting to wake Darren. Tentatively, she wiggled her toes. It wasn't another bad dream; even her toes hurt. Whatever relief Sheila felt at being alive evaporated when reality dawned. Darren hated her for not telling the truth. She'd lost the baby because the Butcher had—

The Butcher. What had happened to him? How had she gotten to the hospital?

Sheila struggled to uncover the answers in her head but all she could remember was blood. Neil's blood. Her blood. Her baby's blood.

"No, God, no." The protest was a silent cry in her broken heart. She turned her head toward Darren and ignored the needling sensation. A different pain lanced her chest and she wondered why he was here. Guilt. He probably felt guilty. Without moving her head, she let her eyes roam over his inert body.

He looked peaceful and she drank in her last look at him. The lowered guardrail allowed his head to rest atop a pillow on the very edge of the bed. One of his hands curled around hers, and she stared down at his bruised knuckles. Before she could wonder how they were marred, a shadow passed in the doorway and she quickly shut her lids.

Someone knocked at the door and she felt Darren jerk. "Excuse me, are you Mrs. Abruzzo?" a male voice asked.

"I'm Mr. Abruzzo."

"Oh, I didn't see you down there. Doris Dickson sent this from your office—"

"Shh," Darren hissed. He released her hand and Sheila opened her eyes to watch him sign for a package. Anger burned in her face. After all she'd been through, he was getting work delivered to her hospital room? He was only here out of guilt. Well, she thought, as soon as the messenger left, she'd free him. She didn't need his pity.

Darren turned around. He stared down at the package with a huge grin and she snorted. "You're awake." He rushed forward. "Oh Sheila, baby I'm so sorry—"

"Don't call me baby," she said and clutched her abdomen. She gasped in pain.

"Take it easy, Sheila. Let me get the doctor."

"I'm here. Hello, Ms. Washington. I'm Dr. Sheridan."

Sheila blinked through the tears and pain and focused on the woman walking toward her. She forced the words out. "Did I lose the baby?"

"Sheila?"

"Andrea?"

Her friend pushed past Darren and knelt beside the bed. "Thank God you're awake," Andrea said. Her hand hovered over Sheila's head, like she wanted to stroke it but she didn't.

"I lost the baby, didn't I?" she sobbed.

Darren moved beside Andrea. "Sheila—" The way his face contorted had her gasping for air.

"Calm down Miss Washington."

"Just tell me." When another person entered the room, Sheila sank back onto the pillow. "Dr. B. Tell me the truth."

"The truth about what, Sheila?" Dr. Baldwin said.

"Get out of my way," a man ordered.

That voice had Sheila fisting the sheets and ready to sprint from the room.

"Oh shit!" Andrea said.

"Dr. Baldwin, I don't want that man in here." Darren turned his face to the side and took a step back. "Not you," she said, and her voice wavered. "Him."

DARREN STARED FOR SEVERAL HEARTBEATS BEFORE RECOGNITION HIT. Sheila's father.

"I'm going to have to ask all of you to leave. This excitement isn't good for my patient," Dr. Sheridan said.

"I'm not going anywhere without my daughter." It was obvious from the tone of his voice Michael Chase was accustomed to getting what he wanted. Power rolled off of him and Darren watched Dr. Sheridan's eyes widen as a wave of it washed over her.

"You don't have a daughter anymore," Andrea said. "She doesn't want anything to do with you, so get out."

He ignored Andrea and turned to the doctor. "Dr. Sheridan, I'm Michael W. Chase. I'm taking Elizabeth to a private facility where—"

Andrea and Darren stepped forward at the same time. "Oh no you aren't!" she said.

"Mr. Chase, Sheila isn't in any condition to be transferred. Besides she can make her own decisions."

"Here's the paperwork," Mr. Chase said. He held out an envelope. "If you try to interfere, I'll slap you with a lawsuit so fast—"

Sheila guffawed and five faces turned toward her. Darren looked between Sheila and Dr. Sheridan.

"See, she's delirious," Mr. Chase said.

Darren's arm drew back to slug the asshole but Sheila's cry from the bed stopped him. "No, Darren, don't!"

"Darren." It was Andrea's voice calling out to him this time. "That bastard isn't worth it. And *I* am Sheila's power of attorney. There's nothing he can do to her." Andrea tugged Darren backwards. "That's not what Sheila needs from you right now," she whispered.

Michael Chase stepped forward and Andrea's nails dug into Darren's arm. "If you don't come with me now Elizabeth, I won't clean this up. You'll be on your own with the media and it won't be like the last time."

"Somebody call hospital security and have this piece of shit removed from my room," Sheila said. "I can't stand the smell anymore."

"Hot damn," Andrea said. "My pleasure." She released Darren's arm and reached for the bedside phone.

"You're making a mistake, Elizabeth. You're going to regret this."

"My name is Sheila," she said. "Sheila Washington."

SHEILA THOUGHT SHE SAW A FLICKER OF PAIN IN HIS EYES BEFORE HER father turned on his heel and stomped from the room. She quickly dismissed the thought. You had to have feelings in order to be hurt. Michael W. Chase was a feelingless bastard. He hadn't even said hello to her.

"I want everyone out so I can examine my patient," Dr. Sheridan said.

Dr. Baldwin was the first to move to the door. "I'm going to call Agatha and tell her you're awake," he said.

"I'll be in the waiting room," Andrea said. "Peach said she'd come back tonight but I'll call her and tell her you're awake now."

"Wait," Sheila said. "How long was I out?"

Andrea and Darren looked at Dr. Sheridan. "You were in and out of consciousness for almost three days," the doctor said.

"Three days?" Sheila tried to sit up and black spots bloomed in her eyes. Darren and Andrea reached for her.

"Out," Dr. Sheridan said "Out now."

Andrea grumbled, "Kinda bossy." Darren lingered at the door and moved only when Dr. Sheridan shut it.

"You're lucky to have so many people who love you," Dr. Sheridan said.

Sheila's eyes filled up. She took the tissue from the physician and grimaced. "When can I get out of here?"

"I'd like to do another ultrasound before we discuss discharging you."

"Ultrasound?" she balled the tissue in her hand. "You mean I'm still... I didn't lose the baby?"

"The babies are—"

"Babies?" Sheila said.

"Yes, Ms. Washington."

"But, but I was bleeding at the warehouse."

"It appears that one aborted but we've been monitoring you and the remaining fetuses closely. The other two—"

"Wait a minute. You mean there were *three*?" Sheila's voice cracked. She'd been pregnant with triplets?

Dr. Sheridan nodded. "I understand multiples run in Mr. Abruzzo's family. Now, given the recent trauma, and your history of hypoglycemia, you're going to have to promise to take it easy for the next six months."

"Does Darren know?"

"I think he is aware of the pregnancy. We had a difficult time keeping him in *his* bed but Andrea evoked the right of POA. She's been adamant that you should deliver the details."

"I bet they've made the staff miserable."

Dr. Sheridan clucked. "As I said, you're lucky to have so many people who love you. How's your head?"

"Great, if you don't count the stabbing sensation every time I move."

"I'm glad your sense of humor wasn't damaged from the concussion. Would you like something for the pain?"

"How will it affect the babies?"

"Well," Dr. Sheridan began.

"Never mind. Maybe a nap will help."

"That's a good idea. I'll tell your entourage you're worn out and no visitors for at least two hours. Sound good?"

"Thanks."

"I'll be off at 6 P.M. but Dr. Obermann will be checking on you. And of course Dr. Baldwin is here too. Rest well, Ms. Washington."

SHEILA CLOSED HER EYES BUT SLEEP ELUDED HER. SHE *HAD* LOST A BABY and that knowledge kept her from feeling excitement over the two who were allegedly healthy. The pain in her chest had nothing to do with the kidnapping. Before the tears dribbled off her cheeks, a hand alit on her shoulder. "Sheila?"

Darren knelt beside her and she cursed her traitorous body for wanting more of his touch. Slowly, she lowered her hands, and her anger flared again. He still carried the package from his office. "Why are you here?"

He flinched from the verbal slap. "I'm hanging on the every breath of the love of my life."

He reached for her hand and the tender words threatened to melt her resolve.

"Right," she said and cleared her throat. She raised her chin and tried for an aloof tone. "Meanwhile you're practicing your opening arguments." Her stomach rumbled and the noise startled her.

The package fell with a thud. "What's wrong?"

"Nothing."

"Are you sure? The doctor said—"

"The doctor said I'm fine, so you can go now. Especially since the firm can't solve the Sanchez case without you."

Darren sat on the corner of the bed. "What are you talking about?"

"The files you're holding. I heard the messenger say your secretary sent them."

He held up the package. "This isn't from my secretary."

"Says Mr. 'I-always-tell-the-truth.'"

"Sheila, look." She let her head fall back on the pillow and her gaze rest on the ceiling.

"How do you think it feels to have someone not believe you? To not even give you the chance to explain yourself?"

Darren stood and moved into her line of vision. "You're right to be angry with me. I'm so sorry I didn't listen to you." He tore open the padded envelope and pulled out a square, velvet box. It made a sharp click when he opened it.

"This is the ring my great grandfather gave to his bride, and my father gave to his bride—"

"You cannot be serious." Sheila stared at the antique filigree ring. It had a large, oval cut stone.

"I called my mother the day before you arrived, before all this..." He took a breath. "I asked her to ship this to me and Doris retrieved it from the Post Office, since I've been here."

"Don't take it out of the box!"

"Sheila, I love you. I made a horrible mistake. I should have given you the chance to explain. I know this is not the ideal time to propose but I don't want there to be any question about my feelings for you."

"Oh, *now* you love me. Three days ago you said, and I quote, 'I can't believe I thought I was in love with you.'"

"I was angry—"

"How do I know you won't change your mind when you're angry again? Now that you know I'm pregnant, you say you love me. But what if I can't make it to term? What if—"

"Wait, what do you mean if you can't make it to term?"

"That's exactly what I mean," she said.

"What?" he said.

"I want you to leave."

"Honey, please talk to me. I'm willing to do whatever it takes to make it up to you."

"You are?"

"God, yes," Darren said. "Whatever you want. We can live in San Diego, or move to Nassau or—"

"Whatever it takes?" she said and smiled. "You promise?"

"Yes!"

"Okay. Here's what I want. I want you to walk out the door. Leave the hospital and leave me alone. I don't want you to call me or—"

"Sheila, no!"

"You promised, Darren."

"Anything but leaving you, Sheila. Please."

"So you lied when you said, 'whatever you want'?"

He turned his face to the side. "For how long?"

Sheila's need for space was about more than being stung by his refusal to listen. She felt like she was hanging on by the last filament and her traumatized mind couldn't take any more.

"For however long it takes." His eyes were glossy when he turned back to face her. He opened his mouth but she cut him off. "If you truly love me, keep your word." He rose stiffly and the velvet box fell from his trembling hand. "You might not want to leave that on the floor," she said.

Darren stooped to pick up the box and Sheila closed her eyes. It took an eternity for his footsteps to reach the door and pass into the hall. When they finally dissipated, she gasped at the black box balanced on the corner of the bed.

CHAPTER 33

ANDREA LOOKED UP AND SHOOK HER HEAD. "HOLD ON PEA. MATTER fact, let me call you back." She didn't have to run to catch up with the limping man but she did anyway. "Where are you going?"

Darren didn't answer, even after she blocked his path. The faraway look in his eyes made her breath catch. "I've been dismissed."

"You mean discharged?"

"Dismissed. Sent away. Rejected."

"Wait a minute, you went back into Sheila's room after the doctor told us to let her sleep?"

Darren grabbed her shoulders. "Promise me you'll take care of her," he said.

"Ouch, what is wrong with you?"

He shook her. "She made me promise to leave her alone and you've got to promise to take care of her."

Andrea wanted to slap the fool but something in his eyes stopped her. "Okay," she said.

"And call me every day."

"I'm not calling you—"

"Please, Andrea." That something in Darren's eyes grew bigger and it touched the part of her still grieving for her son. She nodded quickly.

"Okay, I'll call you." He released her arms and shuffled away. "Where are you goin'?" she demanded again. Darren didn't answer her and she redialed Peach. "Girl, you need to come get your cousin."

MONDAY, SEPTEMBER 10TH

"IF SHE PLAYS THAT SONG ONE MORE TIME, I'M GOING TO LOSE IT."

"Andrea, settle down," Momma said.

"Settle down? Settle down? I like Prince but I can't handle *Nothing Compares 2 U* ten times in a row."

"She's grieving."

"Momma, she doesn't have to grieve. She could call him."

"So says the woman who turned her back on Anthony."

Andrea jumped from the chair at the desk and it clattered to the floor. "That's not fair! This is a completely different situation."

"Is it?" Momma asked and she blinked to clear her vision. Her mother crossed the room and bent over her purse. "Sheila got these for you, before."

The tickets Momma held were for a fashion event on Rodeo Drive. Anybody who was somebody in the industry would be there. But so would the paparazzi.

"Take Sean," Momma said, and pressed the tickets and a wad of cash into her hand. "I'll talk to Sheila."

TUESDAY, SEPTEMBER 18TH

DARREN SHIFTED THE PACKAGE UNDER HIS ARM AND FORCED A DEEP breath into his lungs. He listened to the doorman's side of a phone conversation. "There's a man here, claiming to be Darren Abruzzo. He fits the physical description but he didn't provide the correct answer."

Darren didn't argue. He *had* answered the question correctly. When

Sheila had phoned him, finally, she'd warned him about the security measures at her downtown San Diego apartment building.

He studied the man on the phone. The doorman wore a uniform with dozens of brassy buttons but Darren guessed from the way the dark jacket fit his muscled frame, he was overqualified for the job. Or it was his second job. A gold, rectangular name tag, bearing the name, Benson, was pinned on his left shoulder.

"Very good sir, I'll ask him," Benson said. He lowered the receiver into the cradle. "Mr. Herrera said to ask you—"

"Herrera? What is he doing here?"

Benson folded his arms across his chest. "He's Ms. Washington's head of security."

Darren clenched his teeth. Sheila needed security, no doubt, but *that* creep? Calling on the new techniques he learned to calm his temper, the attorney drew in another breath and counted to ten.

"You must tell me how to say, 'call you a taxi,' in Italian, as you told Ms. Washington on the night you met," the doorman said.

The paper bag rustled under Darren's arm and heat flooded his face. On the night they'd met, he hadn't told her he'd call her a taxi. He'd told her he wanted her. "*Io te voglio,*" he bit out.

Benson nodded. "Right this way." He unlocked a door to the left and allowed Darren to pass through before closing it and inserting another key into the elevator. He stepped inside and the elevator rose quickly to the penthouse.

The doors opened with a chime and Darren got a face full of Angel Herrera when they opened. "Hurt her again, and you'll be pissing red for the rest of your miserable life," the head of security said.

The package fell and Darren's hand shot out. Before it closed on the man's thick neck he stopped abruptly. "I can only assume you're here because Sheila wants you here," Darren clipped out. "Why she trusts *you* is a mystery." He bent to scoop up the package and thought he glimpsed disappointment in the Latino's eyes.

"I could say the same thing about you," Herrera said. They stood rigidly before Darren closed his eyes and chanted his new mantra, *I can choose peace over this*. When his breathing returned to normal, Herrera opened the penthouse door.

Darren spared little attention on the posh décor, it seemed overdone for Sheila's tastes, and followed Herrera down a long hallway. He heard Sheila's voice and his pulse quickened with his footsteps. Every nerve ending in his body hummed and he had merely heard her voice. He didn't hear an answering voice and assumed she was on the phone. His cock surged to life at the thought of being alone with her.

"It's lovely," Sheila said. "I hope we'll only be here a couple more—" she laughed softly. "Yes, Coop, I promise. I'm done running and hiding. I'm grateful for you reaching out."

Coop? Darren searched his memory banks and quickly placed the name. He'd been reading up on the Chase family and Sheila's middle brother was named Cooper. So this was his place? Herrera knocked on the open door and Darren counted to ten again. The mindful breaths and counting helped with his temper but he doubted it would do anything about the banner in his pants.

"Come in," she called loudly, then continued. "I've gotta go Cooper. He's here. Yes, I hope so too. Thank you."

Herrera pegged him with another hard look before turning and striding back down the hall. Darren stepped into the room and steadied himself by gripping the door jamb.

Sheila covered the phone and whispered, "Have a seat." She gestured to the sofa but Darren didn't trust his legs to carry him there. He didn't notice the ocean view through the windows behind her. He drank in the sight of Sheila at an enormous mahogany desk.

How could his memory of her beauty be so pitiful? Or had pregnancy transformed her into a veritable goddess? Darren's appraisal halted on a ribbon lacing her bodice. His fingers itched to loosen the knot—

"Hi," she said. Darren stared at her, blinking dumbly until pink dusted her cheeks. She ended her phone conversation, he realized belatedly, and she was now addressing him. "Won't you have a seat?"

"I finished reading *Lonesome Dove*," Darren said. His voice was wrong. He'd made the statement sound like a question.

"Oh. Really? Did you like it?"

"What?"

"Did you like the book?" she said.

Darren swallowed. "Yes and no. Once I got into it, I liked it but I was expecting more from the ending. I felt or rather, *it* felt, kind of... incomplete. Like Call should have claimed Newt, or Gus should have survived. You know?"

"I know," she said softly. They stared at each other for what felt like forever. "There's a sequel but I haven't read it."

"That's not what I meant to say," Darren shook his head. "I've imagined this moment playing out a thousand different ways but that, that wasn't one of them." A smile grew on her perfect lips and Darren stepped forward tentatively.

"How did you imagine this moment?" she asked. Her coy voice washed over him and he closed his eyes for a moment. He was far from cool and collected when he reopened them but he didn't care. Sheila had finally called him and he wasn't leaving this apartment without her. Darren quickly tamped down the thought. He couldn't push her.

He cleared his throat. "I imagined everything from groveling on my knees, to chaining myself to your nipple rings and ravaging your perfect body until you forgave me." At her indrawn breath he stepped closer. "I decided the last option wasn't very realistic because the doctor may have said no sex during the pregnancy." He winked and the pink deepened in her cheeks. God, he'd missed her. "And while I'm not above groveling, I don't think it will win you back either."

"You're right," she said. "I don't want you to grovel. I would like you to have a seat, though." Darren winced at her formal tone and moved in the direction of the sofa. He stopped and held up the package.

"I brought something for you," he said. "It got a little, uh ruffled in the excitement downstairs. It was my fresh pasta, quatrro formaggi, but I think the container might have broken."

"Thank you," she said. "You can put it on the table there." Darren noticed a damp spot on his sleeve where the gravy had seeped through the bag.

"What is this?" He turned from the table with poorly concealed anger and pointed at a black velvet box on the table.

"It's your ring," she said. "It's one of the reasons I asked you to come today. That, and the paparazzi will be going after your family. We need to discuss the pregnancy—"

Darren closed the space between them in two strides. "What's wrong? Are you okay? Is the baby—" He tried to pull her from behind the desk.

"We have a lot to discuss," she said firmly. "I don't expect all of our problems to be sorted out today." She withdrew her hands from his grasp. "But I was hoping we could start over. I mean, try a new way of communicating. Please, Darren. I need you to sit over there. It's hard enough to think with you in the room, let alone when you're touching me."

Darren's brows knit together and she gave him a half smile. Her meaning finally penetrated his fear and he forced himself to back away. She began speaking once he perched on the edge of the sofa.

"I spent the first two weeks after the, uh warehouse, pretty much in bed. I was in too much shock to cry at first and when I finally did, the tears wouldn't stop. Poor Andrea," she said. "I know I drove her crazy because I refused to go to my appointments with Dr. Baldwin or... call you. Thank God Momma came. We had a talk about the last time I saw you, before I was kidnapped—" Darren opened his mouth but she held up a hand. "Please, listen," she said and he sagged against the sofa cushions.

"In the way mothers do, Momma helped me see how similar you and I are. We both drive too fast and we eat too much cheese. We're both loyal and stubborn." She looked down and Darren couldn't see her hands but he was sure they were going to her belly. "That makes me wonder how I'm going to handle a couple of headstrong Abruzzos." She continued without looking up. "You and I are also fiercely protective of the ones we love. It's the passion we bring to our relationships that sometimes make our reactions seem hurtful."

"Sheila—"

She didn't allow him to interrupt. "In the hospital, I accused you of not giving me a chance to defend myself against the information Stan brought. But I treated you no better." Her voice broke and Darren was kneeling at her side in an instant.

"Honey, don't. You don't have to apologize. It was my fault. If I hadn't been a jealous, hot-headed ass, maybe none of this would have happened."

"That's not true," she said. "Oh shit. I thought I could do this without crying." She wiped at her face but Darren captured her hands.

"I'm sorry, Sheila. I should have given you a chance—"

"Wait, Darren. I need to say this. I want to start over with you but I don't know if you can forgive me for what happened in the hospital."

"What do you mean?"

"The proposal. I was hurt and I wanted to hurt you. And I just found out that..."

He waited but Sheila's eyes were squeezed shut and she didn't finish the sentence. "It was a dumb, desperate move to propose then, but I'd do it again. You are the only woman, Sheila." He cupped her face and leaned in.

"Stop!" she said. Darren knew it was too soon but he hadn't been able to resist touching her. He hadn't been able to resist hoping. "Stand up," she said. He recalled how this scene had ended in the hospital and prayed for a different outcome. Then he sent the command to his legs, ordering them to straighten out and it seemed to take forever before they obeyed. Once he was seated, she began in a tense voice.

"My father... is making good on his promise to not help with the media, this time. They're rehashing everything from three years ago, and hounding my brothers. MJ, Cooper, and Sebastian can handle it but it's only a matter of time before the reporters come after your mother and sister. They've been looking for you but somehow you've avoided them."

"I've been hiding in plain sight, here in San Diego, bellisima. Waiting for you to call me."

"And getting updates from your in-house spy, Andrea?" she said. He nodded and Sheila's smile was brief. "They'll dig up Peach's past too, Darren." He shifted on the sofa and hoped they wouldn't. Peach was finally back on her feet. "Angel has some recommendations for other security personnel and it might be a good idea if—"

"Why him?" Darren asked. "Why is Herrera working for you?"

"I heard about how things went down after I left your house. The explanation you didn't get was that Father hired Vasquez when the Bu—" she choked on the killer's nickname. "Well, when *he* broke out of prison in Capetown. Vasquez then hired Angel and, later Sean, to track me and watch for *him*.

"Angel happened to call Vasquez the same night Nnn-neil bribed him. Vasquez slipped and called me a target, and Angel grew suspicious. Neil was counting on the money my father had promised him to marry me. When I refused, and Neil found out Father was having me tracked, he—"

Darren couldn't keep himself on the sofa any longer. He knelt in front of Sheila and covered her trembling hands. "Sheila, I'm so sorry."

"I know, Darren. Me too. Let me finish, please. Angel's a good man and I trust him. He helped save us at the warehouse." Darren snorted and Sheila squeezed his hands. "Angel installed a tracking device on

Vasquez's van. That's how Sean found us and saved us."

"Why didn't your father tell you the Butcher had broken out of prison? Why didn't he try to get you someplace safe?"

Sheila shifted. "The prison break wasn't in the media and I probably wouldn't have believed Father after the marriage thing. I think Mother would have told me if she'd known.

"I hired Angel and Sean for security because the reporters have been brutal. There's this blonde that keeps popping up everywhere and we finally had to get a restraining order against her."

Darren ground his teeth and forced his face to remain smooth. He'd seen the papers, too. However, Sheila's next words made his back stiffen.

"There's a memorial service for Mary Oliver next week and I've spoken with her mother..."

Mary Oliver, the drowning victim. She'd been plaguing his sporadic sleep. Darren could only guess what it had been like for his woman to suffer recurring nightmares for years. Thank God, Dr. Baldwin was helping him, too.

"Are you going to attend?" he asked. Sheila gave a short nod and Darren took a breath to keep his voice calm. "I feel badly about her too honey, but won't a funeral be too stressful for you and the baby?"

Sheila pursed her mouth. "About the baby," she said.

"What?" he asked. She didn't answer right away and Darren's throat tightened when she withdrew her hands from his.

"At the hospital, before you proposed, I found out that I... that we..." Darren watched her brace the edge of the desk. It took forever for Sheila to push back the office chair and stand.

"What's wrong with the baby?" He'd purchased a pregnancy book and he'd read it twice. At 17 weeks, Sheila shouldn't have a basketball-sized swell straining against her blouse. He'd talked to Andrea every day. Why hadn't she told him?

"Nothing's wrong with our babies, Darren, except they kick my bladder constantly—"

"Babies?" his voice was too loud. "Babies?"

"We lost one at the warehouse," she whispered.

"Babies?" he thundered. It didn't surprise him when Herrera's hand landed on his shoulder a second later.

"I warned you, asshole," Herrera said. "Get away from her."

"Angel, don't. We're fine. Right, Darren? We're fine."

Darren shrugged his shoulder but the firm grip didn't loosen. Ignoring the interloper, he took the hem on Sheila's shirt in his hands. They shook as he lifted the material to reveal her belly. He gently placed his cheek against it.

"It's okay, Angel," she said.

"I'll be right outside the door," he said. Darren didn't miss that the remark was directed at him.

Sheila's tears fell onto Darren's curly head. She expected him to move or protest after they pelted him for a minute but several more passed before he spoke.

"Babies," he said again. "Twins?" He looked up and she nodded. "There were three but we lost one?" She nodded again and the way his face crumpled threatened to unhinge her completely. "Are they healthy?"

"Yes. I'm sorry I didn't tell you sooner—"

"Oh Sheila." His arms came around her waist, clasping tightly, and she felt his quiet sobs, vibrating on her stomach. The office door clicked shut.

She ran her fingers over his tendrils, gently at first. When he didn't pull back, she allowed herself to bury her fingers into the black nest, raking her nails against his scalp. She greedily sucked in his scent.

"Let's go to the sofa," she said. Her voice was husky but he misinterpreted it.

"Do you need help? Should I carry you?" he asked.

"No, silly. I don't have any restrictions on what I can do."

Darren jumped to his feet and Sheila brushed the dampness from his cheeks. Her nipples tightened to throbbing points. "Are you saying what I think you're saying?"

She nodded. "I told my doctor I was going to meet with you to see if there was any way we could reconcile. She said I—we—could have sex," her words were swallowed by his hungry mouth. Sheila moaned and snaked her hands around his neck, sucking on his tongue and deepening the kiss. A second later, Darren swept her into his arms and strode over to the sofa. He hesitated a minute before lowering her.

"Where are you going?" she breathed. He reached around the package and she let out a frustrated breath. "I love gifts, Darren, but hello? Make-up sex?" When he turned around, it took her a second to realize the pasta was still on the table. What he held was much smaller.

"I won't make love to you again until you're my wife."

"Darren?"

"I love you, Sheila Washington. Will you make an honest man out of me? Will you marry me?"

Emotion swelled in her throat when he slipped the ring from its box. In the weeks since his first proposal, she had not allowed herself to try it on. Darren knelt and slid the ring onto her finger. It fit.

"Yes! Yes, I'll marry you," she said. He kissed her quickly on the lips then in the corners of her eyes, catching her tears. "But I'm going to make a liar out of you," she said.

"What?"

"We're not waiting until after we get married. You're going to make love to me *now*!"

ACKNOWLEDGEMENTS

I AM GRATEFUL FOR THE FEEDBACK PROVIDED BY MY CRITIQUE PART-
ner, Leslie, and *beta* testers Bev, Karyn, Jinhee, and Suzie.

Thank you, Dr. Bartolome, for the chat about triplets, and Dawn
for help with the triangle choke. Any inaccuracies in these scenes are
my own.

If it weren't for girlfriends, mothers, and take out... well, thankfully
my husband and children are not picky eaters! I am grateful, too, for the
support from my extended family. Thank you, Linda for *turning me,* and
Sylvia, for your endless encouragement. Turn the page for a preview of
the next book in the *Honey Chaser* series, *The Shadowboxer*

THE SHADOWBOXER

TUESDAY, OCTOBER 8TH

PEACH STEPPED ONTO THE ESCALATOR AND SQUINTED AT THE SUN-light glinting off the metal paneling. She shifted her sleeping daughter onto her hip and tried to dig her shades from her purse, then groaned when her fingers encountered applesauce.

An announcement from San Diego airport security blared overhead. It startled Joelle and the child tightened a hand over the tender part of her mother's right shoulder. She gasped at the burst of pain and gripped the railing for balance. Her eyes stung and the reflex annoyed her.

The little hand fell slack and Peach took a deep breath. She shouldn't be carrying Joelle but she could handle it. She'd been through worse pain. Much worse. She could handle a torn ligament and a groggy five year old. But thank God help would be waiting at the bottom of the escalator.

A quick scan of the crowd didn't reveal her cousin. Peach inhaled again and tried to arrange her face into a semblance of happiness for him. The weather report promised the week ahead would be sunny, with high temps of 75°; perfect for a wedding. She still hadn't spotted the groom when the rolling step flattened. She frowned. It was unlike Darren to be late.

"*Hola, cariño,*" Angel said. He stood to the right of the escalator, looking sexier than anybody should in a sweaty t-shirt. The sleeves and most of the sides were cut away, offering a glimpse at bronze muscles. She peeked at his chiseled abs and stumbled for the second time.

"What are *you* doing here? Where's Darren?"

"It's nice to see you, too," he said, peering at her. His eyes were a brown so dark, they were almost black. A weaker woman would get lost in those eyes.

"Excuse us," a voice called behind them.

Angel's hand landed between her shoulders. He guided her away from the escalator, to a set of black suitcases. She twisted away from him and swore. The movement jostled Joelle and her injury. The child groaned.

"Is that my luggage?" She tried not to look at Angel's lips when he answered. Full lips outlined by an ultra-thin mustache. Sinful lips that had kissed her most intimate flesh. Her body warmed at the memory and she stifled a shudder.

"Yes," he said.

She shook off the desire curling in her belly. It was over between them. In fact, it had never really started, after one quickie in the locker room. Fooling around with a customer at the boxing gym she managed had been a mistake. Reaching for the largest bag, she prepared to unleash her anger. Being angry at Angel was a lot safer than wanting him.

"Get your hands off my luggage." She pulled on the extended handle but his hand closed over hers. She recoiled, hoping he wouldn't see her skin pebbling at his touch.

"Relax, *mami*."

"Dammit. Don't call me *mami*. Or *cariño*."

"Okay, Peach. Chill—"

"And don't tell me to chill. Get off my stuff."

Joelle squirmed, her eyes still closed. "Mommy, I need to go pee."

Peach ground her teeth. If Joelle woke up and saw Angel, she'd never get rid of him.

"The ladies room is right over there," Angel said. He pointed to a sign fifty feet away. "I'll wait for you, then I'll drive you to the house."

Joelle lifted her head and blinked.

"No. Gimme my stuff. I don't want you *or* your help."

"Don't be unreasonable, Peach. You need a ride."

Joelle turned toward the male voice. "Angel?"

"*Hola, pollito,*" he said.

"Angel!" The little girl lurched for him.

"Stop it," Peach said. If she hadn't overdone it with the weights, she would have been able to hold onto Joelle. She turned her back to Angel and lowered her daughter, palming Joelle's chin with her left hand. "Hold my hand and do *not* run off. Do you hear me?"

The child's eyes widened at the threat in her mother's voice. "Yes, Mom."

Turning to face Angel, she didn't have to fake her anger now. He'd been out of line, showing up at her apartment after their hookup four months ago. She resented that he'd charmed her daughter in the brief visit. Joelle, who soaked up any male attention, still gushed about Angel when all Peach wanted was to forget about him.

"Why didn't Darren come?" she asked.

"He'll have to tell you that."

Joelle bounced on her toes. "Angel, Angel, Angel. Sing the pollito song."

"Why would Darren ask *you* to pick me up?" Why hadn't Darren warned her that Angel Herrera, a bodyguard, was now working for him and his fiancée, Sheila? In August, Angel hadn't prevented Sheila from being kidnapped. Peach was shocked that they trusted him.

"There's a lot you don't know," he said. "I've tried calling you to explain—"

"I need to go potty," Joelle said. "Angel, will you take me to the potty?"

"No," Peach snapped.